Shep Lee thought he had it all. A successful restaurant, a loving husband who understood his asexuality, and most of all, the ability to be himself, a popular chef in the small town of Cloverleaf, Montana. That is, until his husband, Elmer Eshler, began pushing Shep more on sex.

Elmer doesn't understand why he can't turn his partner on — aren't they perfect for each other? And Shep loves him, right? Shep, meanwhile, while confident with his body, is and forever will be sex indifferent. Why has Elmer suddenly changed his tune? But he doesn't want to lose the man he loves so much. What can they do?

Shep convinces Elmer to try a polyamorous relationship. Elmer gets to have Shep and the sex life he's always wanted. Shep gets a cooking buddy and a chance to experience a relationship and even try sex with a woman as his authentic gender. At first, Shep isn't sure, but finds himself coming around — this feels safer than opening up the relationship. All three of them will be romantically involved, so that should ease any jealousy, right?

But when Willow Saint, a free-spirited, boisterous, and saucy young woman, comes into their lives, neither are prepared for the emotional and sexual rollercoaster that follows. Enthralled by Willow's charm and kindness, Elmer and Shep struggle to understand what this means for their own bond. Can they become one happy family? Or will this ruin everything?

Acing the Game
Copyright © 2023 Carey PW
ISBN: 978-1-4874-3680-3
Cover art by Angela Waters

Published by eXtasy Books Inc

Look for us online at:
www.eXtasybooks.com

ACING THE GAME

BY

CAREY PW

DEDICATION

Asexual relationships are valid.
Polyamorous relationships are valid.
Open relationships are valid.
All relationships are valid.

Chapter One: Elmer

I'm just a nerdy boring square.

For the first forty years of my life, I lived by the book. Growing up in the rural town of Cloverleaf, Montana, a fire burned inside of me to be somebody. I'd been raised in a single-father home with two other brothers. My dad, Bub, was a ranch hand, a seasonal construction worker, and a janitor at the local school. We never had much, but my father had hammered the ethic of hard work into us. I'd spent my childhood days waking at the crack of dawn to ride with my dad to the estate where he'd earned a collection of sunburns, scars, and sometimes even broken bones that he insisted was part of *becoming a man*. By the time I was fourteen and entering high school, I was adamant that I'd avoid any career that required such toil and sweat. In my heart, I knew that I was meant to be a leader.

My household had been the epitome of stereotypical masculinity. The cowboy mentality had been ever-present while living in a home of men with dirty hands, bad backs, and demeanors so tough that one time my brother, Snavis, had accidentally stabbed himself in the stomach with a screwdriver and didn't even blink. Frantically driving him to the hospital, he'd just sat in the passenger seat, smoking and singing along to some Johnny Cash songs. I often envied my brothers' and my father's relentless suppression of their emotions and pain. But I was different.

I'd always known that I didn't want to work with my hands or my body but with my intellect. I studied, I read, I joined the debate team, and I graduated high school as the

1

valedictorian. Also, I had a secret.

When I was ten, I was playing at the local park with a friend of mine named Tony. Tony lived a few blocks from me and would often hang around the playground at all hours to avoid his parents who struggled with alcohol. We were swinging and making horrific efforts to rap a Snoop Dogg song.

"Bitches and hoes." I giggled.

"You're a bitch," he teased me, slapping me on the shoulder.

I jumped off my swing and tackled him, knocking him to the ground. We rolled around on the grass until he managed to wrestle his way on top of me, holding my wrists down with his knees and tickling my sides. I screamed and pleaded for him to quit with tears gushing out. Finally, he stopped, offering me a hand to help me up. Rising to my feet, I brushed myself off and smiled at him. He squinted his brown eyes in the sunlight as he grinned back at me. A minute passed, and we were still grasping each other's hands. Butterflies of excitement swam around chaotically in my tummy. For the first time, I noticed his cute dimples that blanketed his cheeks with charm, and his palm was rough and coarse. I'm not sure how long we stayed like that, but when his hand slid out of my grip, I forever yearned for more. Nothing else ever happened between us. That day, I realized that I was bisexual.

Homophobia had been alive and well in my home. My father and brothers were good people, but ignorant — *very* ignorant. Being the youngest, I'd watched as my brothers returned from school during our teenage years, bragging about their latest *scores* and my dad had congratulated them with a *that's my boy* slap on the back. It had all been so cliché. Snavis had gotten married shortly after graduation to a local girl, and they'd moved to a trailer on her parents' small ranch on the corner of town. My other brother, Kicky, impregnated his girl-friend in his eleventh-grade year. They'd moved into her parents' house, but the relationship had soured quickly. He ended up dropping out of school and working several years with my father in construction until he met a Native American woman from Wyoming and relocated to Missoula, where she worked as a nurse.

When I'd begun high school, the pressure to score with chicks and brag about my sexual conquests created anxiety. I definitely liked girls, but my attraction to boys felt so much stronger. I had decided in the tenth grade that I wanted to save myself for a man rather than lose my virginity to a woman. Thus, I didn't date. Instead, I shoved my nose in my books and in my future.

My father and brothers grew suspicious.

"Why don't you bring home any gals?" Snavis hissed at me one night at the kitchen table. We were feasting on a couple of large pizzas, a dinner staple in my childhood. While he wasn't a cook, my dad was still passionate about family dinners and required our presence at the table each evening until I finally moved out when I started college.

"I don't even see you talking to gals," Kicky agreed through a mouthful of pizza.

"I need to study so that I can get a scholarship," I told them, which was true and a convenient excuse.

"School over gals?" Kicky laughed. "There ain't nothing better than some gals."

"I agree," my father said. "It's not normal to spend all that time alone in your room. Even if you are studying."

"I've got all the time in the world for girls later. I want to go to college. I need to work hard now," I mumbled, staring down at my plate to avoid their questioning glares.

"You sure it ain't something else?" my father probed. His

face looked serious.

"No, it's not," I lied, still evading his gaze.

He stared at me for a few moments just chewing his food with his mouth moving awkwardly since he'd lost most of his teeth. Snavis and Kicky muttered something to each other and chuckled.

"What's so funny?" I snapped at them.

"There's a lot of smart boys who are either gay or can't get anybody. Which one are you?" Snavis snickered.

"I'm just . . . I need to study, that's all." I wasn't good at defending myself against them. My brothers were always big, strong, and confident, never letting anything get to them. Here I was, a delicate bundle of sensitivity who couldn't make eye contact with hardly anybody.

My father leaned over and placed his hand gently on my shoulder. "Stop you two," he instructed my brothers. "If you want to go to school, then I get it. I know it's a lot of work, and I'm sorry that I'm not equipped to help you."

"Thanks." I smiled at him.

"But you're not gay or anything, are you?" he asked.

I sighed. "No."

I had earned an academic scholarship to the University of Montana and fought my way through a bachelor's degree in physical education by working as a grocery store clerk, a bartender, and a student intern when possible. I lived with three or four roommates at times and even on couches when I got really strapped. But I made it, graduating summa cum laude. I had chosen physical education because it sounded easier, allowing myself time to focus on my real goal, which was to become a principal. I landed a job teaching P.E. and coaching track at a local school and remained in Missoula until I was able to complete my master's in educational leadership.

Missoula should have given me the platform to explore my

4

sexuality. After all, I was in my twenties, and college was supposed to be the era for sexual experimentation. But I didn't get far. One night at a small party, a group of us had decided to play spin the bottle. There were only five girls and four guys, including me. The bottle spun, and for the first few spins, it was girl on guy kissing.

"What's going to happen if it lands on two dudes?" one guy asked, nervously.

"Ha-ha, we need to hope it doesn't." Another boy laughed.

The joke continued for a few more rounds before finally it stopped with the bottle head poking at me. As my heart dropped, I looked to see the bottom portion pointing at a young first-year student named Dave.

"Oh, no." Dave cringed, burying his head in his hands.

"Kiss, kiss, kiss!" the group cheered.

Dave grimaced, but my chest, belly, and loins all tensed up in excitement. I was finally going to experience kissing a man. I put my best poker face on and even joked with *ewww* to disguise my internal pleasure.

"Do we have to French?" Dave asked with wide eyes.

"We've all been Frenching," one girl replied. "Come on, it's not *that* big of deal."

When I heard *Frenching*, my heart raced faster. Dave stared at me in reluctance but climbing on his hands and knees, he approached me. I inhaled a whiff of his cologne mixed with some masculine body sweat. I placed my palms on the floor to balance myself and leaned forward. Dave's lips were stiff, and he didn't move his tongue at first. But then he relaxed his jaw, letting his soft tongue dance along mine. I pressed my mouth more against his, ignoring all the cheers and gasps around us. He jerked away, raising his arms up in the air as if he'd won a contest.

"See," he stated proudly. "A real man can kiss another dude. Did that turn you on, ladies?" He flexed his biceps, and an erection popped up in my pants. To my disappointment, the girls did find it attractive, at least in Dave, and he later escaped with one of them for the night. For me, I ended up locking myself in the bathroom to jerk off, savoring the sensations of Dave's tongue inside my mouth and imagining it engulfing my penis.

I could have explored the gay bars. There were lots of LGBTQIA2S hangouts around Missoula. But fear perpetually stopped me. *What would Dad say? What would my brothers do if I brought home a man?* It was impossible. Thus, like high school, I spent most of my college years a virgin, locking myself away to study. Academics was a good excuse for avoiding my life.

After finishing my master's degree, I'd worked several assistant principal jobs around Missoula until one day an opening arose for Cloverleaf High. I desperately wanted to seize a principal position even though I wasn't so keen on returning to Cloverleaf. However, my father had seriously injured his back and was now living on disability. Snavis was there to help but was preoccupied with his home full of five children and two foster kids. I wasn't really utilizing any of the social benefits of residing in Missoula, so I applied, interviewed, and accepted the job. That's when I met Luna.

Luna and I had attended high school together. She'd earned a degree in addictions counseling and worked as a counselor at a local clinic in Cloverleaf. We ran into each other at the grocery store one day when I accidently plowed my cart into hers. Her gaze comprising of two ocean blue pupils fixated on mine and her long black hair fell over them like a delicate curtain. For the first time since Dave, I bubbled with excitement. I was in love.

Luna was like a warm glow. A gentle cool summer evening breeze. I was mesmerized with her smile and her laugh. She always grinned, even on her bad days.

"Just make the most of it," she would holler on her way out the door when she left for work.

I had often come home stressed out during my early years as a principal. Ironically, I was more insecure working in leadership in my hometown than in Missoula. But Luna knew how to comfort me. I would lay my head on her lap, and she would stroke my hair as I released all my anxieties. She never tried to fix it. She listened and was present. During that time in my life, I had really needed her.

Luna and I had gotten married about two years later and bought our own house in Cloverleaf, a large spacious home with three bedrooms so that we could start our family. However, after ages of trying, we learned that Luna had a deformed cervix that would make childbearing extremely difficult — if not, dangerous. That day, I held Luna's little five-feet-four-inches body in my arms as she wept with agony.

Seeing her in such pain, I chose to bury mine. I had dreamed about having children. I loved my father, and I wanted to experience that paternal bond with my own kids. Only after I knew Luna was asleep, I would creep into the bathroom and cry. I sobbed for both our heartache.

We abandoned our dream for children. But that didn't stop me from loving Luna.

Despite her loss, Luna's presence was magnetic. She'd worked with the most vulnerable, sometimes forgotten people in society, yet she remained kind, tender, and empathetic. When I'd come in from work, raving about ungrateful, spoiled kids, Luna's voice was there to guide me.

"You don't know their home life," she would whisper in my ear as she laid beside me, rubbing my back. "They may be acting that way because they've given up that anyone cares. Show them that you care."

Luna had beauty that no other could match. Her skin was

like smooth porcelain, and her black hair was always disheveled looking with its random waves and curls, but I loved it. She could look elegantly wild. When I gazed at her, it was like she was something precious that I somehow won and therefore, must protect. My desires for men still lingered, but I was happy. Plus, it was easier that way. I liked women, so why not just be in a heterosexual relationship. It didn't have all the complexities or dangers to it. Besides, my father and brothers adored her.

Luna and I were married for over ten years before she got ill. It was her cervix again. Luna had worked long hours, continuously pushing herself to the side. After we decided not to pursue children, Luna didn't see any need to keep going to her gynecologist appointments, at least, not as regularly. She'd put it off for several years until she started getting a strange discharge and some pain, especially during sex. By the time all the tests were complete, we learned that she had stage four cervical cancer that had spread to her liver and lymph nodes.

We fought it for a year before she succumbed. My assistant principals were great. They covered things for me so that I could care for her. Luna was insistent that she pass away in her room surrounded by flowers, candles, and me. The day she was dying, she'd fallen into a coma and her body jerked violently as her lungs struggled to breathe. I held her clammy hand in mine and laid my head gently on her chest to relish every heartbeat. She died at five in the morning.

I remained in our home even though everything felt like her. Her smell lingered, and a void remained in the air. I didn't believe that moving would be any better. About a year later, my father passed away from a heart attack. I dived more into work, accepting my plight as a fatherless widower. This process carried on for six years until that one night.

I was lounging on the sofa, scrolling through some emails

and listening to the local news. That's when I heard the name, *The Spare Tire Restaurant*. There on the screen beside the reporter was a tall tattooed man sporting a bowler's hat. It was Shep Lee.

CHAPTER TWO: SHEP

There was nothing more important to my world than food. Researching it, creating it, consuming it, and dreaming about it . . . it all flowed in my veins. The most fascinating part of cooking was taking multiple ingredients and changing them into something new. Chop onions, celery, carrots, and potatoes and get a tasty stew. Process some red peppers, spices, nuts, and oil, and have a scrumptious zesty pesto. There are no limits to creation. As a transgender and nonbinary person, I had gravitated naturally to the notion that anything can break away from its original destiny. Like any cuisine, various flavors ran through me that took turns presenting themselves, proving that I could be everything I wanted to be.

I'd never expected to open a restaurant. I couldn't have envisioned the stress of managing a business, working long hours, and desperately trying to keep things afloat. I'd graduated from the University of Chicago with my teaching degree and had worked in various states as a high school English teacher before landing in Cloverleaf thanks to Tank.

I had met Tank while teaching in Seattle when I was still presenting as a woman and went by the name of Shelly. He was about ten years older and taught math while coaching football and tennis. Tank was his nickname because he stood six-feet-seven-inches tall with a bulky build and had a no-nonsense way of training. The players had often lived in fear of him. Spending my lunch hours reading Percy Bysshe Shelley poems or drowning out the day blasting *Rancid* on my headphones, I'd written Tank off as a jock and me as a geek.

One morning, I was grading papers in my classroom when I looked up to see his gargantuan figure before me. Tank smiled shyly with a red face and handed me a card.

"This is for you," he said before scurrying away like a frightened child.

I opened it. The front showed two crows kissing with a heart above them. I read the inside.

Every time I see you, my heart starts racing, and I feel faint. I have been wanting to talk to you since you started working here, but I get too scared, and no words come out. Maybe we can discuss over dinner?

Is it a joke? The football team was notorious for practical jokes. Yet, a prank like this one seemed too mean to come from Tank. After all, the guy was Teacher of the Year and even offered tutoring on Saturday mornings. *Someone like that couldn't do something so malicious?*

That afternoon, I walked down to the football field where the team was practicing. I didn't have to get too close to hear the grunts of the players as they ran laps or did push-ups while Tank screamed at them to *push it* and *be tough*.

I stepped up to the fence and placed my fingers inside the cage, causing it to shake a little. The noise caught Tank's attention who saw me and immediately turned away. I heard him call the assistant coach over before approaching me.

"Hi," he mumbled without making eye contact. His hands trembled, and I could barely make out his grin under the shade of his baseball cap.

"Hi," I replied.

The silence flooded the air around us as he fidgeted, and I kicked at the dirt under my feet.

"Um . . ." He shyly giggled. "Have you ever been to the football field? Do you want to look around?"

"I've seen the games. I'm good," I assured him, holding up

my hand.

"Oh," he murmured.

After I realized that this guy wasn't going to speak, I broke the awkwardness. "Do you know any good restaurants?"

"What kind of food do you like?" he asked.

"Something authentic. Fresh. I don't do those places that serve the frozen stuff," I insisted.

"Okay."

I squeezed my hand inside the fence and gently pulled his cap up exposing his eyes. They were hazel, and the sunlight gave them a green glow. His shy grin revealed two round cheeks radiating a boyish charm from this colossal man. He was cute.

"You know, if you take me to dinner, we'll have to actually talk to each other," I warned him, leaning my body flirtatiously forward. "Think you can handle it?"

"Yeah," he replied.

"Do you know any good places?" I waved my hand in encouragement.

He nodded. "I know some."

"Tank! Come on! Practice time," the other coach yelled as the players all ran out into the field.

"I've got to go," he stammered, still avoiding my gaze.

"So are we going to *have* dinner?" I asked.

"Yes."

"When? Like some day?"

He chuckled again. "Saturday?"

I sighed. "You can let me know when on Saturday. Have fun at practice." I started walking back up the hill to the school parking lot.

About halfway up, a shadow hovered over me, causing me to turn around to see Tank. His hat was off, and he was sweaty.

"Shelly, I'm sorry," he stuttered. "I'm really shy. Especially

12

with you. I don't want you to think I'm a big dork — or worse, boring. I'm not very good at dating."

"The school hero is shy?" I teased him. "Aren't you the loudest person in the faculty meetings? Everyone loves you."

He smiled, which highlighted his kindhearted spirit. "I know. But it's different with you. I'll pick you up at six, if that's okay? I promise that I'll talk. I wasn't expecting to see you right now. I guess I didn't think you'd respond."

I took his cap from his hand and placed it back firmly on his head, carefully wiping off his brow. "It's okay. Six is fine."

Tank's disabling shyness quickly melted off during the date. He turned out to be different than I'd expected. Tank was a mountain of intellect swallowed up in his enormous physical stature. He'd fallen in love with philosophy in college and enjoyed reading works by academics from many various ethnicities and worldviews. I reciprocated by sharing some of my poems and showing him photos of my special recipes.

"Sometimes I want to quit teaching and go to culinary school," I told him. "But I don't know what I'd do with it."

"You could feed me." He winked at me. "I take a lot of food." He rubbed his round belly that hung slightly over his pants.

"That would make it worth it," I agreed.

We ended up back at my place, talking incessantly and gulping down a bottle of cabernet, snuggling, and holding hands. When the night drew to a close, his expression became serious.

"Shelly?"

"Yes?"

He withdrew his hand and moved a little away from me. "I know this is our first date, but I better tell you something. But please, if things don't work out, don't tell anyone else."

"Okay," I replied, sitting up to give him my full attention.

He fidgeted with his fingers and gulped the remaining wine in his glass. His hazel eyes met mine with a slight flare of moisture that sparkled in the dim lamp light. "I was in a bad car accident when I was a teenager. I got . . . severely injured." He paused and trembled. "It's really hard for me to have sex. Like . . . intercourse. I can do it . . . sometimes. Well . . . not often. It's . . . I understand if this is a deal breaker. I feel like you should know. It's why I don't date much. I like you, and I hope that I can meet someone who doesn't care."

I exhaled loudly. "I'm honored that you shared that with me, Tank. It's a relief, actually."

"A relief?" he asked, jerking away and raising his eyebrow at me.

"Can I tell you something? Please don't tell anyone else?"

He nodded.

"I don't like — well, sex is complicated for me," I informed him. "Don't take this the wrong way, but I don't want to have sex with other people. I've done it, and everything works fine, but I don't get urges to do it with others." I cringed at how strange it all sounded.

At that time, I'd no concept of asexuality. I knew that I didn't experience sexual attraction, and I didn't enjoy sex with people. Orgasms felt great. Yet, it was more natural to masturbate or maybe have someone give me a hand job. The kissing, the touching, and the intercourse part sometimes made me grimace. It wasn't my thing.

I scoured his face, seeing his brows bent in deep thought — or confusion. I held my breath as I waited for him to say something.

"Are you not attracted to men?" he inquired.

I smirked a little. I got this same question every time I tried to talk to anyone about my sexuality. "I'm not gay. I mean, I'm bisexual in the sense that I'm willing to have sex with men or women. But this isn't about me not being attracted to men. I prefer not to do it with another person." I started cracking my knuckles. After Tank shared that he had a physical impairment, I figured he'd accept it and move on.

"So are you not into relationships?" he asked. His eyes darted all over as he gazed at me.

"Yes!" I exclaimed. "I very much want a relationship. Sex is part of that for many people. It isn't the whole thing. I'd be extremely interested in having a relationship with you." I smiled, offering him my hand.

He wrapped his fingers around mine and pulled his body closer to me.

"Does that mean that we can't have sex in other ways? Like other than intercourse?" he asked, slowly caressing my palm.

I placed my head on his shoulder. "I think we can work out anything we want to. Something that works for both of us."

He glanced away. "You're not attracted to me then," he stated somberly.

I pulled his face up and kissed him. His body shivered against mine. He slid his arm around me, squeezing me tight.

"I'm very much attracted to you as a person," I whispered in his ear. "That's what's important. I find you pleasing to look at. It's just not sexual."

"I guess you won't be cheating on me, then," he joked and gave a little chuckle.

His face still looked confused, but we changed the subject and passed out on my couch, snuggling under a blanket. There would be many conversations, but from that moment on, Tank accepted me. About a year later, we got married.

We continued to live in Seattle for another four years before Tank's mother became ill. Tank was an only child and rather attached to his mother whom he either texted or spoke with daily. His mother had been in and out of hospitals with congested heart failure, and Tank was scared that she would die without him next to her. So Tank convinced me to move to a tiny town called Cloverleaf in Montana.

Living in Montana suited me. Roads were empty and wide open, highlighting endless miles of rolling hills and plains. Winters or cool autumn-like days were predominant with only a brief period of three to four months of summer heat. There were no supermarket lines and rarely any traffic jams unless there was construction. Life felt slower . . . easier. I ended up with an abundance of time alone with my thoughts, especially during the long days and nights at the hospital with Tank and his mother.

I watched endless hours of television in the waiting room, including many programs about transgender people. As I sunk into the stale cushions of the couches, my burning internal desire to transition to a masculine form emerged from the depths of my soul where I'd buried it for so long.

The next day, I observed Tank's mother as she struggled to breathe and constantly went in and out of consciousness. I touched one of her hands. It was cold, and the skin felt like silk fabric hardly hanging onto the bones. I studied her face that was wrinkled, pale, and weak. She was only fifty-nine, but years of COPD from smoking and health complications had taken their toll on her. It all seemed so unfair. *Why was this wonderful woman's life getting ripped away from Tank?* An overwhelming hardened ball festered in my gut causing me to explode in tears. It was the first time where I poignantly grasped how short and precious life was.

Tank's mother died during our second year in Cloverleaf, and Tank encouraged me to stay and move into her home, a one-story but spacious ranch home with a huge kitchen. I wasn't too keen on living in such a small town, but I was sold with that perk. Tank's mother had invested in it, and I recalled him even taking a few trips home when we lived in Seattle to help her remodel it. His mother loved feeding people and cooked for just about any local event, funeral, wedding, reunion, anything. The kitchen had a huge, wrap around granite counterspace that hugged the entire room with a large six-foot island with a double sink in the middle of it. Pots hung elegantly from the ceiling. A massive two-door fridge and a separate large freezer sat in the corner. And I inherited all of it.

After Tank's initial grief subsided, I started secretly investigating transgender men. For years, I'd suppressed my desire for masculinity. Growing up in a strict Baptist family, traditional gender roles had plagued me, and there wasn't much tolerance for nonconformity. I wore dresses. I put on makeup. I played the stereotypical girl. Now, I was heading toward forty, and I knew that there wasn't a lot of time left. I could carry on this feminine façade, or I could spend the second half of my life learning how to live as me. The only problem was Tank.

We had had conversations about relating more to men and seeing me as a masculine woman. Tank was always supportive. Most importantly, he never made me feel wrong.

One day, I wrote him a letter informing him of my intentions to medically transition and shoved it in his stack of math papers to grade as he was leaving for work. I probably chewed off every fingernail during my classes. It was common not to see each other during the day, for we had different lunch and planning periods; plus, he still coached after school. But that evening, he came home from practice early.

I pretended to be sleeping on the sofa as if nothing was unusual, but the moment the front door open, my body stiffened into a plank, and my heart raced. I forced my eyes closed. His footsteps softly approached the love seat.

"What's this?" he asked.

I opened my eyes, seeing the letter in his hand and tears in

17

his eyes.

"What does this mean?" he asked again. "You want to become a man?"

My dry mouth left me feeling as if I'd choke.

"Yes," I admitted, squeezing my hands into fists. "I want to transition. I learned how to do it."

"You studied this? Like behind my back?" His words sounded angry, but tears flowed down his cheeks. He slumped down on the sofa beside me. "I don't understand."

I sat up, pulling my knees up in front of me. "We talked before about how I wish I were a man. Well, there's a way to make that happen — medically."

He remained still with his mouth gaping open. "Are you saying that . . . does this mean that you want to leave me? Are you going to leave me for another woman — a woman?"

"No," I corrected him. I saw his hands trembling, so I grabbed one of them, squeezing it tight.

"This has *nothing* to do with leaving you," I assured him. "Or with me wanting to be with a woman. I want to be with you. I don't want that to change."

"You're not really gay? Like . . . the asexual thing isn't—" he stuttered, shaking his head.

"No, I'm asexual," I assured him. "This has nothing to do with that. I'm not asexual because I'm a man and prefer women. I feel that I would be happier if I were presenting as a man."

He stared down, making little eye contact and holding my palm in one hand and the letter in another. Nausea emerged, and I took a few deep breaths to hold it back.

"Are you saying that you're not happy?" he inquired after a slight pause.

My heart sank that he assumed this meant that I didn't love him. "Tank, I *am* happy. But I think I would feel more natural and thus, happier this way. And I also expect that if I ignore it, then over time, maybe I won't be content with my life. Your mom's death made me realize that I'm getting older, and life is short."

"Does that mean that you want a penis?" he asked, finally gazing into my eyes.

I shrugged. "Maybe. Probably. But it's a lengthy process, Tank. I would like to try hormones first. Then get my breasts removed. I want to take it a piece at a time. It won't happen overnight."

He nodded.

"Do those things bother you? Like me having a penis?" I held my breath, dreading that I may not like the answer.

Tank smirked. "I don't think it will impact our sex life much."

Tank and I had a sexual relationship. However, it was a unique arrangement. Intercourse was rare, but we often enjoyed fondling each other or masturbating together, and it worked well for us. Tank felt less pressure to hold his erection, and I was spared the unpleasantness of too much physical contact.

"I could teach you how to jerk it off," he joked, and we both laughed.

"Would that be weird for you," I asked again.

"A little. But you've always been a tomboy. I've loved that part of you." He teared up. "I read this letter, and I thought . . . I feared . . . that you were leaving me. That's what scares me the most."

"I wouldn't leave you," I promised him. "I was so scared that you wouldn't support me. I didn't want to lose you over this." I shook as my heart pounded.

"Would you have? Would you be willing to give up on us over this?" His hand squeezed mine so tight that his anxiety bled into me through my palm.

My throat got dry, and tears welled up in my eyes. But I

didn't want to lie.

"Yes," I admitted with my voice quivering. "I didn't want that. But I was worried that over time, I would regret it. I would get to fifty or sixty and just think back on this moment when I didn't follow my heart. I wasn't true to myself. That doesn't mean I don't love you."

"I know," he said softly. "It's hard to swallow that, though."

"I understand."

"A man . . ." Tank rubbed his forehead. "This will be a tough sell around here. At the school. Parents." He sighed. "It's going to be very hard."

"Does that mean that you support me?" I asked. I clenched my jaw so firmly that I thought my teeth would crack.

"Let me support you a piece at a time. Show me that stuff about hormones you mentioned."

We rummaged through the internet on anything we could find for transitioning from female to male as we consumed two bottles of wine. Tank seemed intrigued every time we caught a picture of a transgender man and would study it carefully. I can't say that his reactions were enthralled, but they weren't repulsed, either.

"I guess this means one thing," he stated as we finally made our way to bed.

"What's that?"

"I'm going to have to learn to be gay," he teased, wrapping me up in a bear hug.

Tank never got the opportunity to fully explore the fluidity of his sexuality. He traveled along with me during my first year of hormones and through my top surgery before getting thrown out of his windshield when a drunk driver crossed the median on the highway when he was driving home from the grocery store one winter night.

CHAPTER THREE: ELMER

Shep looked great on T.V. His petite frame was sculpted in muscle tone that I knew must be from all the running he did around town, and he had blue black, thick hair that was shaggy and often hung slightly over his eyes. But the most seductive aspect of him was his smile. His whole face crinkled up in dozens of wrinkles and dimples, and his eyes sparkled and watered when it got too big. Shep's grin could melt away all the anxiety, sadness, or stress of the day. Seeing him on the screen brought me back to the days of the art club.

Shep and his husband had both worked as teachers at Cloverleaf High. They were great educators and a terrific couple. Shep, who went by Shelly at the time, taught English but organized an art club while Tank took over the football and track coaching. They were upbeat, enduringly goofy, and loved their students. I remembered walking into faculty meetings and immediately laying my eyes on Shep who often instantly returned the gaze with an ambiguous smile. I would shyly glance away, seeing him return his attention on Tank. However, every moment I could, I sneaked glimpses. He always caught me.

One winter day, I was rummaging through disciplinary files when Shep and Tank knocked on my door. The two didn't behave like their typical bubbly selves but were solemn.

"We need to talk to you, if you have a few minutes," Tank stated with a frown.

"Sure, sit down." My throat tightened. *They're quitting on me. How am I going to find another teacher — two more teachers? A coach?*

"We need to speak with you about something," Tank began, looking at Shep. "Did you want to tell him?" he asked.

Shep took a deep breath. "It's awkward saying this . . . but I'm transgender. We wanted to let you know because I'll be changing. We weren't sure how the school would handle it."

Shep's hands were shaking, and Tank placed his arm around his shoulder. Then they both quizzically stared at me for a response. My mind blanked.

"I guess I don't know exactly what that means," I admitted. "I've heard the word transgender, but I don't understand."

"I identify as a man or more masculine to be precise and I'll be transitioning into a man. And I want to be called by male pronouns," Shep informed me. I saw sweat beads on his forehead.

The image of him as a man filled my thoughts. "This is new for me," I mumbled after a long pause. "I thought you two were coming in here to quit."

They awkwardly chuckled before turning serious again.

"We hope that—we're worried that we may lose our jobs over this," Tank told me. "We're not sure how people—parents or students—even staff are going to react. We wanted to start with you."

"Well, I'm okay with it. I don't fully understand it, but it's fine with me." I stared at Shep who mostly gazed out the window. "Do I still call you Shelly?"

"No, I really prefer that you don't. You can call me Shep. It was an old uncle's name," he stated. His blue eyes met mine, making my heart jump.

"You know that it may take some time for people to get used to it. They may make mistakes with your name or pronouns," I said to him. His eyes fell downward again, causing my gut to jump.

"We'll be patient with people," Tank remarked. "But we

also expect people to put the effort in. Or maybe, that standard needs to be set by you."

Fear sent shivers through me. I got along well with Tank, but Shep and I were more than colleagues. I'd often sat in his club because I loved art and did some of my own paintings that contained hidden themes around my bisexuality. It was the only platform that allowed me to explore that part of myself. Now that I thought of it, Shep had responded deeply to my works, even running his finger directly along the images that contained my secret. He'd never revealed if he knew but would simply comment, "I like this part here."

Sometimes we had hung out after the students left, finger painting or writing ridiculously bad poetry. He'd been the only one in the school who made me feel like I could be myself. Now here he was with his spouse requesting my support with a matter that triggered my own internalized phobias around my bisexuality. *What if my support of them exposes me? What if I lose everything?*

The image of me standing before the entire staff and declaring a firm stance on my views about transgender people terrified me. Local parents could be vicious. I'd often remained calm and had rehearsed my responses to parental concerns so that I could keep a situation from escalating while also maintaining my authority. But supporting the transgender community? The religious fanatics in town would flood the next Board meeting, for sure. I'd only been a principal for three years at that time and was still developing my leadership style and credibility. This issue would shake everything up.

"Um . . ." I hesitated. "I can write an email? I mean if you're okay with me disclosing this to everyone. For speaking at a staff meeting . . . I feel someone more educated on the topic would be better to speak to staff directly."

"You're an educated person," Shep asserted. "If you want me to help you with the wording, I can do that. But I think you're the right person to address it."

I shifted in my seat to hide my shakiness. "I know little of it. I'm thinking beyond just the staff meeting, Shep. I may get calls from parents. If I don't have a decent grasp on this matter, I won't be able to respond to them effectively. Do you understand?" I hated resorting to my professionalism. Inside, I wanted to tell them that I was afraid. After all, Shep was my friend.

"I understand, but I still think that it needs to come from you," Shep insisted. I could see his hands trembling as he held them in his lap.

"Leadership's support goes further than just us two or some outsider," Tank agreed. "You set the tone for everything."

"Okay," I conceded. "Could I have some time to think through this? How fast do these changes happen?" The image of Shep as a man with that black hair and those magnetic blue eyes flashed in my mind again. He'd always been androgynous, which may have explained his appeal to me.

"I'm not on hormones, yet, so yes, you have some time before anything visual occurs," Shep replied. "But that doesn't change the fact that I want to be called Shep and be referred to with male pronouns."

"Well, I think it'll be easier for people to do that once you start looking like a man," I suggested.

He sighed, and Tank rolled his eyes.

"Did I say something wrong?" I asked. I shoved my shaky hands in between my knees under the desk.

Shep rubbed his hands together frantically. "I don't know what you mean. I have to look like a man to get people to respect my identity? Who gets to define what a man or masculine looks like? Who determines when I look manly enough?" he snapped, crossing his arms.

My chest hurt. The tension between Shep and I permeated

the air so densely that I almost forgot that Tank was there. "Okay. I'll do it, but I need time. There's a lot at stake here. But there's nothing stopping you from asking people to call you Shep and use male pronouns, is there? You can go ahead and do that without me."

He glared at me. "Yeah, I guess I can. If that's what you need to do, then it's fine."

"You're not going to fire us?" Tank checked, raising an eyebrow.

"No, you're not fired," I assured him.

"What if parents demand it? What if the Board does?" Tank's eyes widened.

"We'll see what happens and deal with that when it arises. I've got another meeting coming now." I stood up and motioned for them to leave.

They thanked me and walked out of the office, but the heaviness lingered in the room. I didn't have another meeting.

The sad truth was that I ended up failing both of them.

I never spoke to the staff and avoided it by dodging Tank and Shep when I saw them, pretending to be busy. I stopped going to the art club. Shep proceeded to change his name, pronouns, and appearance much to the dismay of his colleagues. Whispers consumed the halls, and when I sneakily shot a glance at them in the lunchroom, I saw Tank and Shep off in a corner alone. Everyone had adored Tank, the football hero with a sweet, shy heart. Now, he was an outcast.

For a while, it was just gossip and social isolation, but eventually, they came to me. The parents, the staff, and the Board.

"We can't let a pervert teach in our school!"

"She'll teach the kids to be gay."

"She'll spread the liberal agenda."

"She's teaching against our Christian values."

"This isn't who Cloverleaf is."

Yet, no one ordered me to fire him. They only provided

tons of justifications for why Shep and Tank were bad influences. They may have believed that their concerns were sufficient enough to convince me to get rid of them. But both had golden track records as teachers, which would make terminating them an obvious discriminatory action. Also, I wasn't going to do it. I refused to stare these two people in the eyes and tell them that they needed to leave. Honestly, I had hoped they would just quit so that the pressure was off of me. I waited for it to work itself out while I cowardly hid away in my office.

Shep's classes shrunk as parents demanded that their students weren't enrolled in his or Tank's classes. Some football players wouldn't attend practice if Tank was head coach. He ended up relinquishing the position to the assistant coach in hopes of continuing to work with the team and pacifying the players. However, they still refused to go if he was present. So Tank quit coaching.

The art club resumed but struggled. A parent approached me that her daughter loved the club but that another faculty member should take it over and noted that my lack of attendance in it confirmed that I didn't support Shep running it. My face grew hot, and my stomach sank. But I said nothing.

The once charming, energetic, and devoted duo in the school were now withdrawn, quiet, and becoming more invisible. They never asked me again to speak at a faculty meeting.

Then Tank died. The death vigorously reawakened my own grief considering that Luna had passed away only a year before. Sitting in my dark living room one night, the emptiness in the air consumed me, and I envisioned Shep, all alone now in a town that saw him as an atrocity. Somehow my heart swelled with a deep connection to him in that moment.

When I saw Shep at the school after Tank's death, his once vivacious warm face was now dark and forlorn. He didn't talk to anyone. One day, I was surveilling the hallways, and I crept by his classroom. The door was slightly cracked. I peered in to see him slumped over in his chair sobbing into his raised palms. I wanted to go to him and share the pain inside of me that I knew he must be feeling. Instead, I continued walking down the hall.

That same year, Shep resigned. His letter stated that he was pursuing a new career path and that he thanked me for giving him and Tank the opportunity. I didn't speak to him about it. The year ended, he submitted his grades, he turned in his keys, and he was gone. The school carried on but without the energetic flare of the Shep and Tank years. The art club died.

Shep bought an old abandoned restaurant in town with the life insurance money from Tank's death and had been running it since. His motto was healthy, fresh, and affordable food for Cloverleafers. The restaurant had seemed doomed to fail, but after the first year, the reputation caught up with it. People bragged around town about the cuisine, and when I drove by, the place was usually packed until closing. I guess the townspeople felt that transgender people can't teach their kids, but they can cook their food.

Despite the success and constant urges from people to try the restaurant, I couldn't bring myself to go. I savored the scent of smoked meat in the air when I passed by it, and I even read the menu online. The truth was, Shep never vacated my mind since the day I met him, but guilt over my own cowardness immobilized me. Until I saw him on the news.

Shep's radiant beauty and vitality bounced off the television screen. He laughed, and he shared many stories of his dishes from his southern grandma's family recipes to Asian influences when he did a study abroad in Japan. He even printed recipe cards for any patron who wanted to make the meals at home, but his cooking was unreproducible.

"Is it smart to give your recipes away like that?" the

reporter asked during the interview.

Shep chuckled. "Well, I do what many cooks, especially southern cooks, do. I follow the recipe but then spontaneously add ingredients as I go. It just all works out. For my cards, I keep the directions basic because everyone has different tastes. I think that's the secret to good cooking. You cook from your gut, your heart." He pointed to his chest. "No one can reproduce anyone's heart. So yes, I share, but it's because if they want it my way, they'll come in. If they follow the recipe, maybe they'll create their own version. No quality cuisine should be reproducible. Food is too much of an organic personalized experience. That's what I want people to have."

"Do you cook the dishes exactly like you would at home?" the reporter inquired.

"Oh no." Shep slapped his knee. "My personal rule for my own food is you can never have enough garlic, mushrooms, carrots, or spices. Obviously, not all people will fancy it. So I tone it down in the restaurant. It's safer to cater to broader tastes."

"What's your favorite item on the menu?"

Shep rubbed his chin and gazed upward in thought. "That's a tough one. I alternate my menu by seasons. I would say for fall and winter, anything pumpkin. I do a mad take on pumpkin grits. I make a mean pumpkin cheesecake. For spring and summer, I would say ribs and Asian style veggie noodles. My banana bread muffins are amazing, but I also rock a savory spicy pineapple upside down cake. Captain Morgan's rum, of course. Extra rum," he noted as he pointed at the reported with his two forefingers.

Watching him answer the reporter's questions, Shep acted more like his old self from our days hanging out in the art club, yet he carried a flare of childlike shyness around him that I didn't notice previously. He stared down frequently and giggled. There was some sweat above his brow that made his forehead shine. Otherwise, he looked beautiful. When his blue eyes met the camera, they beamed into me. Butterflies flew all around my stomach.

For the next week, I drove by The Spare Tire every day after work, protruding my neck outward in hopes of getting a glimpse of Shep either inside or even in the parking lot. One time, I parked my car and sat there for thirty minutes staring at the front entrance. *Maybe he'll walk outside and see me?* But that didn't happen.

I couldn't stop thinking about him. Embarrassing social awkwardness plagued my entire life. I'd buried myself in school at the expense of developing social skills. Somehow, the outgoing and charming Luna still fell in love with me despite it. But she was gone. Now, for the first time since her death, my daydreams were filled with images of Shep and me kissing, holding hands, and even making love. I didn't feel uncomfortable around him. We both loved art and bad poetry. We were nerds with a humor that most people wouldn't understand. I wasn't the principal or the clumsy loser. I was just Elmer.

I hadn't forgotten about my secret desires for men. I'd never spoken about it to Luna. I'd figured that we were married and that a relationship or sex with a man was no longer a possibility. So I let it go. Shep reignited those desires. Even on the news, he looked so masculine that I didn't recognize him, but on the other hand, he appeared the same.

My fears about my job or the community subsided as the daydreams of making love to Shep grew stronger. I needed to see him.

A few more weeks passed in which I often parked outside after work and rehearsed a million things to say in my mind. *Hey, I wanted to check out the new restaurant.* Oh, but it had been opened for four years now. *I was just thinking about you and decided to stop by.* Maybe he wouldn't even talk to me. We hadn't spoken again after that day in the office with him and Tank. I had iced him out.

Finally, I mustered up enough courage to enter the building. It was about an hour from closing, and the crowd was dying down, but everything was still rather lively. The smell of smoked chicken, ribs, and roasted potatoes permeated the air along with the clinks and scraps of silverware on plates. The décor contained images of classic horror films, old punk bands, and anime while the tables and seats were diner style with bright red circular stools and silver counter tops. There was an entire glass display of cookies, cakes, brownies, and other treats toward the cash register. I grinned in awe.

He did it his way.

"Seating for one?" I heard a waiter ask.

"Yes."

The waiter escorted me to a booth in the corner by the window. The kitchen door was in front of me, and I could see the steam and hear the clash of pans behind it. I ordered a glass of tea and browsed the menu, never taking my eyes completely off the kitchen.

From the opposite end of the restaurant, a figure moved around the tables, laughing loudly and refilling water glasses. It was Shep.

"Do you know what you want to order?" the waiter asked when he returned.

"Um . . . what's good?"

"Everything is good. Have you not eaten here before?" he joked.

"No." I flushed.

"What do you like? Chicken? Beef? Spicy? Sweet?"

"What about this spicy Thai turkey burger?" I inquired. "It comes with the sweet potato fries?"

"It's excellent," the waiter said with a wink. "Trust me, I was skeptical of the sweet potato fries, but they're so good.

You won't return to regular fries after eating Shep's. He can caramelize them."

"Like they have sugar in them?" I asked.

"No, it's just the way he roasts them. They get a crunchy caramelization to them. You'll see."

The waiter took the menu, and when he walked away, Shep's gaze met mine from a few tables down. I immediately glanced away.

What am I doing? I have the gall to come in here to see him, and now I'm avoiding him?

I forced my eyes up again and saw his beautiful face smiling back at me. He patted a patron on the shoulder before approaching my table.

"Elm? Is that you?" he asked, placing his hand gently on my back. "I haven't seen you in forever. How are you?"

"I'm good. How are you doing?" I was intrigued with how deep his voice had gotten.

Shep plopped down in the seat in front of me and hollered at the waiter to bring him a beer.

"A black one now! None of that light shit! You want a beer?" he asked me. "On the house."

I nodded, and he threw up two fingers to the waiter who bowed and disappeared behind the bar.

"Have you ever visited my restaurant? I don't think I've seen you here." He rested his arms behind his head.

"I just get busy with work. I've been meaning to come." I kept glancing around to avoid direct eye contact.

"What'd you order?" He nudged me in the shoulder.

Finally looking at him, "The spicy Thai turkey burger."

"One of my favorites," he remarked, pounding his fist on the table. "You'll really enjoy it. Hey, Pete! Cook me up a turkey burger, too," he yelled across the room again, making me flinch. The patrons seemed used to his behavior since their attention never left their plates. Or maybe, they were accustomed to Shep. Yelling, cursing, and obscene jokes painted his character, but his blue eyes and award-winning smile let him get away with it. I chuckled recalling the way he would shout at faculty meetings. Of course, being a coach, Tank was even worse.

"What took you so long to come to my restaurant? You don't like tasty food?" He knocked the bottle cap off his beer using the edge of the table. The waiter promptly picked it up off the floor and hurried off. "So what is it?"

I shrugged. "I've just been busy. You know me. I work late a lot."

"More reason to dine out, isn't it? Less time cooking at home. Plus, Randy delivers here. Delivery from noon to nine. No excuses." He waved his finger.

"I guess not. I'll remember that."

"Pick up a menu on your way out. It has all the information." He took a long gulp of his beer. I swear about half of it glided down his throat like a waterfall in one big swig. He belched. "So what is it *really*?" He squinted his eyes at me. "Are we not friends anymore?"

"Huh?" I gasped, choking on my beer.

Shep laughed. "Relax, Elm. It's a joke. I'm teasing you. Can't help myself. You seem so nervous."

"Oh." Sweat beads formed on my forehead. "I guess I haven't been around you in a while. I'm not used to you being so . . . so—"

"Masculine?" He raised his eyebrows.

"Yeah," I replied. "You also seem so . . . loud."

He snorted. "You think I was going to stay the quiet, scared loser forever? I'm not in that high school now." He scoured the walls of the restaurant, pointing up at a large image of a skull with a pink mohawk. "You see that, there? That's my way of saying I don't give a shit anymore."

"It's a rather interesting décor. I bet Halloween is a blast in here." I chuckled as I held my beer bottle up to toast. He clanked his bottle hard against mine, sending a few droplets of beer on my hands.

"Sorry, dude," he mumbled before continuing. "I took a substantial risk opening this place. Restaurants are almost doomed to fail. But it's just money. I can always find something else to do. I wanted to do something . . . important with that money. If it was going to be risky anyway, then fuck. I'm doing it *my* way. This place" — he pounded his fists on the table again — "is mine. I'll be damned if I'm not going to be *me* in my own damn business."

The waiter came with our burgers, and a strong scent of spicy nuttiness sifted into my nostrils. I stared at the golden honey wheat bun hugging a large white burger with chunks of green onions and mushrooms mashed into it and a peanut butter spice sauce seeping out of the sides.

"Wow," I whispered to myself.

"Damn right," Shep agreed. "I make all my own bread, too. None of that tasteless processed shit. Only wheat, honey, and herbs." He cradled the burger in his hands and raised it up as if offering it to the gods.

"Are you going to feed it to Heaven?" I teased.

"Hell no. This burger's too good for even God." He laughed. He bit off about a fourth of it, and his cheeks puffed out as he attempted to chew. "Yummy," he grunted, motioning for me to try mine.

I picked mine up and savored a little bit of the aroma before taking a bite. Immediately, juices exploded in my mouth, and I relished the chewiness of the mushrooms and the crunchiness of the onions. As I munched, a fierce spiciness melted down my throat and proceeded to make my nose run. I grabbed my napkin.

"Well?" He waited, raising his eyebrows.

"It's spicy." I wiped off my eyes and nose.

"It's my restaurant. Everything's spicy. The good kind

anyway. Not that plain intense heat but a flavorful burn. I learned that in Asia." He took another inhumanely large bite of his burger, causing pieces of bread and meat to fall on his plate.

"It's amazing," I concurred.

"I know you were only educated as a PE teacher, but you can do better than *amazing*," Shep remarked.

"I have my Masters—"

"Yeah, yeah, you got a Master's. That doesn't make up for your vocabulary shortcomings."

I flipped him off while sinking my teeth into another mouthful. He giggled.

"That's more like old times." He gave me a fist bump.

I thought while I ate. "It's . . . super moist—mouth-watering, sorry for the cliché. It falls apart immediately. I can feel the different textures. The sweetness in the peanut butter reduces the intensity of the spiciness. This is turkey?"

"Yeah, turkey. That other white meat that goes gobble-gobble. Pete! Beer," he yelled as he held up his bottle and engulfed the rest of his burger. "Patrons! Last call on orders in ten minutes!"

"Oh, are you closing soon?" I asked, eating faster.

"No, we got another forty minutes, but I like to give my crew a head-start in closing up. You can still order drinks. Just no more food. Except dessert, of course. Which one do you want?" He grabbed the small dessert menu from its holder on the table.

"Dessert? I—" I stuttered before two men approached the booth. Shep gave them a fist bump.

"Good dinner, Shep. Those ribs are amazing!" one of the men stated as he rubbed his belly.

"You enjoy your new spare tires, you hear? Come get another one tomorrow," he told them, waving as they left.

"Why does he get to say amazing?" I teased, gesturing

toward the door.

"His opinion doesn't matter as much as yours." Shep winked. "So back to dessert . . . how about my peanut butter and jelly cheesecake . . . yes. That's it. Pete! PB and J slice! A big one!"

"I don't think I can eat—" I objected before he held his hand up.

"Nope, you're eating it. It's on me. You've only come in here once, so I need to get that spare tire for you." He pointed at my stomach that protruded out on top of my belt. I was always self-conscious about my gut.

A few minutes later, a large slice of cheesecake appeared. It had peaks of whipped cream and purple jelly scattered in a brownish cheese sitting atop of a vanilla wafer crust with a hint of added peanut butter as Shep informed me.

"A peanut butter and jelly cheesecake?" I asked in awe.

"Why not?" He grinned, accentuating his boyish dimples. "You can't go wrong with PB and J. I know you love cheesecake."

His words took me back to one of my birthdays. I'd entered my office that morning to discover an Irish cream cheesecake with caramel and chocolate drizzled in zigzags and whipped frosting piped along the edges. It had been the most incredible experience I'd ever had with my mouth. Beside it was a small purple piece of paper.

Happy birthday to the boss, with this cake, your new diet will be a total loss! Love, Shelly.

"The birthday cheesecake." I sighed in nostalgia. "And the bad poetry."

"Oh, you remember that?" He laughed. "I don't have anyone to write awful poetry to anymore. You should come in here more often. I can leave them on your napkins."

I sliced up a large spoonful of the cake and ate it. The swirls of grape jelly, peanut butter, and rich smooth cheese stuck to my tongue and the roof of my mouth before melting its way down my throat. I realized that I'd closed my eyes.

"It takes you to another place, doesn't it?" Shep commented proudly.

"It's amaz . . . it's sweet and creamy. Fruity and crunchy. It tastes like a PB and J," I remarked, immediately devouring another spoonful.

"Yay. My food tastes like what I say it is," he jested. "That's what happens when you use all fresh homemade ingredients. Real flavor."

By the time I finished what must have been a fourth of the entire cake, most people had left, and the staff was cleaning.

"I guess I better get out of your hair," I said as I brushed some crumbs off the table onto my plate. "How much do I owe you?"

He waved his hand at me. "On the house."

"That was *a lot*! You sure? I feel kind of bad." I pulled a few bills out of my wallet and twirled them in my fingers.

"You can leave Pete a good tip. How about that?" He took the money and laid it down on the table. "Hey, guys! Time to get on out of here," he yelled at the kitchen.

"You're kicking your staff out? Doesn't it take a lot of work to close things down?" I asked.

"Nah, I let them go on home a lot of nights. Most have children or they're in school. I take care of the cleanup myself." He leaned backward, rubbing his neck, which showed off his toned biceps hiding underneath his shirt. He caught me watching.

"Isn't that a bunch of work? How late are you here?" I surveyed the dirty tables around the restaurant.

"It's fine," he replied with a shrug. "I don't have any reasons to hurry home. If I need a night off, they cover it. It works. Seems to keep my employees happy and doing a decent job."

"Okay, we're off." I saw Pete and two others making their

way to the door.

"We'll need to get some more bread made in the morning. One of you give me a hand with that?" Shep asked.

"I can," a woman said as she fumbled with her purse.

"Perfect. Be here around nine."

Shep stood up and stretched after they all vacated. He swigged the last of his beer.

"Well, time for me to get this place cleaned up. I hope you come again." He held out his hand to help me up. Feeling so stuffed that I thought I would pop, I graciously accepted it.

"After all this, I want to come back, but damn, I'm afraid of getting a huge belly!" I rubbed my swollen gut.

He chuckled. "It's all in the name, right?" He pointed at The Spare Tire logo on the plates. "Of course, you can give me a hand, if you want."

"Um, sure. I can do that." *He wants me to hang around?* Suddenly, the old me emerged. It was like we were back in the art club, painting absurdities on each other's arms. I felt at home.

It probably could have taken us only a good hour to clean the place up. But we ended up there past midnight. Shep shared stories about the ways he designed the restaurant, the dishes that he was experimenting with, and his plans to enter a baking competition. I talked about delayed flights on my business trips, how I entertained myself in hotel rooms, and just about anything to avoid talking about the high school. I didn't want any reminder of the way I'd acted toward him.

"What about your art? Your painting?" he asked as we were getting ready to lock the place up.

"I haven't done that in years. Not since—" I stopped myself.

"Not since I left," he finished for me.

"Not since I quit coming to the club." All the joy of the evening vanished, and dread took over.

Shep's smile faded, and he looked down. It was the first

time I'd seen him get serious the whole night.

"Well, let's call it a night," he stated, switching off the lights and pushing me outside. The slight chill in the air tickled my skin, causing goose bumps to pop up. I crossed my arms.

He turned to me and smiled. "It was good seeing you. Thanks for the help. And the chat. Come in on Friday. It's catfish day. You'll love my sweet potato hushpuppies and honey butter."

"What's up with you and the sweet potatoes?" I teased. "Is it that southern grandma thing, again?"

"They're orange and sweet. They're really made for butter. See you later." He winked at me and pounced off toward his car, a tiny *Saturn* that I couldn't figure out how it survived in Montanan winters. I proceeded to my SUV, fumbling with my key, but my heart started pounding. I ran over to Shep.

"Shep, wait," I said. "I want to apologize. I can't sit here with this big elephant in the room between us."

"You felt it, too?" he asked.

I nodded.

"I know I let you down. I let Tank down, too. But me and you . . . I shouldn't have done that to us. You were my friend. I was scared and didn't have the guts to do the right thing by you. I'm really sorry." I reached out my hand. He took it.

"I never held it against you, Elm. Things probably would've ended up the same, anyway. That climate wasn't for me. When Tank died . . . I didn't care about it anymore after that."

"I feel like I left you all alone. I wasn't there when I needed to be." We were still holding hands. My whole body fluttered with nerves and desire. "We had so much fun together during those days in the art club. I missed you."

"I know. But I'm in a better place now. I can do and say what I want. I can be the scruffy embarrassingly unclassy dude here. No more facades. That goes for you, too." He

38

poked his finger at my chest.

"What do you mean?" I asked.

He squeezed my hand. "No more fronts between us. I could use a friend right now, Elm."

"So could I," I replied.

CHAPTER FOUR: SHEP

I spent all night thinking about Elmer's hand. Even when we were hanging out in the art club, I'd noticed the soft, delicateness of his skin. But this was the first occasion that I got to touch him for a prolonged period of time. I remembered every time I'd touched Elmer. The ways our elbows sometimes brushed against each other than lingered, using the fact that he was leaning over to read one of my poems as an excuse to get closer. I could never tell who was initiating the contact. Him or me?

I sunk into my leather couch with my orange cat, Myers, on my lap and located the few pictures I had of us back in those days. There was one with both of us smearing purple paint on each other's faces, and I saw the tears leaking out from my eyes as I laughed. I was staring up, but Elmer was gazing right at me with a boyish grin. There was something different between us.

I had loved Tank. I mourned him daily as I paced up and down the empty house where he and his mother once indulged in my culinary masterpieces. Tank let me be myself. But there was a small part of me that wondered if I'd fallen in love with Tank out of convenience. Yearning for someone was new to me. To be so enamored that the thought of someone penetrated my entire being. Infatuation, they call it.

Why had he come to the restaurant? Why had he stayed? Why had he apologized?

Being transgender and asexual, I surrendered hope easily when it came to dating. No matter how attractive I was or how much scrumptious food I cooked, the sex and the genital issue always hovered over me like a dark cloud even though I was quite satisfied in my own body. After Tank died, I stared at the life insurance money for months. We had purchased a two-hundred-and-fifty-thousand-dollar policy, not to mention the left-over funds from when his mother passed.

I'd considered bottom surgery. I had all the money needed to pay a good surgeon top-price for a pristine phalloplasty, including travel and hotel stay and paying for a home healthcare worker to help me. In the end, I had decided against it.

After the top surgery and the continued progress with testosterone, I finally felt congruent in my own body. My relationship with my vagina had changed. The clit had doubled or even tripled in size within the initial month of hormones, leaving me with uncontrollable erections and intensified orgasms for a while. I had never been shy about masturbating, and of course, Tank hadn't complained about my genitals. About a year after he died, I realized that I didn't identify fully with cisgender men. I stared in the mirror and learned to love my masculine figure but feminine vagina. For the first time, I loved my physique for its unique blend of feminine and masculine. Bottom surgery was no longer a goal.

I didn't feel the way that others felt about sex. As a child, I'd watched movies with sex scenes, assuming that people who cared for each other did it. Then I entered high school where it seemed like everyone raved about it. I had planned to lose my virginity in ninth grade to join in the fun. I wasn't impressed with the first time, so I found three more partners and tried it again, just in case the initial one didn't do it right. Then I'd thought sex must be good when people were in a committed relationship and knew each other well. But that didn't work, either.

I had orgasms. But mostly, I wanted it all to end as soon as possible. When I dated, I'd spend hours dreading it, knowing that there would be this expectation for sex hovering over me the entire evening. I tried dodging it by not being in the mood, having a cold, or being on my period. That only worsened things because the more time that passed, the more aware I was—and my partners—that we hadn't had sex in so long, which made me hate it more. I'd longed to escape to the bathroom, jerk one out, and be on with my day if the urge came. Libido wasn't the issue.

Tank had been a blessing in that sense. His unfortunate medical condition that had made erections difficult to hold or even painful had relieved me from that burden. I masturbated in front of him to give him pleasure and didn't mind finishing him off with a good hand job or through the help of a proper sex toy. There had been no pressure.

As I continued to examine the old picture of Elmer and me, apprehension hung on my shoulders. Until now, dating again hadn't entered my thoughts. I'd noticed Elmer from the moment he arrived at the restaurant because I'd seen his blue SUV parked outside of it for weeks. Like every other time I was ever in the room with him, I caught him staring at me. Now, there was no Tank or Luna. I had this urge to touch Elmer's body with my hands and search all the delicate crevices, but I didn't want it to be sexual.

The next day, I knew that I wanted to keep this new momentum going. So I decided to invite Elmer to dinner at my house under the guise of just catching up some more. I didn't have his phone number, and I certainly wasn't going to go to campus again, even though old colleagues frequented the restaurant. So I called the school.

"Wait, I know that voice. Is that you, Shelly?" the secretary asked, who always insisted on not calling me by my correct name yet hiding it under her overly friendly but nauseating tone. Alice was a regular at the Tire.

"This is Shep, Alice. It's Shep. Not Shelly," I said firmly.

"Oh, sorry. It's so easy to get them mixed up. What are you doing lately?" she asked.

"I don't have much time. Can I talk to Elmer?" I insisted. *What if he doesn't want me to call him? What if this is totally weird?*

"Well, aren't we in a hurry? I'll buzz you through to Mr. Eshler."

The phone rang a few times before I heard his soft elegant voice on the other end say, "Hello."

"Hey," I stammered. My chest tightened.

"Shep?"

"How'd you know it was me?" I gasped.

"I recognize your voice. Um, yeah, sorry, I was in the middle of writing out a long email to the superintendent." He spoke in a monotone, making it difficult to decipher his feelings.

"I can call you later. If you're busy." My guts squeezed into a knot. *I'm a loser.*

"No, it's fine," he said in a more relaxed tone. "I just need to redirect my attention. I'm glad you called. I was sitting here thinking about maybe calling you or stopping by the restaurant again, actually. That turkey burger's been on my mind all morning."

"I make some pretty mean scones, too. I can send Randy over with a dozen for the office. Blueberry, strawberry, peanut butter . . ."

Why must I always resort to food?

"You put peanut butter in everything." He laughed.

"There's nothing better than peanut butter. Most everyone likes it, too, unless they're allergic. I'll send some over. Oh, I have ones made with sunflower butter if anyone's allergic."

"That'll only make me think about you even more," he whispered.

My heart fluttered, and my cheeks grew warm. *Is he flirting with me? Nah, he can't be.*

We'd always teased each other. I guess onlookers may categorize it as flirtatious. Maybe it was? As an asexual, I was cautious with my behavior because I didn't want others to misinterpret it as an invitation for sex. Yet, I still very much craved romantic flirtation with those whom I felt a connection.

"I was thinking," I started, fighting the lump in my throat, "I'm due for a night off at the restaurant. Why don't you come over for dinner at the house?"

"At your house? Not the restaurant?" He sounded confused.

I chuckled. "Trust me, I make the *real* stuff at my house. I have to tone things down at the restaurant because not all my patrons can handle intense flavor. My fucking masterpieces are crafted at home. Plus, I don't get a chance to cook for someone often."

Elmer paused for a moment, which felt like agony as I waited, cracking my knuckles, and biting my lip.

"Um, sorry, I'm looking at my calendar," he mumbled after a minute passed. "I've got a meeting until about six. I can head out after that. Sometimes they run over, but I'll try to leave close to six. What's on the menu?"

"Smoked bourbon and vanilla pork chops with fresh corn simmered in a spicy roasted red pepper butter. Sour cream and chive rolls. Peanut butter nice cream for dessert since it's hot today."

"Nice cream?" he asked, skeptically.

"It's a take on ice cream but made with ripened frozen bananas, cocoa, vanilla, and peanut butter."

"How do you know I'll like it? I don't eat bananas." He seemed a little disgusted.

The defensive chef in me awoke. "Of course, you'll like it. I fucking made it. I don't make any gross food. People eat whatever I order for them all the time at the Tire."

He snorted. "I guess I'm eating whatever you force me to, then."

"I was raised up by a southern grandma. You don't make menu requests with southern grandmas. You eat up whatever they bring you. Free your mind, Elm."

"I can do that. I need some mind-freeing. Is there anything I can bring, at least? You like beer?" Elmer offered.

"Yes, as long as it's not any of that light shit or tasteless crap," I blurted out. Sometimes I was too forward in my communication, and I didn't want to turn Elmer off. But back in art club, I'd talked that way.

"Um, okay. I'm not much of a beer person. What should I get, then?" Elmer asked.

"If it's black, you can't go too wrong," I replied.

"Black beer?"

"Stouts work," I suggested.

"Stouts? Let me write that down. Black . . . stouts," I heard him mumble, and the sound of a pen writing on paper. "Didn't you say that you had bourbon?"

"The bourbon's for cooking not drinking," I informed him.

"Okay. Is this your cell number?" he asked.

"Yes." *He knows my number now.*

"Good. Yeah, I'll text you when I'm heading out. Thanks." Elmer's voice turned serious. "I felt a little nervous after the conversation last night."

I took a deep breath. "You shouldn't. I thought it was pretty darn cool of you to say what you did. The only thing you should've done is talked to me sooner."

In reality, the romantic inside of me was secretly wishing that the elephant in the room that he'd mentioned last night were feelings for me. Elmer's avoidance of Tank and me at the school had hurt. However, he betrayed me more when he stopped coming to the art club. I could've easily sympathized with his reluctance to take an affirmative stance to support us.

After all, he was working in a rural conservative school in a town of only 10,000. But when he stopped attending the meetings, I assumed that *he* didn't want anything to do with me for being trans.

"Elm, I have one question about it," I began, fighting the shakiness in my voice. "I know why you were afraid to publicly support us. But why did you stop coming to the club? Why did you stop talking to me?" My stomach rumbled with jitters, triggering a wave of sadness and lingering betrayal that had been buried there.

He sighed. "I shouldn't have done that. I'm sorry. I purposefully blew it off . . . I didn't want to face you. To have to admit that I failed you." He groaned. "I should have been there for you when Tank died, too."

"I worried that you were . . . I thought you didn't want to be around me anymore for being trans," I confessed as my voice choked up. "I figured that maybe you felt like everyone else."

"No, not at all," he assured me. "I don't care if you're a man or a woman. I'm bisexual . . . um . . ."

My stomach dropped. *Why did he tell me that? Maybe he wants me to know that he's LGBTQIA2S, too? Or maybe it's because he likes me? Is this a disclosure to let me know there's a chance? Nah, can't be.*

My heart sunk as it dawned on me why he wanted to reconnect. There wasn't a visible LGBTQIA2S community in Cloverleaf and being *out* was highly risky. It was clear that he didn't want to be alone. I was being friend-zoned.

"Okay," I replied. "I guess you appreciate what it's like to be different then."

"I see what it's like to be unique in a clandestine way. In fact" —he paused for a few moments— "you're the only person I've ever told that. I can't imagine having to be visible like you've been." He sounded emotional now.

"Thanks for understanding," I said to him. "It can't be easy being bisexual in your position. I'm sure that's hard, too." I tried to sound empathetic while also hiding my disappointment that this dinner wasn't a date.

"I wasn't good to you, Shep. But I would never reject you," Elmer said before we ended the call.

"I know."

I spent all morning envisioning preparing my seductively savory porkchops. It was important to put love into food because it absorbs the energy invested into it. Through cooking, I could express myself with total artistic freedom. I wanted to share it with Elmer.

But as much as I craved getting excited about having Elmer in my home, I had to remind myself that we were just friends. I also wondered if I was capable of that kind of relationship because my heart seemed to have different plans.

CHAPTER FIVE: ELMER

For the rest of the workday, I merely sat in my office chair, nodding and saying *um-hum* in the spaces needed. Really, Shep's food consumed my thoughts. I had no idea what bourbon vanilla porkchops were, nor did I eat pork. But if they tasted as mouth-watering as that turkey burger . . . my stomach already churned and growled. I would be alone with Shep in his home—in his and Tank's house. I wasn't sure where he was in his mourning process even though Tank died years ago. I didn't want to move in too soon.

I finished my meeting, grabbed my papers and keys, and tried darting for the door, when my assistant principal, Karen, entered my office.

"You still need to decide if you want to hire this teacher from Denver," she stated, swinging a human resources packet at me.

I nodded. "Sure, hire him."

"It's a her," she corrected me, squinting at me.

"Oh, yeah, hire her." I bolted for the door, scurrying her out so that I could close and lock it.

"Did you even look at it?" she asked as she pulled out the resume.

"I trust your decision."

She raised her eyebrows. "Since when?"

Karen was right. I never let anyone else make choices because at the end of the day, it was my butt on the line. However, my stomach wanted those porkchops like someone craving heroin.

I snatched the papers from her hand. "What are your concerns?" I asked, flipping through it but not reading anything.

Karen gently removed the documents from my hands, giving a slight covert grin. "It can wait until tomorrow." She smirked.

"What's so funny?" I demanded.

Karen blushed. "You must be seeing someone. I can tell. Only being in love would make you tell me to hire a teacher that you haven't even reviewed. Who is she?" Karen stepped closer with hungry prying eyes.

"No one," I denied.

"Ah-hah." Karen winked at me.

"We'll look at the resume tomorrow."

"I'm just glad to see you dating again," she commented, giving me that look when people think they know what's best for you. "You're so young. You can still have children and a family—"

"I've got to go now. I'm late," I interrupted before hearing the typical rant about the need to hurry up and remarry so that I could have some babies. I didn't require the painful reminder that I was childless.

I flew home to freshen up, throwing off my tight ugly gray suit and slipping into jeans and a David Bowie t-shirt. I often wore my shoulder length brown hair in a neat ponytail for work but decided to let it fall freely along my shoulders. In a matter of five minutes, I transformed from stiff uptight conformity to the scruffy artist that I wished I could be.

As I approached Shep's doorstep, the aroma of smoking wood chips filled the air circulating near his house. My stomach growled, and my mouth watered. I knocked on the door.

Shep opened it but immediately turned around and walked away.

"Hurry up and come in," he yelled. "Don't let my cat out."

I followed his voice to the kitchen where a pan full of fresh ears of corn drizzled with red pepper butter and a basket of rolls sat on the island. A black serving tray with protruding skulls on the sides contained a display of crackers, cheese, and hummus.

"I don't want you to ruin your appetite, but that hummus is homemade. Beats the hell out of store bought," Shep informed me, motioning for me to try it. His hair was shoved into a beanie, and he wore an apron covered in classic horror movie characters tied snuggly around his petite frame. His androgyny fueled a fire inside my chest.

I stuck a cracker into the hummus, scooping up a hefty chunk, and as I placed it on my tongue, Shep threw a beer bottle at me, almost causing me to drop it all over my shirt.

"Oh, shit. I was supposed to bring beer. I totally forgot," I said with a mouthful of food.

"That's okay. I figured you wouldn't buy anything good anyway. I always keep a proper stock for drinking, cooking, whatever. You never know when you'll need a decent beer," he claimed as he grabbed another from the fridge and slammed the top against the side of the counter to open it.

"I guess you don't like bottle openers," I noted, pointing to the cap on the floor.

"Too fancy," Shep remarked. "How's the hummus?"

"Amaze—very flavorful. It's a little sweet." I ate some more. I hadn't ever eaten hummus. It had intimidated me when I saw it in the market. But this tasted phenomenal.

"Caramelized onions," he said.

"Oh." I scooped up another large mound. "I could pig out on this alone."

"Good because I made some for your lunch." He grinned.

"You made me lunch?" I froze. I wasn't used to someone taking care of me like that. At least, not since Luna died.

He slapped my back, causing me to cough. "You'll eat it."

He arranged the food on the wooden dining room table.

Skull napkins and salt and pepper shakers sat in the center of it. I picked one up.

"There's nothing in it," he told me.

"You don't use them?"

Shep held his finger up at me. "You better not butcher my cooking by drowning it in salt and pepper. My patrons can do that, but *you* better not!"

"Okay, okay." I set the shaker back down and stuck my hands up in surrender.

I sliced into the inch thick porkchop. Juices bled out onto the plate. I held the piece up, examining the layer of spices that thickly coated it. Shep stared across the table at me with his arms crossed and an amused smile on his face.

"Go ahead," he instructed. "Flavor won't kill you."

I placed the meat on my tongue and felt more juices squirt out as my teeth cut into it. The spices immediately tickled my nose and throat, making my eyes water. Before I knew it, the piece seemed to dissolve away.

"Wow," I muttered. "It's—"

"Try this now." He shoved a corn cob in my face.

I bit into the fresh crunchy kernels that released an ooze of spicy red pepper butter that dribbled down my chin. As I chewed, he tossed a roll on my plate.

"Eat that," he ordered.

I swallowed the corn down, sneaking a gulp of beer before biting into the roll. The moist dough basically smushed and crumbled as soon as I bit down. It was light but savory with a slight crunch of fresh chives and a creaminess to it.

"Anything else you need to force me to eat?" I teased, taking another drink.

"Not for now," he replied, cutting into his own porkchop.

"Do you want me to tell you how it tastes?"

"Nah." He waved his hand in dismissal. "I know it's amazing." He winked. "I can see it on your face."

I ate two porkchops, three ears of corn and five rolls, feeling my stomach press tighter into my belt with each helping. After finishing two beers, I was stuffed.

"We're not done, yet. The nice cream," Shep stated as he grabbed a cylinder container from the freezer. He scooped three massive helpings into one bowl and a single large spoonful into another. He plopped the enormous one down in front of me.

"I don't think I can finish all this," I whined, holding my belly rolls in my hands.

"You'll eat it," he insisted as he ate a mouthful.

I dug my spoon into the nice cream. A swirl of dark chocolate and banana squished between my teeth and around my tongue. It tasted better than any ice cream I'd ever eaten. Easier on my stomach, too.

"Why are you feeding me so much?" I asked, giggling. "I think I gained ten pounds."

"I figured you probably don't eat enough home-cooking. And I don't get a chance to share my food. Not the blander restaurant safe stuff."

"It's really good. I thought about it all day since you called." Thinking about it only gave me reason to fantasize about him.

"Maybe we can do this more often?" Shep suggested. "I don't ever hang out with people. Not outside the restaurant, anyways."

Butterflies swam frantically in my chest and abdomen. "I'd like that," I agreed.

After dinner, we moved to the living room and chatted about the years since Shep quit his job at the high school. The teacher who replaced him never restarted the art club, nor did she ever offer much help to students who needed it. Our writing scores on the graduation exam had decreased.

"I guess you should've convinced me to stay," Shep joked,

as we stretched out on his sofa, rubbing our tummies as the food digested.

"I should have," I said somberly. Shep had been a valuable employee, but it was more that I missed seeing him every day. The guilt of my own cowardice hung over me.

"You wouldn't have been able to. I was done. I wasn't hanging out there without Tank," Shep remarked. "I was completely isolated."

"How are you doing with that? With him gone?" I asked. I wasn't sure how to ask someone about grief. I wasn't certain what to say when people asked about mine.

"I got used to being alone, I reckon." He shrugged while running his finger along his stomach. "Hell, before Tank, I didn't even think I'd ever marry. I was alone *a lot.*"

"Me, too." I purposely placed my hand close to his that was laying on the couch between us. "I was too gutless to try to date or flirt. Luckily, Luna was the assertive one. She just took charge of it."

"You like that?" he asked. "I figured you were the principal type. I thought you'd be more forward."

"In dating, yes. I'm not one to make the first move. I spent too many hours using studying as an excuse *not* to socialize. I'm surprised I have the skills needed to be a principal." I agonized over rehearsing everything I said to anyone at work. Being around Shep was easy. My whole body relaxed.

"So . . ." He pulled his legs up on the sofa and faced me. "Have you dated men? Secretly? Are you on the down low?"

I choked some on the beer I was sipping. "No. Only a little kiss one time in college during a game, so it didn't mean anything."

"What stopped you?"

"I was too scared about my family . . . my job . . . other people. I was too anxious to —"

"Come out?" he asked.

I nodded. "Yeah. Honestly, I prefer men. Even though I haven't had sex with a man, I think I would favor it. Those feelings have always been stronger."

"Me, too. But I'm open to girls. Romantically, anyway," he told me.

"You're bisexual, too?" I turned to him. Suddenly, the attraction to him intensified.

"Yes." He smiled. "But I haven't dated any women. Not since some high school experimentation."

"Do you even date?" I asked. I held my breath as I waited for his response.

"Nope. I spend my time managing and cooking in a restaurant." He smirked. "When you think about it, food is more erotic anyway. The way it awakens your entire body and seizes your thoughts when you get that whiff of decadence up your nose. The high. The strong urge to overindulge, and the constant battle not to. Also, the reluctance. Some people struggle to fully let go in bed just as they struggle to give in to unknown culinary pleasures. It's strange how people find trying new foods so risky."

His eyes sparkled in the lamp light as I admired his philosophical comparison of sex with food. "I guess it *is* a lot like sexuality," I agreed, grinning. "Do you ever wonder if more people are bisexual or may discover that they like sex with some people, but they refuse to try it?"

"I think that all the time," Shep stated.

I'm not sure how the routine began, but I ended up having dinner nearly every night with Shep. Sometimes it was late into the evening if he needed to close the restaurant. On those days, I stopped by to help him in which he continually proceeded to send me home with a lunch for the next day from whatever leftovers he had around. For three months, I experienced cumin-infused dry rub ribs, smoked catfish, corned beef and cabbage, and even boiled cow tongue in a savory thick vegetable sauce. I consumed strawberry sandwich cookies, lemon meringue pies, spiced banana cupcakes with chocolate buttercream frosting, and orange cream-sickle cake. I had probably about twenty different exotic dark beers to wash it all down. By that point, I wasn't positive if it was love or food addiction that left me helpless against my infatuation with Shep.

CHAPTER SIX: SHEP

The more that Elmer hung out at my house, the more that nothing happened, only reinforcing my friend-zone status. We ate, we drank, and we spent hours late into the evening sometimes talking. We chatted about our childhoods, our dreams, our fears, everything. I needed a friend. But every night that he left, my heart fell into a void. I constantly fought against my thoughts as I entertained fantasies of Elmer holding me in his arms or kissing me.

One evening, we decided to drag out some old art supplies. Finger painting was our method of choice, and Elmer created a landscape scene with a river flowing through a valley, but it was all in tones of red and purple.

"I think people look at river scenes and think about cool colors. Relaxing hues," he said as he examined his picture. "They miss the heat that's there but often ignored. The energy swirling all around it. What did you do?" Elmer asked, peering his head at my canvas.

I held it up revealing a large green cucumber isolated on a plain brown countertop with its shadow shaded in.

"What's that mean?" he asked.

I studied the image for a moment. "I think cucumbers are misunderstood. My cat is terrified of them. You don't find them as common ingredients unless it's a sandwich or salad. Hardly ever in hot dishes. They're lonely. The lonesome cucumber. Yes, that's the title for it." I wrote *The Lonely Cucumber* on top of the canvas.

"Why do you think they're left out of hot plates?"

"Because maybe they don't like the heat so much," I guessed. "Maybe they're meant for the cold recipes. But you can serve lots of cold dishes that aren't just salads and sandwiches. If you put some imagination to it. That's the problem. Not many people are that imaginative. They only want the spicy stuff. A cucumber may not be able to give you that."

"I never thought much of cucumbers before. Do you feel like a cucumber?" Elmer inquired, holding my canvas up to the light.

I glanced at his picture. "Do you feel like a hot stream?"

"Maybe sometimes." He compared our canvases side by side. "I think people look at me and only see the cool colors. What they want to see. They don't see me."

"What do you mean?" I asked him.

He stared at his painting. "I have to play a role most of the time. I have to be professional. I get judged by a different standard. So people see the coolness. They don't see me as a . . ." He hesitated.

"Go on," I encouraged him.

"A man. An artist. Someone passionate. Someone . . . sexual."

Sexual. My chest tightened.

"I guess people overlook me because like a cucumber, they see no use of me," I stated. My cucumber looked lonelier to me now. *People prefer the hot dishes. The sex.*

Elmer laughed. "Use for you? With all that incredible food you cook?"

"I don't fit in with the lifestyles of other people," I confessed. I stared down.

"Good, neither do I." Elmer nudged me with his elbow and smiled.

I swallowed hard, feeling my Adam's apple rise and fall. "What I'm trying to explain is that I'm asexual." *Why did I just say that?* I feared that Elmer would freak out, even as a friend.

"Asexual?" His forehead wrinkled in confusion. "Like you . . . don't have relationships with people? Isn't that what asexuals are? They don't want to date people?" Elmer hammered out questions with a surprised but concerned look on his face.

"I have relationships with people. Aromantic is when you don't have romantic attraction," I corrected him. "I'm asexual. It means I don't experience sexual attraction." *He told me how erotic he is. This is definitely going to sabotage any chance between us.*

Elmer stared down at the canvases, picking at the ends with his fingers. His face looked tense.

"You don't have the desire to have sex?" he questioned after a few moments but still evading my eyes.

His avoidance of looking at me filled me with dread. "I get horny sometimes. I can have orgasms. I guess you can say that I'm okay with having sex with myself. Just not so much with others." It felt good to get it off my chest, but at the same time, my heart was racing.

His wrinkled forehead indicated that he was thinking hard about this "So like . . ." His hands trembled. "You wouldn't want to have sex with *me*, for example? If we were in that situation?"

My soul lit up. *He's referring to us having sex.* "Are you propositioning?" I teased him, giving him a slight shove in the side to lighten things up. He grinned slightly but mostly remained serious. "It's hard to explain." I flushed. "It took a lot to bring up the asexuality. I wasn't ready for a convo about *us* having sex."

He continued to fiddle with the canvases.

I took a deep breath and clinched my fists. "Okay, yes, I'd do it with you." *Oh my God, I said it!* My stomach exploded with all kinds of jitters. "But it wouldn't be because I look at you and think that I physically want you, like sexually — or for your body — ugh, it's hard to explain. I'd want to because . . ."

58

My words trailed off as I realized that this meant exposing my feelings for him. The night's dinner rumbled in my gut, sending a wave of nausea up into my chest.

"I'll try this again," I pathetically continued. *Damn, things didn't feel this complicated with Tank. Why does he make me so nervous?* "Um . . . I've had sex with people because I have feelings for them. So on the one hand, part of it is making them happy. But I feel closer to the person, too, so it has an advantage for me. I appreciate the intimacy, even though I don't enjoy it the same way." I held my breath after I said it.

"Well, what do you do?" he inquired. "Just . . . lay there? Or, sorry, I guess . . . make yourself hump someone?" His shoulders tensed up.

"Okay, we're getting *that* personal. Um, I don't hump people. I haven't done that. I haven't gotten the other surgery," I told him, motioning toward my crotch. "Honestly, I can't say that I participate much in it compared to maybe other people. I don't care for intercourse. I'm more comfortable with other things. There's other things, you know."

"Does that mean that I can't . . . touch you?" Elmer asked finally making eye contact but now forcing me to glance away.

My mouth dropped open. "Do you want to touch me?"

"I mean," he stuttered. "You wouldn't want me to, right? You're not attracted to me."

"Is this about asexuality or about you and me?" My heart fluttered but also sank.

"Both," he responded.

I exhaled slowly and placed my palm over his hand. He looked at me with his long hair flowing over his eyes. He turned his chair to face me and wrapped his fingers around mine. We sat still, staring into each other's eyes.

"Oh," he said suddenly, pulling out his cell phone. "I didn't realize it's so late. It's nearly two."

"Yeah, it's pretty late. You look tired. Do you want to crash here?" *Did I just ask that?* He only lived a short walk away, so sleeping over didn't make any sense.

"Sure." He smiled. "That'd be great. I didn't even realize how sleepy I am. You want me to sleep on the couch?"

He said yes. I adjusted in my seat to hide my jitters. "You can sleep there," I answered after gathering my composure. "You're welcome to share the bed, too. If you're not weirded out by that kind of thing," I suggested.

"I'm not. I shared beds with friends in school."

He called me a friend. My hope dissipated.

We put all the art materials away. I had a large Texas King mattress to fit Tank's massive body. So there was plenty of room for two platonic people to rest peacefully.

"Do you mind if I sleep in my boxers?" I asked him. "I get hot, but if it's weird—"

"No. I sleep in mine, too."

I stole glances at him undressing. Even though it wasn't sexual, seeing Elmer, the big principal, in his boxers excited me. It was a side of him that no one saw, and I was drawn to that.

We climbed into bed, which was quite messy since I didn't plan to wash the sheets until the next day. Elmer turned on his side, facing me.

My heart was thrilled to hear him breathing beside me, but my nerves were all over the place. *Should I do something? No, he's just a friend.*

My thoughts raced and my heart thudded until finally, after an hour, I drifted off. I don't know what time it was when I heard Elmer whispering.

"Shep?"

"Hmm?" I moaned, opening my eyes. "Something wrong?"

"Can I kiss you? Is that okay?"

I sat up a little on my side, and he followed.

"Yes," I answered. I wasn't sure if I was dreaming or awake.

Elmer gently pressed his soft dry lips against mine. He pulled away slightly, trying to make out my facial features in the darkness. Then he kissed me again.

"Good night," he said as he laid back down and closed his eyes.

I froze. *Is he sleepwalking or something? Sleep-kissing?* He snored. *Yes, he must be dreaming. Who the hell does this?*

I spent another good hour staring at him, trying to see if he would wake up and randomly kiss me again. But Elmer continued sleeping and occasionally kicked me in the shin with his feet.

I woke up first the next day. It was Sunday. The Tire only opened for lunch and dinner, so we usually didn't show up until a little later in the morning to prepare. Elmer didn't move. I got up and decided to find something to make for breakfast. Opening the fridge, I found some shredded carrots, milk, and eggs. I decided to make scrambled eggs with carrot cake pancakes.

Elmer didn't emerge until the pancakes had scented the house with cinnamon and nutmeg, and the aroma from the few pieces of bacon I mixed in with the eggs perfumed the kitchen. He still only had his boxers on, and with his hair all disheveled, he looked like a teenage boy. He stood only about five foot seven, a few inches shorter than me, so he was far from the behemoth that Tank was.

Rubbing his eyes, he said, "That smells great."

"Good, I hope you're hungry."

"You didn't have to go to the Tire?" he asked as he began cutting his pancakes with a fork.

"Not until after two today. Pete and Sal will be there until then." I usually went to the Tire every morning, but I'd texted

Pete and Sal to see if they would cover for me. I didn't want to leave Elmer.

We sat on the barstools of the kitchen island, chewing, slurping coffee, and not saying a damn word. Elmer hardly looked at me. My stomach was so tight that I almost gagged on the food.

After we finished, I collected the dishes and started cleaning up. Elmer remained silent.

"About last night," he began after a few minutes.

My shoulders rose with tension as if to shield my face even though my back was turned to him.

"Yeah, what about it?" I asked coolly.

"I guess I shouldn't have kissed you. I'm sorry about that."

My heart pounded in my chest, and I squeezed the kitchen cleaner spray so hard that my knuckles turned white.

"I didn't want to . . . how do you feel about it?" he asked. The words came out slowly as if he was scared.

I turned around and threw the kitchen cloth in my hand at him, letting it hit him in the chest.

"I think you shouldn't kiss people if it doesn't mean nothing," I shouted.

"Huh?" Elmer stood up with his eyes wide open.

"You heard me. You don't wake folks up in the middle of the fucking night, kiss them, go back to sleep, then tell them the next day that you shouldn't have done that. You're playing games," I accused him, fighting off tears. I turned away from him and leaned against the stove.

"Wait, Shep," he pleaded, walking over to me.

"You don't do that. Even if you just want to be friends, you don't play mind tricks with your friends like that," I said, still not facing him.

"I'm sorry, Shep. Fuck," he stammered, placing his hands on my shoulders. "I was worried that I forced you to do something that you didn't want to do. You haven't said anything all morning about it. So I thought . . . I was wrong. It wasn't a mistake. It was . . . what I always wanted."

I swung around. Elmer's hands shook timidly, and his face was forlorn. I gazed into his deep brown eyes that stared back with yearning.

"It was?" I whispered.

"Yeah. Ever since I met you. I know we were both married, but . . . I got this feeling with you. I wanted to be close to you all the time."

"What are you saying that you want, Elm?"

"I want to be with you. I want us to be together. A couple. Is that what you want?" He searched me with his eyes.

"I'm dying to be with you," I confessed with a huge relief in my chest. "I had felt something for you, too."

Elmer smiled and leaned forward, moving some of my thick hair away from my eyes. "May I kiss you?" he asked.

This time, I slung my arms around his neck and yanked him into me, nearly causing both of us to fall over. Elmer grabbed my waist and squeezed me tight. The kiss was so passionate that I thought we might suck each other's faces off. Elmer's hands slid all over my back and hips.

We parted, both gasping for air and grabbing the gray granite countertops to balance ourselves.

"Wow," he panted, "What was *that*?"

"I have no idea. I ain't never kissed no one like that before. It's a little . . . arousing," I admitted. My whole body awakened with a thousand balls of excitement ricocheting everywhere. Romance intoxicated me, and I wanted to feel him pressed against me again.

"Do you want to do what I want to do?" He waited for consent.

"Do I want to have sex?" I blurted out.

"If you put it that bluntly, then yes. I mean, we can do it whatever way you want or feel comfortable with."

I grabbed his hand and led him back to the bedroom. The dream of holding Elmer and having him all to myself inebriated me so excessively that I don't know how much attention I paid to the sex itself. I was too inundated with romance and the ideal image of him that had lingered in my mind for so long . . . and in my heart. When his smooth warm skin rubbed against my bare chest, butterflies swooned all through my body in ecstasy. As he thrusted inside of me, resting his forehead on mine and staring into my eyes, I burned from my loins up to my chest. I pulled him closer, squeezing his butt. I kissed him, held him, and cherished him.

I called into the Tire that day, and Pam was accommodating in taking care of things for me. Pam was basically my assistant manager, and Pam and Bank, our other cook, knew all the recipes well enough to oversee the dinner service for an evening. Besides, I never missed work, and Pam agreed that I should enjoy some slack time. Elmer and I laid in bed, pressing our naked bodies together.

"I'm surprised that you're comfortable like this," Elmer commented, running his hand along my abdomen.

"I said I'm asexual. I didn't say I had problems with nudity. Look at this body." I flexed my arm muscles. "Would you have a problem with being nude with this build?"

"I love your body. I love that you . . . is it strange for me to say that I love that you're a man with a . . . you know . . ."

"A man with a pussy," I finished for him.

Elmer laughed and blushed. "God, I forgot how raunchy you are."

"No, it's cool," I told him. "I'm nonbinary anyway. I've grown to love my physique as it is. The perfect balance between the two genders harmonized together in this beautiful physique. It's like a work of art." I sat up. "We should fingerpaint our nude bodies. Commemorate this moment."

Before he could speak or move, I leapt from the bed and

retrieved the paint from the night before. Elmer threw the sheets off of him.

We played around, drawing assorted designs all over each other, and giggling profusely. Then we rubbed our bodies together to mix the different colors.

"I thought you'd be way more against this," Elmer stated.

"I said I struggle with sex. I didn't say I had a problem with nonsexual touching. I'm not uptight."

A pang of insecurity ran through me with that comment. I was unsure if Elmer truly understood the meaning of asexual. Examining him, he looked so beautiful in his own nudity with his little tummy that protruded out, his long hair, and his boney legs with gobs of curly hairs. The blues, the reds, the greens, and all the unusual shades of paint covered him.

"What will work say?" I asked him. "About us. It's a small town. I figure that eventually, people will know."

"I'll deal with it. They can't just fire me," he assured me. His confidence surprised me given his previous behavior.

"That place does a damn dandy job at making you want to leave, though," I argued, placing my hands on my hips. I knew Elmer loved his position. I didn't want to be selfish in doing anything to jeopardize it.

"But I'm the boss. I have authority." He took my hand. "And I'll use it this time. I promise."

"I guess that was mine and Tank's whole point," I blurted out before realizing that I totally killed the mood. "We thought you'd protect us."

"I know. You two were right," Elmer agreed, rubbing my cheek with his palm. "I'm not allowing that to happen again." He threw his arms around me. "Shep, let's move in together."

"*Now*?" I gasped. I was letting the day's events sink in. Moving in together wasn't even on the radar.

He shrugged. "Why not?"

My mind blanked, but my heart pounded. "Because we

became a couple like two seconds ago."

He grinned, which revealed the lovestruck naivety in him. "We've been a couple way longer than before this. I want to do it. I'm over here every night. I only go home to sleep and get ready for work the next day. Plus, I dreamed about this for so long. I always wanted you. I longed to be with a man. Let's dive into it."

My mouth gaped open. I hadn't pictured Elmer as this adventurous person who would jump into a relationship without precautions. He'd seemed so reserved and even fearful. I didn't know where this side of him came from. But I agreed. He had his own house if things soured. *What harm could it do to let him move in here?*

Three months later, we flew to Las Vegas and got married.

Chapter Seven: Elmer

I fell madly in love with Shep. Being with a man felt more natural to me and even made me feel more masculine myself. We moved into Shep's house since he adamantly refused to abandon his kitchen, and I rented mine out, fully furnished, to Snavis' wife's little sister and her children. I felt weird living with him in the same home that he shared with Tank, but he was cool about it. We bought new furniture, painted the walls black and purple, and changed it into *our* home the best we could. He hung a large poster of David Bowie in the bedroom for me, which eased a lot of my discomfort.

Not many people commented about our relationship until we got married, especially when I took Shep's name. I mostly dealt with whispering and glares, but it wasn't too bad. I kept a picture of Shep holding up a pineapple upside down cake on my office desk, but otherwise, I didn't talk about it. It wasn't anyone's business. And since I didn't bring it up, it was easier for people to ignore it.

One day I was monitoring the hallways and overheard two teachers gossiping around the corner.

"How could he shame Luna like that? She was such an angel. She would die if she knew what he's doing," a woman's voice stated.

"Maybe he's confused," another voice replied. "He may have a harder time since her death than we thought. It's too bad. Just think, he'll never have any children."

I turned down their hallway, and the two teachers jumped before hurrying off to their classrooms.

It wasn't the first occasion someone mentioned the impact that my new marriage would have had on Luna. People had frequently reminded me that I was childless as if I was doomed because of it.

Luna hadn't known that I would hide away in my office in the evenings, crying about the kids that we couldn't have. There were other means to fulfill my life, but I wanted to experience the parent and child bond, and I wanted my *own* biological children. I craved to hear a little mini-Elmer scream, *Daddy, Daddy,* at me. I wanted to hold their hands while we trick and treated around the neighborhood, even finding ways to scare them on Halloween. I fantasized about Christmas mornings where I could spoil them with lavish toys. But I'd loved Luna, so I'd written it off as a dream that wasn't meant for me. So marrying Shep didn't make any difference. And I craved to be with a man more than anything.

In the beginning of my marriage, our sex life didn't seem extraordinary. Or maybe it was because I hadn't had a sexual relationship with anyone for so many years, so *any* sex felt like a lot. It was about a solid year into things that I started noticing that Shep wasn't into it. We did it a few times a month, but it finally dawned on me that he never initiated it. In fact, he didn't show much affection aside from hugging, cuddling, and some kissing. The first time we made love, it was the most sensual experience I'd had. But I began to wonder if perhaps I wasn't very good at it. Or worse, perhaps he didn't love me like I loved him.

We were eating dinner at the Tire one night after everyone left before beginning the nightly cleaning routine. It was pizza night. Shep offered many diverse types of homemade crusts, such as garlic herb, spelt flour, and spicy wheat. Customers could choose any toppings with a choice of his signature marinara, pesto, or alfredo sauces. I'd selected the white pizza, topped with fresh mozzarella, asiago, and parmesan cheeses and arugula. Shep chowed down on Hawaiian pizza with pineapple, Canadian bacon, and mozzarella. We consumed the entire pizzas by ourselves. They were *that good.*

"I feel a little awkward bringing this up," I stated after swallowing my last scrumptious bite. "I don't want to make you mad."

"When do I ever get mad?" Shep remarked, as he started to pick up the dishes. I grabbed his arm to stop him.

"Can you sit for a minute?" I asked. He set the plates down and plopped down in his seat.

"Shep, I love you."

"Of course, you do! Who wouldn't?" he joked, throwing his arms up in the air.

I took a deep breath. "I don't want to make you feel bad, but . . . I guess I don't understand why you don't want to have sex."

"Oh, we're having *that* convo." He groaned as he slumped forward. "Okay, well, I did tell you that I'm asexual from the very beginning."

"I'm not sure what exactly that means," I admitted. A lump formed in my throat. I needed to talk to him, but I also didn't want to start a fight.

"Have you looked it up?" he asked.

"No."

"Read any books?" He raised his eyebrows at me.

"No."

"Joined some *Facebook* forums?" He leaned forward, placing his elbows on the table.

"No." A sense of shame burrowed deep inside my abdomen.

Shep snorted. "So how much effort have you put in to try to understand what that means? Don't you think you should've tried to get it before Vegas?"

"You're getting defensive," I accused him. I didn't

appreciate his smug response, but I understood. He was *very* sensitive about sexual discussions.

He rubbed his forehead. "Fine. Sorry, my bad. What are you confused about?"

Frankly, I was stupefied about *everything*! Shep had said that he didn't feel the urge to have sex with other people. At the same time, he still got horny and masturbated. I didn't know how he could get aroused but not want to make love to me. I would choose a partner rather than doing it alone.

"Like, how often do you masturbate?" I asked, clamping my hands together.

He shrugged. "I'm not sure. Maybe a few times a week. Sometimes less. Sometimes more. I don't keep count. Do you know how much you masturbate?"

"So you're horny a lot?"

He stared at me a moment. "Sometimes. I do it occasionally to relax. I found Monday morning masturbations in the shower as a pretty helpful way to begin the week," he told me nonchalantly.

I scrunched my face up in confusion. "But . . . like even when you're in the mood, you don't feel the urge to come get me? I can help you with that, too."

Shep's expression turned serious, and he peered at me for several moments. "We have sex. To me, I think we fuck regularly. Do you not think we do?"

"I would love to do it more," I replied. His gaze intimidated me. "Besides, don't you think that you might feel differently about it if you didn't always refer to it as *sex* or *fucking*? That makes it sound so mechanical. I see it as making love. It's because we love each other, right?"

He sighed. "I guess it's making love because I love you, and I'm doing it for you."

"You don't feel like you're making love to me?" I asked jerking away and placing my hand over my heart. The concept that he only had sex with me to appease me filled me with dread.

"It's hard to explain, Elm. I enjoy seeing you happy. I like holding you. Honestly, I don't know." He ran his fingers through his shaggy hair and rubbed his temples. "Sex seems so . . . basic compared to all the other ways I can love you. It isn't the only way to love someone."

"Why don't you approach me when you feel horny?" I wasn't letting him avoid the question.

He shielded his eyes with his hand. "It's just a physical urge. It has nothing to do with another person. Body parts become aroused. People get horny sometimes." His voice sounded a little shaky.

I sat with my mouth gaped open. "But why don't you come get me?"

"Because, Elm, I'm kind of sex averse. Some aces can still be sex positive and even enjoy it. I'm certainly not saying when you go down on me or touch me that it doesn't feel good. It does." He looked upward as if searching for the right words. "It's like if you had to force yourself to have sex with an ugly person . . . someone you're really not attracted to. You could do it. Your orgasms should work. But it isn't something you necessarily want to do."

My hands trembled slightly, and anxiety circulated through my body. Shep noticed and took my hand.

"Is that how repulsive you find me?" I asked, fighting back tears. "You have to force yourself? Was it that way with Tank?"

He squeezed my hand. "Elm, I didn't mean it like that. You're beautiful and incredibly attractive."

I just wasn't grasping the disconnect. *How could I be attractive but not sexy?* I was a little shorter with a big belly and no sense of style. *Maybe I'm not sexually alluring? Am I the problem?* Staring at Shep, he was naturally exotic. His black hair was long enough that his bangs draped across his almost turquoise blue eyes. His lips were full, covering his pristine white teeth that shined along with his dimples when he smiled. A near perfect six-pack covered his abdomen, and I could see all the muscular hills and crevices that aligned his thin frame from all his early morning workouts. I had no idea how to control myself around someone so exquisite.

"Maybe I need to lose some weight," I suggested, pinching my stomach.

"You don't need to do anything," Shep assured me, placing his hand on my abdomen. "It has nothing to do with that."

"I only slept with one other person. Perhaps I'm not very good at it. Like what if we bought some toys? Would that help?" I offered. I couldn't resist the notion that enhancing our sex life was the answer. Maybe we were both inexperienced.

"If you want to try toys, I'm fine with it," he agreed. "But it's not going to change the fact that I'm ace. We could do the most spectacular fucking imaginable, but I'm still me at the end of the day. I don't want you blaming yourself for this." He brushed my chin with his hand and gave a slight smile.

"We don't do much when we make love. We should try something new," I encouraged him. "You never let me do it doggystyle, and I always wanted to try it."

"You're not fucking me like a dog," Shep snapped. "I'm sorry that I can't satisfy your sexual interests. It's hard enough for me to do it already. Acrobatics in the bedroom . . ." He groaned. "That'll only make it worse."

"We can do something else then."

"There's nothing else to fucking do, Elm!" He stood up and stomped off behind the bar, grabbing a beer. He kept his back to me.

I stayed glued to the seat of the diner booth, fiddling with a fork, and absorbing the vast distance that hovered in the air between us. I wanted to go pick him up in my arms and make this all vanish. Instead, I sat there.

We didn't talk about it again for weeks. At work one day, I typed in asexuality in *Yahoo*. One of the first results was the Asexual Visibility and Education Network or AVEN. The line at the top of the page read,

An asexual person is a person who does not experience sexual attraction – Learn More.

I clicked the *Learn More* button that took me to an overview page.

An asexual person does not experience sexual attraction – they are not drawn to people sexually and do not desire to act upon attraction to others in a sexual way. Unlike celibacy, which is a choice to abstain from sexual activity, asexuality is an intrinsic part of who we are just like other sexual orientations.

A sexual orientation? I'd never heard of anything beyond being gay or bisexual. I continued reading the page, coming across the section entitled *Arousal*.

For some asexual people, arousal, sometimes interchanged with libido in asexual dialogue, is a fairly regular occurrence, though it is not associated with a desire to find a sexual partner or partners.

It said exactly what Shep was telling me, yet it was strange to see it in writing. A later paragraph went on to clarify that asexuality was not the same as medical conditions concerning low sexual desire because in those cases, the person faced distress for not having sexual needs met.

Was Shep distressed?

He hadn't initiated sex, but he certainly never seemed

bothered by it. He hugged me, kissed me, and cuddled with me, but otherwise, he did his Shep thing. I didn't notice any anxiety or negative feelings from him about it. All I knew was that *I* was unhappy.

He was right that sex wasn't the only way to show love. Shep was a funny caring person. He often provided seniors discounted meals, even having Randy deliver them in the winter so that they didn't need to leave their home. Living in a low-income community, he offered coupons in the weekly papers, two-for-one nights, and free dinners on birthdays. He sometimes worked seven days a week and gave his employees generous leave time and health benefits, which drained a great deal of his profits. Once a month, he provided cooking classes at the local college to promote healthy eating.

Shep was also a wonderful spouse. He not only cooked me fancy delectable dinners, but he paid close attention to my likes. He surprised me with a smoked beef brisket on my birthday when he never ate beef, but he knew that I was fond of it. He rubbed my temples when I got headaches. My clothes were cleaned and ironed for work even though I had no clue when he found the time to do it. Yet there on Monday morning, my fresh suit and shirts were ready. More importantly, he made me feel great about myself. I admired him and wished many nights that I could be him. In many ways, Shep was my hero.

We were taking a short walk around the neighborhood one late evening. In Montana, summer sunsets were long with sunlight often stretching out into the ten o'clock hour. We loved our walks because they gave us time to debrief from the day.

I held Shep's hand in mine. There weren't many people nearby as we walked through some of the back ranch roads near our neighborhood.

"So I read some about asexuality," I told him.

"Oh?" He mumbled.

"I'm sorry about not approaching it the right way. Honestly, it just seemed so abnormal to me like something must be wrong. I didn't realize it was a sexual orientation."

"So you get it?" he asked, staring off into a field.

"I don't know if I *get* it, necessarily. I think I understand it more. There's still this part of me that wants to believe that I can change it somehow or that you can. It's hard to wrap my mind around it." I squeezed his hand. I didn't want him to become angry with me again.

"I know. I'm sorry I get so snappy about it," he apologized, looking down. "I guess I'm insecure about it sometimes."

"You are?" I knew that Shep had uncertainties, but he also hid them very effectively. To me, I thought he could do *anything*. So seeing him scared felt strange.

"I wish I wasn't," he shared with me. "But we live in a sex-crazed world . . . or at times it feels that way to me. I feel like people . . . well, more that *you* won't like me because of it."

I put my arm around him.

"I love you. That's not going to change," I assured him, kissing him on the cheek.

"Are you happy sexually? Be honest with me." He stopped walking and turned toward me.

I froze. I certainly didn't want to hurt Shep or make his insecurities worse. At the same time, I wasn't satisfied. We did it a few times a month, and it seemed that he was merely tolerating it. I wanted to have more sex, but I also didn't want to make him uncomfortable in the process just to fulfill my own needs.

"No," I replied.

It was the longest word ever uttered from my lips. Surrounded by never-ending open space, a heavy weight pressed down upon us. I grabbed his small hand in mine, he appeared so far away. His fingers tensed up in my grasp.

"Shep, I don't want to hurt you. That's not the intention."

He clearly avoided my eyes, gazing off into the prairie. I caught a tear trinkling down his face. I wrapped my arms around him again, pulling him closer. We stood silent. The evening crickets and moos from the nearby cows filled the air. Feeling the burning desire inside of me and the desperate clinging from Shep as his arms squeezed my torso, I knew that our hearts were in the same place, which gave me hope.

"I don't want you to be unhappy," he told me. "You deserve better."

"There's nothing wrong with you. I deserve you." I gripped him tighter.

He sighed. "I know. I mean that you deserve to be happy. If you're miserable, that's not good."

I kissed him. "You make me so happy," I insisted. "You're the first person who ever made me feel like I could be myself. You're helping me learn who I am. You're amazing."

"There you go again with those empty nondescriptive words," he teased.

I placed my hands on his cheeks and tilted his head to face me. "Shep, you're a talented cook. You put your soul into it. You're also awkward as fuck and scream across the room, but people seem to like it. You were a loving caring teacher. You're an attentive and supportive spouse. You think that I don't notice that you've been having sex to make me happy?"

"So what do we do?" he asked, searching my face for reassurance.

"I don't know," I said, holding his hand up to my lips and kissing it. "But we'll figure it out, okay? That's what we'll do."

We continued strolling down the vacant dirt road, looking out to an infinite horizon that was fading under the setting sun. Darkness began to cloak us when we turned to head home, and I could barely decipher Shep's face anymore. By the time we reached the house, blackness befell us.

CHAPTER EIGHT: SHEP

I can't say that I've ever been a jealous person. Dating had always been difficult for me. I had the looks but not the personality. Many times, when I didn't get suspicious about my partners talking to other people, my dates had viewed it as indifference then dumped me. I hesitantly approached relationships because I didn't know what the sexual expectations would be or if my asexuality would ruin everything. My timidness also left my ex-boyfriends seeking greener pastures. Tank was the only one who pursued me, and his insecurities around his own sensual issues had been comforting. Reminiscing, I appreciated a spouse who, like me, feared rejection from others from being sexually different.

I wasn't angry because Elmer had sexual needs. However, I couldn't satisfy him. Worse, any physical affection challenged me. A short kiss here and there was tolerable, but if it turned into making out, disgust emerged. The monotonous motion of opening the mouth and moving tongues generated a feeling of invasiveness. *How long is this going to last? How much longer do I have to pretend that I like it?*

Hugs and cuddling were nice unless they started to morph into the sexual realm. Elmer and I could snuggle under a cozy weighted blanket on the couch, but then his hands would start touching my body. He would make these moaning sounds, which were probably more related to love but to me, felt sexualized. Sometimes, my face would instinctively cringe, and I would pull away when he reached for me. Immediately, guilt, shame, and embarrassment flooded over me. The last thing I wanted was for Elmer to feel like he repulsed me. I hated it.

I'd first come across asexuality when I randomly watched a documentary one night called *A-Sexual*. Initially, it was a strange concept to me. However, when a man shared his experience of cuddling with another person and enjoying it until kissing became involved, a light went off in me. I enjoyed sex at times, but it was more about the romantic high than anything else. In the few somewhat lengthy relationships I had prior to Tank, sex had occurred early and frequently but then faded away. I guess I'd viewed it as a means to progress intimate connections. Then once those were formed, the naïve part of me wanted to believe that it wouldn't matter anymore.

I had finally accepted that asexual fit me. *What did that mean?* After all, there are some asexuals who remain virgins. I wasn't. *Did that make me an imposter?*

When I'd had sex with people I loved, I didn't feel violated. However, I laid there, inactive, and sometimes squeamish from the juicy noises, kissing, and pounding on top of me. The pressure to linger in bed snuggling afterwards tortured me as my genitals sat marinating in bodily fluids, and I feared that my partner would want to do it again.

I had tried with Elmer. He had made me feel like a middle school kid with his first crush. I'd fallen head over heels. The romantic attraction had burned inside me, allowing me to ignore my aversion because pleasing him and feeling so close to him fulfilled me.

After we'd surpassed that phase, my true nature reemerged. However, Elmer seemed more confused.

One night, I was preparing dinner. It was a simple meal of farro, blueberries, carrots, fresh lemon, and walnuts toasted in butter. As a cook, the mixture of textures fascinated me. There were few non-meat dishes that didn't include a chewy sweet fruit mixed with roasted crunchy nuts.

"Wait," I said to Elmer as he sat slumped over on the bar

stool, sipping a stout. I'd gotten him addicted to high-quality dark brews. I grabbed some cinnamon from the spice cupboard.

"This," I said, shaking the spice container. "Why haven't I thought of this before. Nuts toasted in butter and cinnamon. It will add some luvin' sweetness to enhance the blueberries." I scooped a heaping teaspoon on top of the walnuts in the skillet. "You can't use too much love, or in this case, too much cinnamon."

"You're not shy with the spices." Elmer laughed.

We sat down at the table to eat. To maintain my leanness, I consumed a conservative portion, but Elmer heaped a mountain of food on his plate, often returning for seconds. I couldn't help but adore his protruding gut. It was like a trophy for a chef.

"How do the walnuts taste with the blueberries and farro?" I asked.

"That was a clever idea," he mumbled with a mouthful. "I like the warmth of the cinnamon with the sweetness of the blueberries and the saltiness of the feta. The spiciness and lemon really pop."

"So the addition didn't overpower the bond between the other ingredients?"

"No, it doesn't." He smiled.

"Good," I affirmed. "Cinnamon is a strong spice. You can't miss it. My favorite part of this dish is the citrus, though. Add a little lemon zest to a recipe, and it explodes with freshness. But in this case, the cinnamon was able to join the others and maintain harmony." I took a bite. "I think it complements the fruit while still allowing the lemony flavor to shine through."

"It's like it gives the dish something it needs. A little extra to enhance that flavor," Elmer agreed, shoving a huge spoonful into his mouth.

"But the lemon is okay?" I checked with him. While I

absolutely savored my food, I needed to know that others relished it, as well.

"Yeah, I love it. That's the best part." He leaned over and squeezed my thigh.

After dinner, we stretched out on the sofa. We often enjoyed either a good walk when the weather was warm or a nice evening conversation while we lounged on the couch. We both worked long days, so this time together with no distractions from gadgets or T.V. was sacred to us.

"Elmer, I have a strange question for you." I took a deep breath. "Have you ever dated two people simultaneously?" I asked, feeling my gut tense up.

"Like cheating?" His eyes grew wide. "No. Of course not. I couldn't hardly get anyone to go out with me. Let alone, two people."

"Not cheating." I swallowed hard. "Like both partners know that you're dating them."

"One of those open-relationship things? Swingers?" He asked, searching me with a raised perplexed eyebrow.

"Well, kind of. I mean, yes, that would count." I nervously played with the string of my pajama pants.

"No. I wouldn't even know where to start with that. Wait. Have *you*?" His eyes looked like they'd pop out.

"When I was in high school, I had a girlfriend and a boyfriend one time," I admitted. My cheeks grew hot as he stared at me.

"And they knew about each other?" Elmer's mouth hung open.

"Yes, I was very upfront with the guys I dated that I had a girlfriend. I dated her for two years. We never had sex, though."

Elmer remained quiet for a few moments, staring up at the ceiling. "Does that count?"

"Count as what?" I snapped. "A relationship? Yes, it counts. Anything romantic matters. I loved her. I cared about her more than the guys."

"So she was your girlfriend, and you had an agreement to date guys, too. Did you have sex with the guys?" he asked.

I nodded. "Yes, I did. I was still learning and wanted to understand what the big whoop was about. But maybe that was why I loved her and not them." I flinched. As much as I'd learned to accept myself, I feared Elmer's rejection.

"Did you ever have an open-relationship again?" he asked, putting his arm around me. He must have sensed my insecurity. I took his other free hand in mine.

"No. Just high school. I sort of retreated into myself after that."

We sat in silence for a few minutes, sipping beers, holding hands, but not looking at each other.

"How confident are you about us?" I asked, squeezing his hand tight. "About our bond?"

"What do you mean?"

I pushed through my anxiety to get the words out. "Do you think our bond is strong enough that nothing would shatter it?"

"Yeah. God." He grinned a little, pushing his hair back from his forehead. "I'm the luckiest guy in the world. Nothing's going to break us." He kissed me.

"I'm confident, too," I lied. Secretly, self-doubt hovered over me like a dark cloud. But all I had was my trust that his words were true.

"I think that since we're both sure," I proceeded despite the dryness in my throat, "I have an idea about resolving our sexual dilemma."

I got down on the ground and knelt between his legs so that I could see his face. I placed my hands on his knees, rubbing them gently with my thumbs.

"We could find a third," I muttered so softly that I wasn't sure he heard me, and my fingers now pinched him, causing him to jerk.

"Sorry," I apologized.

"A third *what*?" He cringed.

"A third person," I suggested. "Another person to join our relationship . . . not our marriage."

His eyes stared blankly ahead, not looking at me but off into space.

Finally, after several moments, he asked, "So you want to find someone else to date? Or you want me to? Like your high school thing?"

"Well . . . yeah." My stomach tightened, and my mouth was like cotton.

"Wait, which one is it? You date someone else or I do?"

"You do," I said. I sounded sad, so I changed my tone. "It would give you someone to have sex with. Of course, I'd still want to be your first preference and priority. What do you think?"

He stared down in thought. "I don't think I want to find random strangers to do it with. That's not my thing. Shit, I've only been with two people."

"I don't want you to go around fucking a bunch of other folks, either. I'm talking about finding one person who's okay with this arrangement."

Elmer released a long sigh and gulped down the remainder of his beer. "Shep, I don't think I can feel right about that. I can't go off and cheat on you. It wouldn't be fair. I'd feel like an asshole."

"Well . . ." I thought to myself for a minute. "What if I dated them, too?"

"How would that work?" he inquired, scrunching his forehead up even more.

I shrugged. I hadn't considered that I would get involved

with someone else. But if it meant making Elmer happy, maybe I could think about it. "I don't mean that I would fuck them. But we'd have a romantic relationship. Kind of like if my girlfriend in high school also dated my boyfriend. A three-person couple."

"So what does the other person get out of it, then? Who wants to join a relationship where they're second best?" he argued.

"That's not necessarily the way it is, and they can always leave if it isn't working. What if they really like us? Maybe some people are happy in this kind of dynamic." I wasn't sure if it made any sense. I didn't know much about polyamory. I had only read online that some aces tried it in their relationships with allosexuals.

A worry hovered over me. The idea seemed logical, and I wanted to believe that our love was strong enough that nothing could break it. However, the notion of Elmer finding someone else whom he would spend separate time with intensified my insecurities. At least this way, we would both be involved.

"Where's this coming from? I didn't think you'd be the type to go for . . . this stuff," he questioned me.

"That sounds judgmental," I retorted.

"I'm not trying to judge. You seem to keep to yourself like me. I didn't picture you . . ." He leaned closer to me. "*Are* you polyamorous?"

I'd honestly never considered it. *Why couldn't I be in a multi-person relationship?* "I don't know," I replied. "I mean, I guess I kind of was in high school. I haven't tried it."

"But you want to have relationships with other people?"

"*One* other person," I said holding my forefinger up. "Like I said, we love each other. This other person is . . . a bonus. Similar to a good friend," I informed him, climbing into his lap and straddling his thighs.

"A good friend that fucks us? I'm supposed to do it with this person . . . in front of you? With you?" he stuttered, twisting his face up in utter bewilderment.

"You can have sex with them alone. Fuck, I'm asexual. The purpose of this is to have less sex, not *more*," I corrected him. As the words came out, images of Elmer screwing someone else gave me the willies.

"We're *not* doing a threesome . . . three-way thing?" he asked.

"No." I wanted to barf.

"Good." Elmer sighed in relief. "I'm not *that* sexually confident. It would be too awkward. And to do it in front of you . . . so weird." He slapped his forehead and giggled.

"Are you indicating that you *could* fuck someone else?" My heart stopped as I waited for his response.

"But it isn't just fucking. You said that you'd date them? Romantically?"

"Yeah, I'll try it."

Elmer rubbed his chin with his right hand, something he did when he was anxious or insecure.

"But . . ." he started. "What we have is a passionate bond. You're going to build that with someone else? That feels like it would be cheating."

I sat up. "But you form romantic bonds through sex. Why wouldn't it be the same thing?" I contended. "You told me that you show affection through it. I don't think you're a casual sex person. So technically, we'd both be unfaithful."

"That's because nobody gave me the opportunity," he admitted. "I couldn't ever score before."

"Would you have a one-night stand?" I asked.

"No," he snapped. "That'd be weird to me. I can't sleep with a stranger."

"Then sex is not just sex," I pointed out to him, tugging on his long hair.

"Okay, I guess not. But I don't want this to turn into . . . cheating. I don't want to lose what we have or jeopardize it. This all seems so risky, Shep."

I pondered his concerns while I fiddled with the curly hairs on his chest. Elmer frowned, which made him look like a pouting kid. I hated it when he did that. Normally, he emitted an air of authority and respectful reservation, but when he sulked, it stank of immature indecisiveness.

"What if we found a girl?" I suggested.

"A girl?"

"You prefer men. So do I. Maybe a woman would balance us out a bit. Add something different that we don't have to worry about competing with."

He returned to stroking his chin.

"I think you want to do it," I asserted. My body was on fire.

"What makes you say that?" he asked, moving away from me.

"Because you haven't said no or absolutely not. You're asking all these questions. Be honest. You're considering it." I poked him in the chest with my forefinger.

"I don't know what I'm contemplating, Shep. Are you really serious?"

"Yes, I am." Inside, I wanted to tell him to forget about it. But I was too scared that he would eventually leave me unless we improved his sex life. So I proceeded. "I'm not saying it's forever. We can just try it. See if it helps with the sexual stuff."

"You're okay with me fucking someone else?" His expression looked surprised and even a little hurt.

Put on your poker face. "Yes, I am. As long as you love me, and things don't change with us."

What am I doing? But he hasn't said no. Maybe this is what he wants. Frankly, I was bound to lose him anyway with the sexlessness hovering in the air.

"How do you feel about me forming a romantic connection with someone else?" I inquired, pulling his chin upward with

85

my palm to see his eyes.

"It scares me," he mumbled. He stared worriedly at me.

"Like I said. We should try it, and if things sour, we'll stop. We can end it any time," I assured him.

"But then there'd still be situations that happened that you can't just erase. We can't go back. If I sleep with someone, it's going to change things. There's no way for us to predict what that will look like."

I agreed. I had no idea how this venture would impact us. "From what I understand, a lot of couples in these situations make rules."

"Rules?" He perked up.

"Boundaries. What we can and can't do with this other person so that there's some sacredness. Or I think that some people in open-relationships do. I'm unsure about polyamory."

"Like what would that be?"

I thought a moment before snapping my fingers. "No I love you. No talk of love with the other person. At least, not without discussing it with me."

"What else?" he asked.

"No unprotected sex."

"No cuddling," Elmer suggested, nudging me in the chest with his finger.

"Hmmm, I'm okay if you want to cuddle. I realize that I'm not particularly good at it."

"I mean you," he corrected me. "Because I know that you don't do it much, so I wouldn't want to see you doing it with someone else."

"That's fair," I consented. "But most importantly, we communicate. We talk about it. How we're feeling. What we're thinking. We stay honest with each other."

"How am I not supposed to get jealous?" he asked.

"I suspect we both may struggle with that at first. It'd be normal. I think we'd get used to it after a while." I'd never had that issue. But at the same time, I'd hadn't been in a multi-person relationship.

"I don't know . . ." Elmer said as he looked down.

"We should experiment. Whose somebody that you can kiss?"

"Huh?" His head popped back up.

"Someone that you assume would be okay if you kissed them. There's got to be somebody." *What am I doing?* I wanted to make myself stop. *But you'll lose him if you don't do this.*

"I don't know. I don't walk around assessing who will kiss me and who won't," he remarked.

"What about Stacy? I think she's had a crush on you."

Stacy worked at the school for a few years as the front office assistant before quitting and becoming the town clerk. She crushed on Elmer since they were kids but was overly clingy and borderline obsessive, which scared him and most other men away. She'd just divorced her fourth husband and was rumored to linger around the bar in the evenings searching for a new partner. She was short, stocky, and caked in red blush but was fairly attractive until you spoke to her.

"You want me to walk up and kiss her?" Elmer's eyes grew wide with shock.

"Go talk to her and ask to kiss her. Tell her you're experimenting with women again."

"Oh, god, she'll stalk me all over town if I say that." He covered his eyes with his hand.

"You can say afterwards that you're gay. The kiss proved it."

He laughed. "I'm sure that's what every woman wants to hear. Hey, this man that I've lusted for my whole life finally kisses me only to have it affirm to him that he's gay. I don't think we need to abuse this poor lady for our own personal agenda."

"Yeah, you're probably right." I ran my fingers up and

down his chest as I thought. "What about a bar? Like one in another city where folks don't know us. You can hit on someone. We both can and see how we feel about it."

"Do *you* know how to hit on people at bars?" he questioned as he pointed at me.

"I don't go to bars."

"Neither do I."

We both giggled. We certainly had socially awkward nerdiness in common.

"All we need to do is talk to people. You're a good enough looking guy to get someone to agree to kiss you," I encouraged him, rubbing his cheek.

"*You're* the hot one. Look at me. I've got this receding hairline and a beer belly," Elmer stated, squeezing his stomach rolls in his hand. "They'll all probably want to date you. Then they'll find out that I'm the person that they have to fuck."

I snorted.

"I'm not even that good at it," he continued. "I think this third is going to get a raw deal with us."

"No, baby, because they're getting a loving school principal who knows how to please a woman sexually and a world-class chef." I kissed his forehead.

"I'm not dating anyone here," he said as he shook his head.

"No, it'd be too risky," I agreed.

Elmer leaned forward and kissed me before wrapping his arms around me, pulling me closer to him. Suddenly, things felt light. The conversation wasn't concluded, yet we'd finished one of the most intimate conversations ever. And feeling his body pressed against me, I couldn't get close enough to him. The fear that I just fucked up our relationship and that he may learn that he'd be happier in a sex-full partnership hovered over me. Nevertheless, a feather of hope fluttered in my gut, telling me that somehow, this was going to all work out.

CHAPTER NINE: ELMER

Shep's suggestion of adding a third lingered in my mind. I'd always considered myself monogamous. Finding someone who actually wanted me was difficult enough, so I'd certainly hadn't imagined that I would find two people. I didn't want to jeopardize my marriage. The whole idea terrified me.

How important is sex?

I'd lived a sexless life for many years. Without a partner, anyway. Sitting alone in my room with a good porn video had defined my sexual endeavors until I got with Luna, and our physical intimacy had been great. It hadn't been this super exciting sex where we constantly shook things up with new positions or toys, but it was consistent and nice. There had been lots of days when Luna crept up behind me, nibbling on my ear and sinking her hand down my pants. Or times when she'd crawled on top of me in the morning or surprised me in the shower with a succulent blow job. Luna had made me feel desirable and attractive.

Shep never approached me sexually, nor did his touch ever indicate that he physically desired me. Deep inside, I'd yearned to be sexually craved. I wanted a partner who would spontaneously approach me in the kitchen, seduce me, and roughly have his way with me. For years, I'd wanted to be with a man, and I guess I'd assumed that men would be even more hypersexual. I thought we'd be doing it all over the house. I loved Shep, but he hadn't provided the relationship that I had hoped.

But do I want to have sex with someone else? A girl?

Finding a woman felt safer. A stereotypical super-sexual male suitor would be way better, but likely would heavily strain my marriage. I probably couldn't control myself if I found that kind of man. Men were my preference, so in that sense, Shep would forever be my number one. *Or would he?* I enjoyed sex with him. But not having a partner who reciprocated the pleasure, love, and fascination with the flesh disappointed me.

But am I ready to share Shep?

Sharing him threw another monkey wrench into things. I fantasized about sexual endeavors with this imagined girl, but conceptualizing Shep forming a romantic connection quickly severed any arousal. I was open to *me* having the girlfriend. But if I had to see him cook for someone else, I wouldn't be special anymore. Jealousy consumed me just watching him in the Tire sometimes as he charmed the patrons, even offering his regulars free slices of pie, cheesecake, or leftovers to take home. He made people feel noticed, heard, and valued. So I dreaded that perhaps, I wasn't so cherished after all.

I stopped by to see Snavis one Saturday to help him put together some new furniture he'd purchased for his kids' room. I'd never talked to my brothers about sexual matters, but they freely bragged about their own. But despite their relentless teasing, I wanted to talk to *someone,* and Snavis lived the closest.

We were assembling some dresser drawers, drinking cheap beer, and listening to some classic Leonard Skynyrd, Snavis' favorite band.

"Since when do you drink beer?" He joked when he handed one to me. "Is that part of that gay culture you're into now?"

"I finally discovered good tasting beer," I informed him. "Or at least, Shep taught me about it."

"That hard black stuff he drinks?" He grimaced. "Too

bitter for me, man. But your dude has some pretty decent brews at the Tire. Some good pale ales. Of course, I get the family discount."

Snavis and Kicky had been weirded out when I first came out to them. While I knew that they weren't comfortable with it, we'd lost dad, and Luna died, so I think their priorities in life changed. "Dude, can I talk to you about something? Something important?" I asked him after we finished the dresser.

"You can always talk to me, little bro." He winked at me.

"No, I mean seriously. Like can you not make any jokes or tease me? And definitely don't tell anyone about this conversation," I pleaded. "I need your advice."

He jerked his head up in shock. "You need *my* advice? Mister Ph.D."

"I only have a Masters. Yes, I want your input." My throat tightened, and my mouth went dry.

Snavis left the room, returning with two beers and motioning for me to follow him. We stepped outside to the backyard, and he pulled up some chairs for us. He lit a cigarette and popped open our drinks.

"Well, this is a first, bro," he stated. "What can I do you for?"

"You promise you won't tell *anybody*." I wasn't used to being vulnerable with him. I was unsure if he could even handle it.

"Your secret's safe with me, bro." He slapped me on the thigh.

"Shep is asexual. It means that he doesn't feel sexually attracted to people," I told him.

Snavis looked confused. "What does that mean?"

This is going to be harder than I thought. Here I am explaining asexuality to Snavis who catcalls and always wants to share nude pictures of girls that he seemed to collect on his phone.

"He doesn't see a person and feel like he wants to do it with them, to put it simply. We still have sex, but he mostly does it for me."

He stared at me with a puzzled look as he toked on his cigarette.

"I don't get it. But what do you want from me?" he asked after a few moments.

I took a deep breath. "Shep recommended that we find a third, like another person—a girl—to join our relationship. That way, I can have a sex life but still be with Shep. He'd be my number one."

Snavis' eyes swelled so big that I could see the zig zags of tiny spider-like veins in them. He gulped more of his beer down and pulled his chair in front of mine to face me directly.

"You're going to have a threesome? Wow! You're suddenly the coolest person ever," he exclaimed, punching me in the shoulder.

"No, no. I'm not having sex with Shep and this girl at the same time. She'd be my girlfriend, and we'd have sex. But she'd be Shep's girlfriend, too," I explained.

He thought for a moment. "Ummm . . ." he muttered. "An open marriage? Swinging?"

"No, not swinging." I wasn't describing this well at all, or maybe it was too weird for him to understand. "This girl would be *our* girlfriend. It's three people who all are in a relationship."

"So you're not gay then?"

"I'm bisexual. There's a difference," I corrected him. "It's not about getting with a woman. We thought it'd be safer that way. We both prefer men, so we'll stay each other's first priority."

"Wow," Snavis remarked, leaning back in his chair. "I didn't reckon your life was so . . . exciting. Have you been hiding this from me the whole time?"

I glanced away. "It's not that thrilling. I've never done this stuff before."

"What do you want from me?" he asked.

"I want to know how you would feel if Belle proposed something like this to you?" I asked him. Belle was his wife.

"If Belle suggested that we bang another chick? Sounds pretty awesome." He chuckled, lighting a fresh cigarette.

"Not just that. Both of you date her. Would it bother you to see Belle in a relationship with a woman?"

Snavis smirked. "I think I can get over it if it did. Fuck, I'm getting turned on thinking about it. You ever watched lesbian porn?"

I rolled my eyes and sipped my beer. He sensed my frustration.

"Sorry, bro," he said as he leaned forward again. "I guess I don't understand what you want me to say. It sounds pretty fucking awesome to me. You get to go out and find some hot chick to screw, and Shep doesn't care. Most dudes would be in heaven right now. I don't know what the problem is."

"I worry about it hurting me and Shep. You *really* wouldn't be jealous? What if Belle spent more time with her than you? What if you saw Belle doing things for her that she does only for you? Or worse, you see Belle do things that she *doesn't* do with you? What if Belle likes her more?"

He laughed. "That wouldn't happen, bro. Me and Belle . . . we're tight." He crossed his fingers. "I could fuck ten girls. She could fuck ten girls. We'd still be glued together."

"Have you slept with other girls?" I inquired.

"Nope, no desire to. I mean, if she was encouraging it like Shep, then I wouldn't refuse. But she's the one for me, bro." He winked at me.

"So you think that you can have sex with other people and still be in love with your wife?" I asked. If he felt that he could love Belle after knowing she slept with other people, maybe it wasn't a big deal.

"Sure. Sex isn't love, man," he told me as he tossed his cigarette butt to the ground.

His words rang in my brain. He was right. Engaging in some hot steamy sex with this girl in no way would erase my love for my husband. *I can do it.* Shep seemed confident that we could handle it. Perhaps I was letting my naïve insecurities overwhelm me.

"So who is she?" Snavis asked. "Is she hot?"

"We don't have one, yet."

He laughed. "Let's see." He rubbed his chin. "Who's on the single scene in Cloverleaf right now."

"We're not dating local. Too many rumors and gossip. We want to keep this between us . . . and you." I stared at him dead-on to show him that I was serious.

"How do you even ask a girl about this?"

"I have no fucking clue."

A few nights later, I returned home late from a schoolboard meeting. Shep had prepared portobello mushroom burgers topped with homemade pistachio pesto and Swiss cheese served on toasted wheat buns. He served them with parmesan crusted zucchini fries. As I prepared to sit down at the table, I noticed his laptop open. We always talked over dinner, so the presence of the computer puzzled me.

"What's this?" I pointed at it.

Shep set all the plates down and poured us some cabernet before taking his seat.

"I've been researching dating sites for couples," he told me as he bit off about a fourth of his burger, which made it impossible for him to chew with his mouth closed. He always inhaled his food in a few gargantuan mouthfuls.

"They make dating sites for that?" I asked, nearly choking on my wine.

"Well . . . sort of," he responded, sliding the computer over to me. "Look at it."

I saw a webpage for couples dating. I didn't scroll far until images of erect penises, wet vagina selfies, and naked breasts consumed the entire page.

"What's this?" I gestured at the pictures. "You can't even see their faces." I searched further. "Wow . . . it's just a hook up site."

"There all hook up sites. At least, that's what it looks like," he agreed.

"Aren't there sites for polyamory?"

"I found one," he told me. "It's the same. And apparently, they call girls who are willing to date couples unicorns because they're so hard to find. I think we'll be sifting through tons of penises, boobs, and vaginas to find one. Unless this looks like what you want."

My eyes were still glued to the screen in disbelief. "I think these people might scare me," I admitted. "I'm not ready for something so . . . aggressive or confident. I'll probably disappoint these folks."

Shep nodded. "Yeah, me, too. I don't think hooking up with a socially reserved dude and his asexual husband are what they're looking for."

"I don't know if my sexual appetite is *that* big. There's got to be something else."

He pushed his empty plate aside and finished his wine. "I think we should post a profile and see what happens."

"On this?" I snapped. I feared getting myself into a situation that I couldn't handle. These profiles terrified me. I didn't want to re-experience rejection similar to the old days.

"It was recommended as the best site with the most people on it. There may be a person willing to be a third lurking around here. It's not like we have to respond to messages for hookups," Shep suggested.

"You want me to post pictures of my penis?" My mouth dropped open in horror.

"God, no." He slugged me in the shoulder. "Just regular pictures. I guess we should try to post something kind of sexy . . . or appealing. What's sexy?"

Tall, muscular, and hairy . . . me? How am I sexy? "I don't know."

"You're the allosexual. What makes people sexy?" he demanded, pounding his fist on the table.

"I know what makes other better-looking people sexy." I stared down at my gut. "No one's going to think *I'm* hot."

Shep laughed, pouring us some more wine.

"You've got to get some better self-esteem than that, dude," he said, handing me my glass. "Stand up and show me sexy."

I got up and removed the hair tie from my hair, letting it flow around my shoulders. I was still wearing my work clothes, which weren't erotic at all. I yanked off my tie and unbuttoned my shirt a little.

"Unbutton all of it and show your chest," he recommended.

"Well, what are you going to wear?" I asked.

"Black eyeliner . . . something black. What I always wear. Nothing like those stale boring clothes like you have on," he teased, winking at me.

"Of course, you have a style. You should be the one showing your chest. You've got the six pack," I argued.

"I don't want them to want to fuck *me*. Come on, you've got to show them what you have to offer, dude." He motioned with his hands for me to keep undoing my shirt.

I sighed in shame. "I don't have anything to offer. I don't even have a big dick. Did you see those guys on that site?" I pointed at the computer.

Shep chuckled again, walking over to me and throwing his

arms around me. He moved his hands under my shirt and rubbed my back.

"You're beautiful, Elm. I'd do you."

"Yeah, says the asexual." I snorted.

"I still find people attractive. If you want to do this, then flaunt your sexual appeal," he ordered me.

I stepped away and straightened my torso to make my gut smaller. I finished unbuttoning my shirt and forced the sides of it behind my arms and shoved my hands in my pants' pockets.

"Now give me a sexy look," Shep coached me.

"How?" I'd been way too shy to seduce anyone and didn't see myself as tempting.

He shrugged. "I don't know. What do you normally do when you try to be sexy?"

I covered my face with my palms. "Maybe that's why I only slept with two people. I have no idea." It was all starting to feel like work and pressure.

Shep walked out of the room, returning with some black eyeliner and a classic bowler hat.

"Sit down," he instructed me, holding up the eyeliner.

"You're going to put that on me?" Shep sometimes wore eyeliner around the house or on the rare occasion we ever ventured outside of Cloverleaf. I'd never felt *that* confident.

"It'll make your eyes pop. Plus, I think it adds some eroticism . . . or least some style," he encouraged me with a smile.

He carefully painted the edges of my eyelids with thin pristine lines. He pulled my hair back again with a hair tie and placed the hat on me. Then he wrapped my wrists with some studded leather bracelets. He ran out of the room, this time returning with a red plaid button up shirt and a pair of black dress pants.

"Dress pants?" I flinched. "Isn't that too formal?"

"They won't be able to tell that they're dress pants. The

black pants will look better. Put this shirt on but leave it un-buttoned." He tossed it to me.

I followed his instructions, then went to examine myself in the mirror. It wasn't bad, and actually, it was a vast improvement. The blob in my midsection still gave me reservations, but I looked attractive and even a little exotic. When I returned to the room, Shep had changed into a pair of fitted dark blue jeans with a tight black t-shirt and a studded beanie. His eyeliner highlighted the deep blue of his eyes that almost matched his jeans.

"I think if we're going to look like this, we better find a goth girl," I suggested.

"That's what I'd want anyway. I certainly don't want anyone boring." He grinned.

"Where should we take the picture?" I asked.

He examined our house, searching for the most potentially sexy space. We settled on the spare bedroom. Shep had painted it black with hanging blue icicle lights, creating a psychedelic atmosphere. We turned a few lamps on for adequate lighting and opened the curtains a little. We stood against the wall with Shep slightly in front of me to help cover my belly while still revealing a glimpse of my hairy chest. I circled my arm around his neck, and he placed his hand on my thigh, holding his phone in the other for the picture. We probably flashed thirty photos. We tried different poses. One had us kissing. Another had Shep hugging me. Some we looked serious, while others we smiled. We selected five that made us feel sexy enough.

"So we post them now, and that's it?" I asked, watching as he uploaded them.

"Nope, then we got to complete a profile. What are we looking for?" Shep read the website's directions. "It says to be honest because it'll help you find the right match. Let's try, two married dudes seeking a female third, preferably goth or punk, to join us in a polyamorous relationship. We've got money, food, and humor to offer. We're not searching for a mere hookup, and we're not interested in threesomes. Does that make sense?" He looked over at me. "I'm not sure how to write this."

"Wait," I interjected, placing my hand on his to stop him from typing more. "Are these people even living near here? I don't want anyone around here to see a profile of me on something like this."

"Don't need everyone to know what a sexual adventurer you are." He laughed, punching me slightly in the shoulder.

"Do you want folks to know it?" I asked him. While Shep had more freedom working at the Tire, everybody in Cloverleaf was a target for scrutiny or at least gossip.

He snorted. "I gave up on giving a shit what people here think of me years ago. I'm already trans. I can't get more taboo than that."

"But I'm a principal. I could get into a lot of trouble with this if people saw it . . . if students looked at it." My eyes bulged out suddenly in horror. I snatched the lap top up. "No, we can't do this. It's too risky."

Shep smiled. "Boy are you going to struggle with this."

"There's got to be other options," I insisted, tossing the computer on the sofa.

He thought for a moment. "Float around the bar scene and try to seduce girls to follow these two creepy dudes home for a non-threesome? Come on, girl . . . we got what you need," he joked, making his voice sound evil.

"Well, wait." I held my hand up as I pondered other options to find the elusive mythical unicorn. "Didn't you say that you use *Facebook* groups for trans guys?"

"Yeah. I'm on some for nonbinary and aces, too."

"Wouldn't there be one for polyamory or finding a third or something?" I suggested.

Shep stared at me for a few seconds before taking out his phone to research it. He grinned.

"What is it?" I demanded, trying to peer over his shoulder.

"Shit, aren't we in luck. There's several here specifically for unicorns. One's a group and two are pages."

"Try the group," I urged him with a nudge.

"Ha-ha, it's in Alabama . . . or at least, I guess the admin is."

"Alabama?" I repeated.

He chuckled. "We're way behind on freakiness, man. Oh wow. I clicked *Join Group,* and it sent the request. No screening questions. Says they get about twenty posts a day. About five hundred members. Locality may be a problem, though." He kept scrolling. "Here's a page. It's for unicorns. Damn, it's for UK folks. Shit. Wait."

"What is it?" I nagged, pulling my chair up beside him.

"This page is linked to a site about finding a unicorn . . . eh, but it looks like it redirects to another hook-up thing."

I leaned back and groaned, running my hand through my hair. "Why can't we be better at hooking up with people."

"Well, dear, there ain't going to be many women who want to date two men, let alone an ace and a shy dude." Shep wagged his finger at me, continuing to search his phone with the other.

"Maybe this is doomed." I didn't know why I was disappointed.

"Not if we went local. I'm sure there are women around here that wouldn't complain about two guys with jobs, a good house, a home chef, and oh, one spectacular body," he joked as he lifted his shirt, revealing his toned abs.

"They're not even going to have sex with that, though," I reminded him while also suppressing my envy.

"I didn't say sex was off the table, I guess," he said, pulling his shirt back down.

I flinched. "What are you talking about? I thought the whole point was for you to have less sex and me to have more?" My heart sank. *Shep was going to have sex with her?*

He nodded. "It is. But I make love with you to fuel our bond. If I have a connection with her, then . . ."

"Then it would lead to love," I finished for him.

I didn't want Shep loving anyone else. Somehow the concept of me having sex with a woman who was also my girlfriend seemed fine. But for Shep to do it . . .

"God, don't frown so much," he assured me, rubbing my chin. "I'm an ace. I'm not going to be fucking all over the house. It *might* occur. Anyway, we don't know if *any* of this will happen."

I sat still, staring down. Shep returned to his phone.

"It looks like that request to join the unicorn group was approved," he told me. I leaned forward again to have a look. He scrolled down the page. There were people from all over the country and lots of women. I could see their faces and not only their breasts or vagina, which was a relief.

"They're not bad looking on here," I commented. "Hmmm . . . there's some couples like us. Should we post our picture? Our location? That seems to be what they're doing."

Shep posted two of the best pictures from our photography session and wrote a comment.

Hey, any fellow Montanans? A manager and professional chef seeking a super sexy goth girl to join our marriage. One will feed you well, the other will discipline you when you're naughty!

"Why are you writing *that*!" I pulled his hand away from his phone. "I'm not into S & M."

"Come on, it's a joke. You're a principal. We got to make that sound sexy somehow." He jerked his hand back.

"You want someone who's super sexual?"

"I don't know. It sounds good. I'm posting it. Aha—" He

continued to type.

Feel free to comment below or DM us.

He posted it.

Suddenly, I froze. "Oh, god, what did we just do? Did you look at the member list? What if somebody we know is on here?"

Shep laughed. "I don't think anyone here knows what unicorn means or that there would be a *Facebook* group for it. I think we're safe." He tossed his phone down on the table. "Let it lie. We'll see what happens."

CHAPTER TEN: SHEP

After our experimentation with couple dating sites, my expectations were low. Part of me felt intrigued to explore this dynamic in our marriage, but mostly, I was relieved. I tried the idea, and it didn't seem possible. Elmer didn't act too disappointed, either. Until a few a days later when someone commented on our original post.

Hey, I live in Great Falls. I'm down with getting to know you. Feel free to check out my profile. If interested, DM. Willow Saint.

I clicked on her name to pull up her *Facebook* page. She was only twenty-five with curly dark brown hair that was short, making it look more like an afro. She wore glasses and had many selfies showing off her collection of unique frames. Her face was round and plump, and she had a curvy figure. She had more of a rockabilly fashion style with her poofy skirts and tight corset tops. Her about page said that she worked as an office assistant at a dental clinic.

I saved one of her pictures to my phone and sent it to Elmer with the following text.

Hey, sexy principal. I've been really naughty and feel like I need detention after school. My mom says you should give me a good paddle with your big stick.

He responded with a question mark. I informed him about our new potential girlfriend who lived in Great Falls and that she'd showed interest in our post. He told me to wait until he got home to reply to her.

In between firing up the smoker for the Tire's barbecue night and completing payroll, I snuck in little opportunities to stalk Willow's *Facebook* profile, scrolling through what must have been thousands of artistically designed selfies. Willow dressed in a range of styles from goth to punk to even Victorian. Dressing up and playing roles seemed to be her forte with different colored wigs, makeup in shades of greens, blacks, and purples, and a variety of outfits including corsets, ballgowns, pantyhose, pink and yellow tutus, ripped t-shirts, floral sundresses, and bellbottoms. There were photos of Willow reading by a large willow tree. Willow in a black one piece with red skulls, curling up her body in the sand by the ocean. Willow in the subway, hugging a rail and lifting her leg up, exposing a cherry-colored garter belt pinching green fishnet hose. Willow laying in a bathtub of floating strawberries bobbling over her breasts. The photo that captivated my attention the most was Willow in running shorts and a tight crimson tube top hitting a volleyball. She wore no cosmetics, her forehead shined with sweat, and her kinky curls protruded from a ponytail on her head. I gravitated to that image because it was authentic. She wasn't hidden in all the costumes.

I obsessively read all about her. She was from Spokane, Washington and had attended a beauty school out there. I perused her photos searching for evidence of anything that appeared to be a relationship. But most of her pictures were either selfies or her hugging men and women, making it difficult to determine if any of the people in those photos were boyfriends or girlfriends. Willow's profile also showed an interest in cooking. She'd posted pictures of juicy charred steaks topped with mushrooms and blue cheese sided with garlic cheddar mashed potatoes. There were pink strawberry flan cakes with fresh strawberry syrup, blackened lemon chicken with roasted new potatoes, cheesy pulled pork quesadillas, and grilled spinach, mozzarella, and artichoke Stromboli perfectly golden brown in a light butter and egg wash. Her ability to plate her food with such pristineness for someone who saw cooking as a mere hobby impressed me. Having someone else to connect with over the culinary arts was appealing. I figured it would be nice to have something that only she and I could bond over since her and Elmer would have this sex life that I wouldn't be a part of.

Elmer came over to the restaurant after work since I was closing. I served him a smoked pulled pork sandwich, slow-cooked Brunswick stew, crispy homemade potato chips, and a *Rogue* chocolate stout to wash it down. I watched him scarf it up hungrily as I tended to the few remaining patrons who were relishing blueberry and chocolate cheesecake, savory apple pie topped with cinnamon ice cream, and dark bitter chocolate eggshell candy cookies decorated with crunchy baker's sugar. I saved a large slice of the cheesecake for Elmer, slamming it down in front of him as soon as he tried to rub his round belly to indicate that he was stuffed.

"You'll eat it," I assured him with a slap on the back.

"I thought I was supposed to be trying to get sexy not more overweight," he complained before reluctantly spooning up a generous bite of the succulent dessert. "Wow," he moaned.

"I told you," I teased him. "Besides, you're fine. So you got a little tummy. Lots of men do."

"You don't," he argued.

"That's because I'm a freak of nature," I replied. "I don't gain weight." While I ran regularly and watched what I ate, I'd always been a small person. My body metabolized food quickly. I envied Elmer's adorable round stomach.

105

He helped me clean the tables and dishes while we waited for the remaining patrons to depart. He never whined about it. He enjoyed these simpler tasks rather than the complicated drama that he dealt with all day. Plus, it was a convenient way to feed him and give us some time together.

"I looked at her page," he said as he started placing the chairs on top of the tables to clean the floor. "She's cute. She looks like you."

"She looks like me?" I snapped.

He held up his hand. "I don't mean it like that. I'm talking about your style. I think you two would get along well with that goth stuff you're into."

When I'd presented as a woman, I'd loved adorning my face with various shades of eyeliners, eyeshadows, and lipsticks, anything to make my features pop. Presenting as a man, I still relished the occasional black eyeliner that I only wore in my home or if we traveled to Portland or some other liberal city. As much as I wanted, I'd failed to work up the bravery to be the man in Cloverleaf with makeup. It was already difficult getting people to gender me correctly.

I walked over, throwing my arms around his neck and playfully pinched his belly rolls.

"So what do you think?" I asked. "Should we message her?"

"I think you should do it. She responded to you anyway. I don't want her to see me and then flee."

Elmer had the most boring *Facebook* page complete with a banner of the high school for his cover photo and a profile pic of him in an ugly brown suit attempting to put forth his most professional face. He never posted unless it was about school events. It read like a profile for a stale piece of bread.

"Okay," I agreed. I took out my phone, opening it to messenger.

Hello there! I read through your profile. You're quite an

interesting chick.

"Chick?" Elmer objected. "That's not polite, is it?"

"I'm trying to be flirty." I dismissed him with my hand.

"You can be flirty without being a dick." He nudged me in the shoulder.

"Whatever, man. Look. She responded. That's a good sign."

"What'd she say?" he asked as he tried to grab my phone.

"She called me cutie. She's says I'm pretty sexy myself." I rolled my eyes, which was more of a knee-jerk reaction. *Why can't people comment on my interests? Hey, I own a restaurant. What about that? What about my love for running? What about my musical tastes?*

"What is it?" Elmer asked seeing the annoyance on my face.

"I'm already sexy," I grumbled, plopping my chin down in my hand as I pouted.

"There's worse things to be in life." He winked at me.

"I know that." I sighed. "Ugh, here we go. Sex talking."

"You don't have to talk about sex. Ask her something about herself," Elmer suggested, rubbing my shoulder.

I wrote that I liked her style and that I was dying to know about all her favorite recipes. She responded that she loved to cook and that she thought it was so cool that I owned a restaurant. She said that she'd checked out the menu from my website.

"She said my food looks amazing," I stated.

"What's wrong with amazing?" Elmer remarked. "You suck at compliments, man. At least let her come and eat your food before you expect her to give you some professional critique of it."

"Uh, oh," I muttered.

"What?"

"She wants to look at your *Facebook* page."

"So give her my name."

His name is Elmer Lee. He's a principal. That's why his page sucks so bad.

"Shep!" he snapped at me.

I laughed. "Well, it does."

"I didn't create it for dating. I'm a principal." He pointed to himself with his thumb. "You were a teacher. You know that we have to present ourselves differently."

"I was still cool when I was a teacher."

He glared at me until the phone beeped to indicate that Willow had responded. She commented that Elmer looked way different than me. I couldn't refrain from teasing.

Don't be deceived. Elm's a real partyer when he lets loose. He's a pretty wild thing underneath those rigid principal clothes. Do you like men with authority?

"A wild thing?" Elmer asked, shaking my shoulder.

I snickered. "Don't worry. She says she likes guys with careers. She wants to meet us."

Our eyes nearly bulged out of their sockets.

"Who just meets a bunch of strange dudes?" he insisted.

"Well, Great Falls is only like an hour and a half away," I reminded him. "I'm sure that we'll meet up with her in a public place. Why not? Are you a phone talker?"

"No," he replied.

"Exactly. I'll see if she wants to suggest somewhere." I typed it in and waited. The phone beeped. "Oh. She says that she has a sister here in Cloverleaf and wants to come here. She wants to meet us at the Tire." I wrote that we'd be happy to welcome her at the restaurant and that I couldn't wait to feed her a bunch of scrumptious food.

"Why don't you write LOL like she does," Elmer asked.

"You don't want to sound old."

"I'm not. Do you put LOL in things? Sorry, not doing it." I waved him away from me.

"She's a generation or two ahead of us in texting culture," he noted.

"Texting is beyond us, man," I corrected him. "She says that she'll meet us on Friday. She wants to bring her sister."

"What for?"

"Probably to make sure we're not a bunch of weirdos. Can you blame her?" I wrote that I couldn't wait to spoil her and her sister with an assortment of tasty Tire food and that I hoped they had good appetites because I was going to stuff them.

"That sounds sexual," Elmer accused, pointing at my phone. "You going to do her sister, too?"

"I'm being friendly. And flirty. If y'all read sexy junk into it, then that's your deal, not mine," I defended myself. "I'm here to win her over with my sensational cuisine. Yes, it will be green curry pork with red potatoes, carrots, and onions all served up with homemade garlic parmesan naan and coconut rice."

"Why that dish?" he asked.

I closed my eyes, picturing the food before me. "The juiciness of the pork melts in your mouth like butter before a kick of subtle but poignant spice creeps up through your nostrils. It's not that heat that just burns. It warms you up from the inside, where you can fill your pores releasing it. It brings your whole body to life. I want them to get awakened. To taste something they've never devoured before."

"What if they don't like curry?" he asked, shrugging his shoulders.

"They'll eat it." I winked.

I laid in bed that night fantasizing about the right dessert to add to the curry. I settled on orange cream sickle cake. It was an unusual dessert that I pounded full of orange zest, with a whipped marmalade-like jelly in the middle and blanketed with citrus buttercream frosting and a touch of orange blossom honey. Orange was sweet, fruity, and fresh tasting while also carrying a bit of sourness to it. Its aroma consumed the air around it, leaving its scent in my clothes. With these two magnificent dishes, I knew that Willow couldn't leave without a lasting impression that would linger inside her nostrils, clothing, and stomach for hours.

When Friday arrived, Elmer was a mess. He rummaged through all his wardrobe, searching for an outfit that appealed to women — or just anybody for that matter. I encouraged him to leave his hair down. He didn't wear it that way outside the house because he feared that he'd look immature and thus, less principally. I found an older pair of frayed jeans and gave him one of my studded belts. I picked out a black fitted t-shirt that hugged his body while also camouflaging his stomach.

"This shirt's too tight," he moaned, tugging it away from his gut.

"Here." I tossed an old flannel at him that had belonged to Tank.

"Wait . . ." He fumbled it around in his hands. "I can't wear this. It's . . ."

"It's a good shirt worn by a great man that deserves to be worn by another good man," I retorted, giving him a side hug and a kiss on the cheek.

"Thanks," he replied. It was quite baggy on him. "Wow, this takes me back to the nineties grunge days."

"You weren't cool enough to be a part of that period, honey." I surveyed him with my eyes. "You make a good Eddie Vedder, though."

"Pearl Jam?"

"So you *do* know something."

Elmer threw a sock at me. "Am I really that square? She's not going to be into me at all." He sighed. "You'll get all the attention."

"Is it a competition?" I asked him.

He groaned. "I don't want it to turn out that way. I don't need us getting jealous . . . especially over her."

I sat down beside him on the bed as he put his socks on. "What do you mean?" I asked.

"I figure that there'll be some jealousy over you and me. It's not going to be easy watching you with another person, even if it isn't sexual. But that's all right . . . I guess it's okay. It means that I love you and sharing you is hard, right?"

I hadn't mustered enough courage to visualize Elmer having sex with Willow. Each time the vision entered my brain, I immediately suppressed it. *Was that love?*

"Right," I replied.

"But if we start getting jealous over who she prefers, then . . . then . . . well, that means something else?" he stammered, picking at his nails, a behavior he did when he was nervous.

"What would it mean?" *Is he backing out?* Relief washed over me.

He turned to me with a sad look. "I don't want us to feel the way about her that we do for each other."

Tears swelled up in my eyes, but I buried them down. I was scared that he would fall in love and worse, adore her more than me. But at least I wasn't alone in that fear. I hugged Elmer, resting my head on his shoulder.

"I don't want that, either," I whispered in his ear.

"Can we promise each other that no matter what happens, it's us first?" He stared into my eyes. "If that changes, then . . . we end it, okay?"

"Okay," I agreed.

"Promise?"

"I promise."

CHAPTER ELEVEN: ELMER

"Why y'all all spruced up?" Danny, Shep's nephew, asked when we walked into the Tire. "Going to a rock concert?"

"No. What's wrong with what I'm wearing," I stuttered, making a ponytail with my hair in my fist.

"You just look . . . you know . . . less . . ."

"Like a principal."

"That's it." He chuckled, slapping me on the back. "You finally got him to loosen up, Shep. Hell, you should do it more often. I bet no one will recognize you in here."

"Danny, have you been simmering the green curry," Shep inquired, glancing at the kitchen.

"Patty's tending to it. Been stewing for eight whole hours." Danny stuck his nose upward, inhaling a big whiff of the spicy goodness permeating the air of the diner. "Smells so good, it'll clean your nostrils out." He laughed, whacking me again.

"Ow!" I yelled.

"Oh, sorry," Danny apologized. "He's one of those extra sensitive types," he whispered to Shep.

"No, he's not," Shep corrected him, punching me in the side.

"Ow!"

They giggled together as Shep threw his arm around Danny's shoulder, leading us to the best booth in the place. It was in the far corner, giving patrons an entire view of the restaurant and the kitchen while also nestling against a window that peered onto Highway 2 outside. We sat down, and Shep ordered two *Chimay* beers that he often kept hidden in the back cooler, reserved only for himself and his special customers.

"Only the best for good taste," he would say.

Shep looked exceptionally handsome. He wore a black bowler hat with rings dangling from the side, a fitted long-sleeve black t-shirt and a pair of worn bell-bottom-like jeans. The eye liner he decided to wear really accentuated his blue eyes.

"Are you nervous wearing that in here?" I asked taking a big gulp of my beer.

"Kind of," he muttered.

"Do you think someone will say something to you?"

"I don't give a fuck," he asserted. "See if they can find cooking this good at the prices I offer somewhere else. Nah, when it comes to food or prejudice, the belly always wins . . . or at least, it should."

We didn't talk too much but rather just sat there, sipping beers, and constantly scrutinizing every car that pulled into the parking lot. Danny came by to take our order, but Shep instructed him to tend to the table when our guests arrived and that the whole party would be having the green curry pork with the orange sickle cake, all specifically reserved for us only.

"Mayor Dean sure has been commenting and asking about that curry. He keeps begging for a bowl," Danny informed Shep.

"Tell him he should have been a girl." Shep smirked.

"Huh?" Danny asked.

I kicked Shep from under the table. "Let him know that Shep will make some more next week," I told Danny.

"A whole pot for him and a party of ten on Wednesday," Shep agreed, dismissing Danny with a wave of his hand.

"Are you going to remember that?" I asked.

He grinned. "I recall all my promises. Besides, part of the way that I can survive as a trans person in this tiny town is by keeping all the residents happy and full."

Just then, a small grey car pulled in with two girls inside. Shep and I both leaned toward the window. My heart stopped, and my throat grew dry. A tall lanky girl got out of the driver's seat. She had a pixie haircut and wore a blue t-shirt with an extra-long flowery white skirt. The other woman who climbed out of the passenger side had to be Willow. The bob of kinky hair gave her away. She sported glasses with hot pink frames and a tight-fitting indigo dress with cherry flowers on it. In her hair, a lone daisy protruded out from the left side.

My eyes met Shep's, lingering there as if we were both making the final decision to go through with this endeavor. My heart thudded violently inside my chest, and my gut knotted up so much that I felt queasy. I was sure that he could see my fear, yet he stared blankly at me.

After what seemed like an eternity, Shep gave me a slight smile and got up to meet the girls at the door. I sat there, twisting my fingers in and out of knots. I grimaced at my own nervousness about whether a girl would like me when here I was married to Shep, the love I had wanted for so long. Something inside me felt dirty . . . even wrong.

"Are you feeling okay?"

I looked up to see the pixie haired girl grinning at me but also with a look of concern. I touched my face, wiping away sweat.

"Um, yeah, uh, hello." I offered her my hand.

Shep motioned for them to sit and took his seat beside me.

"What kind of drinkers are you?" he asked. "Wine? Beer? Spirits? It's on me."

"I like wine," Willow replied.

Shep flashed her his most boyishly cute smile and winked. "So the real question is . . . red or white?"

"The only wine worth drinking is blood red." Willow winked back.

"Danny!" Shep yelled, causing Willow and the pixie girl to jump. "A bottle of cabernet from my special stash. And bring out my naan."

The girls giggled at him.

"So who's your friend? Sister?" he asked.

"I'm Oak."

"The family of trees," Shep joked.

"Yeah, I suppose." Oak smiled as she took the glass of wine that Danny poured for her.

"I like trees," he continued. "They're strong. They're big. They make their presence known. They also provide shade and shelter. Trees are good. There's worser things to be named after."

"What's Shep?" Willow questioned, taking a piece of the hot garlic naan.

"It's basically the stuff you sweep out your front door at night," he answered, shoving a huge chunk of naan in his mouth.

"You're putting yourself down?" She sat back in surprise.

"Nah, that junk is everywhere. It gets on everything. No matter how much you clean it, it'll still return the next day. You never get rid of it."

"So you're hard to get rid of? Is that it?" she teased, tilting her head and raising an eyebrow at him.

"Let's just say that I encapsulate your world," he remarked, making a circle with his hands. "Eat my food, and you'll see."

He was so much better at flirting than me. I could already observe the sparkle of interest in Willow's eyes that never left him. They proceeded to pull out the menu and engage in deep discussion about ingredient choices, cooking methods, and presentation techniques. Shep hung on Willow's every word as she shared concepts that he'd never considered, and I might as well have been invisible. Occasionally, Oak would give me an encouraging smile but then she'd turn to gawk at Shep's menu or Willow's *Instagram* food pornography.

Danny served us our bowls of curry along with salad, rice, and more naan. He leaned over and whispered into Shep's ear.

"I've got to go take care of something in the kitchen. Ladies," Shep excused himself and stormed off.

"So . . ." I mumbled. "Y'all like curry?"

"I haven't had curry like this," Willow said, stirring it with her spoon. "Smells amazing."

"We should all try some together. The first bite of Shep's food is special. You should savor it," I suggested, heaping up a large spoonful and blowing on it.

The girls smiled in agreement, digging their spoons in. We all nodded our heads before indulging in the first taste. The aroma of the spices tantalized my tongue and nostrils, and the juices oozed down my esophagus into my belly, like a warm hug. I'd closed my eyes, and when I opened them, I saw them laughing at me.

"You make it look orgasmic," Willow joked.

I flushed.

She chuckled more. "Take another bite. I want to watch you enjoy it."

I obeyed, closing my eyes again and this time, unintentionally letting out a slight moan. The girls laughed.

"Wow," Willow said. "So Elmer —"

"You can call me Elm."

"Do you like food and sex?"

I nearly choked on the sip of beer that was heading down my throat. I grabbed my napkin, coughing into it.

117

"He's the principal," Oak told Willow.

"Oh, I guess you don't get to talk about sex much, or at least as openly, huh?" Willow asked.

Finally getting my voice back, I said, "It's okay. I'm sorry. Well, you're right. I kind of have to keep my composure a lot in public. There're not many leadership positions here, and I'm in one of them."

"But you're all right with the town knowing you're married to a man and that you have a girlfriend?" Oak questioned me. "Can I have another glass of wine?" She dangled her empty glass in the air.

I poured her another from the bottle Danny left on the table. *Is she already my girlfriend?*

"I guess—well, yes." I nodded. "I'm cool with it. It's my personal business. It's not like I stand around talking about my private life at work." I hadn't really thought it through. Anyone finding out terrified me.

"But in Cloverleaf, everyone knows your personal shit whether you want them to or not." Oak grunted, rolling her eyes.

"I do my job well," I proclaimed, finishing off my beer and waving for another. "That's not going to change. My private life is my business."

Willow grinned, her eyes sparkling the same way they had with Shep. My stomach exploded in butterflies.

"I think professional men, especially leaders, are so sexy," she commented. "You seem so shy right now. I adore guys who have so many different sides to them. It makes them mysterious. I'd love to see you work."

"I guess we're both leaders. Shep owns the restaurant."

She peered across the room at Shep. "Yeah, but he doesn't have an entire school under him. That's a lot of pressure. That's really hot." She licked her lips.

Oh my god, she's flirting with me! I shifted my position so that my legs were spread apart, and I slung my arm around the empty space where Shep sat. *I need to act desirable. Sexy people sit like this.*

I proceeded to tell them both about my journey to become Cloverleaf High's principal and threw in some exciting stories of bomb threats and mask mandate decisions. Both girls leaned forward, intrigued, as they slurped their stews hungrily. Shep returned, handing me my second beer, and opening one for himself.

"Sorry, ladies," he apologized, as he plopped down beside me. "Sometimes they can't make the recipe right without me."

"Your curry is probably cold," Willow stated.

"I'll get Danny boy to put a steaming spoonful on top of it to warm it up. Danny!" he screamed, causing the girls to jump again. "How is it?"

"Well, I don't guess it's possible for anyone to love it as much as Elm here, but it's amazing. Wow. So flavorful," Willow raved, finishing up the last of her stew.

"Better than chili," Oak agreed.

"Another helping?" Shep asked.

"Oh, I don't think I need to eat all that," Willow stated, pinching her stomach. "You can tell I already eat too much."

"No, I can't. Danny! More curry," Shep yelled. "Besides, I like people with meat on their bones."

"But—" Willow tried to object.

"You'll eat it." He winked at her.

"He loves making everyone plump," I informed the girls.

"Plump is happy. I don't have the appetite to enjoy my food like everybody else. So I savor it vicariously through others. Willow, you're perfect. I wouldn't let you change one inch of that tummy." He pointed at her waist.

"He won't even let me get rid of mine," I joked, tugging at my own gut.

We finished off the curry, and Shep ordered us four generous slices of orange sickle cake.

119

"I know it's a weird choice," Shep told us. "To pair this cake with curry. But considering this is our first date" — he reached across the table and gently rubbed Willow's palm — "I had to give you the best. Otherwise, you may never come back." He looked at me with his seductive devilish grin. "Dig in."

"Wait, Shep, before we do," Willow interrupted, grabbing his hand with hers.

"Um-hum?"

"Can I kiss you?"

His body tensed up beside me causing the booth to squeak. His whole face froze. My mouth dropped open. I tried looking casually back down at my cake.

Shep glanced around. It was near closing time, and there were only a few regulars hanging out, but they were seated on the other side of the restaurant. He then looked at me, but I didn't remove my eyes from the dessert. He put his hand on my knee in a clandestine fashion, squeezing gently, before turning back to Willow.

"How do you want to do this?" he asked.

Willow got up and placed her hands on Shep's shoulders, pulling his legs around to face outward from the booth. She sat on his lap and drew his chin up to her lips. I thought the kiss would be a little peck, but she wasn't an amateur. I watched her tongue move in and out of his mouth passionately . . . sexually. I saw him slightly pinching her stomach, the way he often did to me when we kissed. I wondered if I should knock her off of him or slap him. But seeing someone using Shep in such a sensual manner filled my loins with excitement. I loosened up my belt buckle.

After it was over, Willow sat back down and took a big bite of cake, slowly licking the icing from the fork. Shep casually started eating, too.

"Oh my god," Oak gasped. "This cake is so fucking good."

"Come on, Elm," Willow teased me. "I want to see you really enjoy this dessert."

Glancing down at my erection made me feel like one bite would make me come in my pants. Yet the confusion from all the mixture of emotions that I was feeling also caused me to worry that I would just vomit.

I spooned up a heaping forkful of cake. I closed my eyes and took a bite, moaning with pleasure as the citric sweetness exploded on my taste buds.

"If there's one thing I learned about you two is that you guys sure can have some fun with food. I want to lay in bed feeding Elm all day." Willow giggled, pointing her fork at me.

"It's gotta be *my* food," Shep mumbled with his mouth full.

"Don't speak too fast," she challenged as she crossed her arms. "You haven't had mine, yet. What's your favorite dessert?"

"Cheesecake," both me and Shep answered.

"I'm going to make you two a Mississippi mud cheesecake tomorrow night, and we'll eat it at your place. What do you think?" She smiled fiendishly, winking at us.

"I have to work tomorrow night," Shep stated.

"It's Saturday. You won't be working, right, Elm?" she asked.

"No," I replied. I froze. *I'll be alone with her? What will happen? Am I ready for this?*

"Then I'll come over and feed you cheesecake." She turned to Shep. "Besides, how late do you work?"

"We close at ten, and it takes another hour or two to clean and prep for the next day," he responded, pushing his empty plate away.

"How about this," she said confidently as she shimmied her body in the seat. "I show up at your place to feed you cheesecake." She tapped my hand. Her gaze moved to Shep. "Later, I'll come here to close this restaurant with you."

Shep and I stared at each other like two kids caught with

their hands in the cookie jar. I don't think either of us expected things to progress this fast, nor did we expect to have alone dates.

Too scared to mess it up now, I stuttered, "Okay."

Shep shrugged. "Okay."

Chapter Twelve: Shep

Elmer and I didn't say much on the walk back to the house. I only recalled the nightly hum of various insects in the late summer air, the cool breeze brushing up against my bare arms, and the poignant urge to grab Elmer's hand, to hug him, to kiss him — to do *something*.

I slept in the next morning so that I could prepare for working a Saturday at the Tire, our busiest day of the week. I didn't have much time to engage in a discussion about the past evening's events with Elmer. He merely sat around the porch, sipping coffee, and reading as normal, as if pandora's box hadn't just gotten blown open. I resented the nonchalant silence.

By the time I got dressed and ready to head out, Elmer was watching a football game and eating hummus while wearing an old *Guns-N-Roses* t-shirt and boxer shorts. I sat down beside him, clicking off the T.V. and removing the food container from his hands.

"That's about over twelve hours . . . *twelve hours* that we haven't talked about this. That's not a good start," I admitted.

"I know," he mumbled, evading my gaze.

"What are you thinking?" I asked hesitantly. My throat tightened.

Elmer sighed and fumbled with the waist band of his boxers, revealing the black patches of curly hair that lead down toward his privates, a spot that I didn't find *sexually* appealing but charming, nonetheless.

"Go on. Tell me," I encouraged him. "Are you mad at me for kissing her? I didn't know what to do. I thought you wanted me to." My heart hung heavy.

"It's more like I'm upset with myself," he responded solemnly.

I widened my eyes and raised my eyebrows. "What for?"

"Because a part of me liked it. *Sexually* liked it." He finally looked up at me, and I could see his fear in his frown.

"Oh . . ." I took his hand and curled my fingers around it. "That's fine. The whole point of doing this was to let you explore your sexuality. So I guess that's okay."

"There's this jealous feeling, too," he continued. "Because she picked you. Envious that you kissed her back. So when it turned me on, it felt wrong."

"I know what you mean," I agreed. "I felt so guilty after kissing her. You didn't say anything. I thought you were mad at me for it."

Elm put his arm around me and pulled me closer to him. "I'm not. We both agreed to this going into it. It feels so . . . weird."

"Do you want to move forward with it today? We can always back—"

"Yes, I do," he interrupted, nodding his head gently. "I don't want to spaz out like I typically do. If you're still okay with it, I mean."

"I'm all right with it," I lied. I had no idea how seeing Elmer kiss Willow would make me feel. The dreary feeling twisting in the pit of my stomach suggested that I didn't want to find out.

"You're not going to have sex with her, right?" he asked. "I know that sounds hypocritical, but it would really mess with my head. If you're not into sex—"

"You mean sexual attraction," I corrected him, holding up my forefinger.

"Yeah, but then if you're intimate with her . . . I guess it feels like an ultimate romantic betrayal because if it's not sexual, it has to be something more . . . something deeper." He glanced desperately at me.

"I understand. I don't have any urge to get it on with Willow," I promised him. I certainly didn't want to do anything to hurt Elmer. That was the last thing I expected. Especially since it was *my* idea.

"Did you like her?" he asked.

"Sure, she seems nice." The truth was that I *did* really like her. I didn't expect our conversations about food to be so intriguing, and I had already started fantasizing about cooking dates with her. It felt good to share a bond over cuisine that involved more than me cooking it and the other person eating it. We felt more like equals.

"I want something from you," I told Elmer.

"Yeah."

I ran my finger up and down my thigh. "I want to know everything you do with her . . . sexually. No secrets. Most importantly, and do not fuck this up, but you make sure you use protection. I don't want any STDs or babies . . ." My voice trailed off, and my stomach dropped. I knew how badly he wanted children. I hated myself for being so insensitive.

"Yes, of course," he concurred. "I'm not going to have unprotected sex."

I kissed him goodbye, but a feeling of distance and dread lingered in me as I walked away from him. We were both going to be alone with her. The real challenge to our relationship was only beginning.

The school year was about to begin, so the Tire was packed full of patrons out school shopping or enjoying the final days of summer. I was hosting the last fish fry of the season, browning pounds of southern style catfish, hushpuppies, and crawdads. My dessert special included multiple varieties of homemade fruit sherbet, vanilla sugar sandwich cookies with raspberry cream cheese filling, and fresh strawberry short-cakes.

Despite all the distractions from the customers' voices, the clicking and scraping of silverware on plates, and the sizzle from the kitchen, I constantly checked my phone.

It's seven PM. She'd be over there now. What are they doing? Why hasn't he texted me.

As closing approached, a twinge of fear emerged in my gut that Willow wouldn't show up at all. Perhaps she was having too much fun with Elmer that they'd forgotten the time and decided to spend all night together. *What if I come home, and they're in bed?*

A part of me wanted to run out of the restaurant, stomp into my house, and stop it. But like Elmer, I was also curious. I wanted to see if this would make him happy and if it could work out for me, too. At least, I loved him enough to hope so.

It was ten thirty. I was alone, wiping off tables and refilling napkin holders. I'd ordered my staff to leave, for I certainly didn't want to initiate any rumors when this young girl showed up to meet me. But she was thirty minutes late. *Maybe she isn't coming . . .*

Maybe her and Elmer are tangled up in our bed with their legs wrapped around each other, grinding and moaning in ecstasy . . .

Just then, I heard a knock on the front door and saw Willow smiling and waving. I let her inside, and she stumbled in wearing only a pair of cut-off jean shorts, fishnet thigh highs, and a tight black tube top with skulls painted on it in silver glitter. It looked like she'd been wearing lipstick. The remnants of it outlined the outer corners of her lips. Her curly hair stuck out wildly around her round dimpled face.

"Sorry, I'm late. We lost track of time. I'm not usually as fortunate to have two dates in one night." She took a seat at the bar.

"Can I get you something," I asked. "Wine? Beer?"

"How about some of that wine from last night. That was

good."

I opened up a bottle of cabernet and set out some pita bread and hummus, a staple appetizer that I always kept fully stocked and handy.

"I don't know if y'all ate," I said as I placed it down in front of her.

"Thanks, this is great," she stated as she began eating. I wasn't sure what she fancied, so I laid out a sample of my most popular ones. Sundried tomato, caramelized onion, and roasted red pepper. I poured us both a generous glass of wine.

"Wait," Willow stopped me before my glass hit my lips. She cupped my chin and pulled me toward her, kissing me as passionately as the previous night. "Sorry, Shep. You know, you're really cute. I can't help myself."

"Thanks." I'd never felt insecure about my looks. I liked my style that I sometimes dressed up a little with some makeup and cool hats. Maybe it was because of my asexuality, but I didn't worry about other people finding me hot.

"I feel really attracted to you. Like I just want to kiss you and touch you." Her hands rested on top of mine.

I laughed shyly. *When is a good time to tell someone you're asexual? What if I tell her and mess everything up for Elmer? Should I get her to like me first? Is that deceitful? Do I need to tell her I'm trans? Does it matter?*

"Are you attracted to me?" she asked, taking a big gulp of wine.

"Um, yeah. I like your style. It's unique." I found her adorable, even if it wasn't a sexual attraction. I also liked her forwardness. I thought it would do Elmer some good.

"You seem shy," she remarked, peering into my eyes.

"No, I'm not," I assured her.

"Well, you seem shyer than you did last night." She giggled. "You two are like opposites. In public, Elm's shy, but you're not. Alone, Elm's not shy at all, and you're as quiet and tense as you can be."

So he's not shy at all now? Alone . . .

"I'm not . . . oh, shit," I stammered and guzzled down my wine in one shot.

"What's wrong?" She stared at me with a raised eyebrow.

I took a deep breath and twirled my glass around in my hands. "Look, I'm not good at keeping secrets or hiding things. So I'm just going to tell you. But I'm sorry if it's awkward. It's complicated." I hated it when I rambled.

"Tell me what?"

A heavy long pause hovered in the air between us, and I poured myself another hefty glass and topped hers off. I took a large gulp, nearly choking on it. I clumsily shoved a piece of pita in my mouth, causing parts of it to fall onto the counter.

"I'm waiting," she urged me, crossing her arms.

I braced myself against the counter. "Look, Willow, the reason that Elm and I are looking for a girl—"

"A beautiful unicorn," she emphasized with a wink.

I nodded. "Yes. A beautiful unicorn who obviously knows how to dress and how to cook. It's that . . . I'm asexual."

She rubbed her chin. "Asexual? I've heard the term before, but I haven't met anyone who was asexual."

"It means that I don't feel sexual attraction to people, mostly."

"You don't like sex?" She looked more disappointed than puzzled.

"I don't hate it," I informed her. Even though I'd promised Elmer that I wouldn't have sex with her, I feared giving her the impression that it was completely off limits—at least, for now. I didn't want to chase her away. "But honestly, sex with another person isn't my thing so much. But if I love someone, it's okay. I'm still very much a romantic. I don't know if any of this makes sense."

Willow ate a few pieces of pita and sipped her wine, processing the information. "So why did *you* seek a unicorn?"

"Because I thought Elm would be happier if he had

someone to do it with who likes it the way he does." I immediately regretted my words. She probably expected to have super-hot and sexy adventures with us only to find out that she was basically a lover for one and a cooking buddy for the other. I was fucking it up.

"So what do *you* get out of it?" she asked. Her tone carried an air of regret but also curiosity.

"I get . . ." I examined her for a moment. Despite a few confused looks and apparent surprise, she seemed unflappable, just sitting, eating hummus, and sipping wine as if she was at a cocktail party. She hung on my every word.

I walked over to the side of the bar and sat down next to her. Her face lit up with a grin so bright that my heart fluttered, and my face grew red. Willow swiveled her stool to face me, and I reached forward, putting my hands on her hips and pulling her closer to me so that my legs sandwiched hers.

"You sure you're asexual?" she teased as she leaned over and kissed me.

I smiled shyly like a teenage boy. "I think I like you," I told her. "While I may not feel this physical attraction toward you, I do feel attracted to you. But there's more."

"Yes," she answered eagerly stroking my thighs with the palms of her hands.

I stared down for a long time, trying to muster up the best words to say. She grabbed my hips and dragged me closer to her, whispering in my ear, "I really like you, too. Maybe one day, you'll like me enough to not mind sex."

"There's more to it than that."

"What is it, Sheppy?"

I glanced away from her. "I'm a . . . I'm trans. I was assigned female at birth."

"Really? Wow, I've never met a trans guy before." She smiled, rubbing my back with her fingers.

"I consider myself nonbinary, really. I don't necessarily

identify with cisgender men, but I definitely feel more like a man than a woman. Transmasculine is what they say . . . or at least, what seems to fit." I figured if she was bisexual, then maybe it wasn't a big deal. But then again, people had unique sexual preferences. Maybe being with a man with a vagina was a turn off.

Willow chuckled. "Is *that* all? I don't care. Whatever you were before doesn't bother me or change how irresistibly cute you are now. God, do I seem like someone who would mind?"

I grinned in agreement, realizing that it should've been obvious that someone like her wouldn't care. It was my fear of rejection from someone who I actually liked. This time, I yanked Willow toward me and kissed her passionately. Moving away, I couldn't stop giggling.

"Sorry," I stuttered. "I'm not a big kisser . . . unless . . ."

"Unless?"

"I'm feeling this strong connection with someone." I flushed. *Did I just say that to her? This is so fast.*

"You mean, this crazy scary but giddy feeling? Like I don't ever want to leave this place. I want to lay down and hold you all night long." She pinched my thighs and placed her forehead against mine.

Wow, cuddling and no sex. She does get asexuals.

"You don't care that I don't have . . . you know." I indicated by pointing at my groin area.

"I'm bisexual . . . well, I guess now, I'm technically pansexual. No, that don't bother me at all, Sheppy."

"You're okay that our relationship isn't about sex?" My whole body froze as I waited in anguish for her response. I didn't want to get pushed to the sidelines because I wasn't sexual.

Willow shot me a devilish grin and threw her arms around me. "Nope. As long as we can do this," she stated, hugging me tight. "And we can cuddle up, maybe naked sometimes." She pulled away suddenly. "Does it mean that we'll never do it? Not even sometimes? You said that you don't mind if you like someone."

I finished off my wine, and my Adam's apple felt like a hard rock lodged in my throat as I recalled Elmer's insistence that I not have sex with Willow. *You've been honest up until this point and all is good. Might as well not stop now.*

"So." I sighed. "Elmer and I have these agreements going into this. He prefers that you and me don't have sex."

"Oh," she muttered quietly, leaning away from me.

"I'm sorry," I told her, holding her hand. "I guess it sounded good when we discussed it with each other, but after telling you, it doesn't sound fair." My feelings confused me. Seeing her move away caused an emptiness in my chest.

"Sheppy, if we're all three going to have a relationship, don't you think that I should be part of these agreements? Or am I some sex toy for Elm so that you can salvage your marriage?"

My mouth dropped open, and a sharp pain burned in my chest. It was the first time that Willow grew serious and even sounded insulted. My gut told me that I didn't want this new tantalizing sensation created by her to vanish.

"No, not at all. And you're right." I slapped my hand on my forehead. "We're lousy at this."

She sighed, fumbling with a crumb of bread on her leg. "Do you want to do this, Shep?"

"Yes," I answered because I wanted her arms around me again. "I didn't get to finish from before."

"Finish what?" She raised her eyebrow at me.

"When you asked me what I got out of it. I didn't finish."

"Okay, go ahead," she urged me.

"I never got to be with a woman as a man . . . since presenting as more masculine. The way you look at me and touch me . . . like a man . . . I want to experience that. And I'd really like to do it with you, Willow." My heart pounded. *How can I feel this with another person? Am I betraying Elmer?*

131

She smiled and threw her arms back around me. "Wow," she whispered. "It's like dating a virgin. What an honor."

We kissed, and I pulled her on top of my lap, as if I were in control, letting my masculinity flourish.

"I'd love to let you be a man with me," she said breathlessly in my ear.

Chapter Thirteen: Elmer

Shep always cooked us breakfast on Sunday mornings. That day, it was Belgian waffles with caramelized pearl sugar topped with baked cinnamon apples, cheddar scrambled eggs, and turkey sausage. I was already in bed when he'd returned from the restaurant the previous night, even though I wasn't asleep. I had sat on the sofa until one, processing my own evening and imagining what was happening at the Tire. It was too late to talk about it, so I laid down. It was typical of my ongoing urge to avoid anything complicated.

I waited until we got ready to eat before bringing up the subject. I had this burning excitement exploding through me, yet also this dreadful feeling that I cheated and would offend Shep. Or worse, that he would hurt me. My stomach rumbled in conflict.

"So," Shep began, knowing that I'd never say the first word. "What happened last night?" he asked casually, eating but staring down at his plate.

"I feel very nervous about this conversation," I admitted, burning my tongue on the coffee. I ate a large piece of waffle to soothe it.

He nodded. "Yeah, I know what you mean."

"You do?"

He must have done something. The thought sent a piercing sensation down my chest. Naively, I pictured them hanging out, swapping recipes, and becoming friends. Watching Shep as he chewed, I admired the beautiful crevices of his cheekbones and the spotted dimples around the corners of his mouth. I was foolish to think that Willow wouldn't feel attracted to him. I guess another part of me wanted to convince myself that he only did it for me. *He couldn't really enjoy it, right?*

"What did you do?" I asked him.

He continued eye-balling his plate, stabbing his eggs with his fork and stroking his coffee mug with the other hand. "I was home late," he remarked after a few seconds.

"Yeah, I noticed. I heard you come in." His silence scared me.

"She was late with you, too. Guess that's a good sign," he stated matter-of-factly.

"Good sign?" *He's upset. I knew this was all a mistake.*

"That she likes us, and that she wants to be our girlfriend. That's the goal, right?" He glanced at me for reassurance, but there was still an air of distance to him.

"What did y'all do?" I cautiously inquired again. "I mean, you stayed late, too. So . . . you had a good time?"

"So did you, I assume," he retorted.

"Are you avoiding the question?" I snapped, feeling my irritation bubbling up in me.

"Don't accuse me like that," he responded, throwing his fork down. "You said this conversation was uncomfortable, and well, it's difficult for me, too." He stared down, resting his head in his hands.

"I'm sorry," I apologized, holding up my hand in a truce.

"We kissed," he admitted, still pouting. "We talked. We ate a lot of hummus. We kissed."

"Did you make out?" Something inside of me wanted my questions to stop, but I was also dying to know.

"Yes," he mumbled.

"Like . . . taking off clothes, or just kissing?" I clarified.

"Kissing. And cuddling."

I wasn't sure which would have been worse. Naked petting would have made me worried, yet snuggling was intimate. I struggled picturing Willow nestling next to Shep. Shep holding her. A wave of sadness flooded through me.

"Did you like it? You like her?" I asked with a shakiness in my throat that he must have sensed, causing him to finally look at me.

"Yes. She's really cool," he replied.

My heart sank. Somehow, I expected to have this new exciting fling in my life while also being able to keep Shep all to myself. I figured they'd be friends like the wives on that *Sister Wives* show. Companions who offered support but were mainly focused on my happiness and keeping the home cordial. The pain in my spirit only poignantly drew my attention to what Shep must feel by letting me fuck another person.

"What about you? What'd y'all do?" he asked, now glaring at me.

"We ordered pizza—"

"Oh, god, you fed her shit," he moaned, slapping his forehead. Shep despised anytime anyone ordered takeout or fastfood because he firmly and spiritually believed that all people deserve only the freshest cuisine. Giving them anything less was the equivalent of poisoning them.

"We ate pizza," I continued. "Had her cheesecake . . . which is pretty damn tasty! It's in the fridge. You should totally try it."

"Get on with it," he demanded.

"We had some wine on the sofa. I talked about growing up here and being a principal. She chatted about her art. She does paintings. They're really great. She showed me a lot of pictures of them." I knew that I was only prolonging the story to avoid getting to the physical part.

"Then?" Shep pushed me to go on.

"Then . . ." I hesitated, fidgeting with my hands. "We started making out."

"Clothes or no clothes?"

135

"There were some . . . clothes removed, yes," I admitted. I wanted to vomit.

"What exactly?" he pressured as he leaned back and crossed his arms. His face had no expression, making my confession harder because I couldn't assess his emotions. He was much better at hiding them than me.

"Shirts. No pants. Just shirts." Even though we'd agreed to this, it felt like I was confessing to cheating and that any minute, Shep would slap me and walk out. I picked at my fingernails.

"Bra?" Shep asked.

"She wasn't wearing one—" I blurted out, immediately gasping at what I said.

"Did she touch you . . . in the pants?" he went on, gazing at my crotch.

"Yes."

"Did you touch her?"

"Yes."

"Where did it stop?"

I took a deep breath and finished off my coffee. I stared at the remaining Belgian waffle that was so scrumptious a second before but now the smell and sight only made me nauseous.

"Elm?" Shep pushed.

"We . . ." I choked. "We gave each other hand-jobs. We got each other off. That's why we lost track of time." I wanted to get down on my knees and beg him not to leave me for what I had done.

He stroked his chin, pulling on his few strands of facial hair.

"Are you okay," I asked, moving over to the empty chair beside him.

His face tensed, and his eyes appeared watery. He wiped them with his napkin. Shep wasn't a visibly emotional person, so seeing him hurt only caused me to cry. He looked over, watching me sobbing, causing his own tears to pour out more. Ironically, we both started laughing at the sight of each other.

"I'm okay," he assured me, after our giggles subsided. "I mean, we agreed to this, so I can't be mad at you for it. That wouldn't be fair. I guess it's a little hard, though."

"It is," I concurred, giving him a hug and a kiss on the forehead. "Maybe it's because we love each other. And that's a good thing."

He nodded. "Yeah. I'm sure lots of couples in their first outside experience feel this way when things progress, right?"

"Probably." I was still in disbelief that I was doing this. I hadn't even considered how other couples who explore polyamory would handle it. Maybe it was all normal, and we would work through it.

"I think I need some time to process it all. To get used to it," he told me.

I squeezed his knee.

"Did you enjoy it, Elm? It wasn't sex . . . or it was . . . but you get what I mean. Did you get something you needed?" He took my hand, which was encouraging.

"I don't know. Yes, I enjoyed it. Needed . . . ." I wasn't sure about that part. I felt selfish.

"How did she make you feel?" he asked, rubbing my cheek with his hand.

I gulped hard. "Um . . ."

"Be honest. You can tell me," he urged me.

"Desired. It felt good." I knew how insecure Shep was about his asexuality. So I hated informing him that someone else was giving me something that he couldn't. While we were still close, a distance was there.

"Okay, then," he said, as he got up to start cleaning the table. "That's what I wanted for you."

It was clear that Willow had had a good weekend with both of us and was interested in becoming our girlfriend. Great Falls was only an hour and a half or so away, making it easy for her to visit. She could take the transit that ran to and from Cloverleaf to save gas. It wasn't long before she decided that she wanted to stay over.

Willow and I had been texting each other all morning when I arrived to work that following Monday. I had never dated much, so I was unsure if this was how women acted. Were women so forward and free in their sexuality, or was this just Willow? I was still processing the images of Shep and her making out and cuddling. Now, I thought about her staying the night with us.

Where would she sleep? With us? Or would me and her stay in the bedroom with Shep on the couch? Would we walk into the other room when we wanted to have sex, leaving him alone with some kind of instructions that would let him know when we were done? Would he watch?

I texted Shep that Willow preferred to stay at the house when she visited that weekend. He agreed.

Shep was right. Willow's request for separate dates had taken us off guard. We preferred more transparency. So her staying at home was the only logical way to proceed. But it all seemed too surreal. I carried all the guilt of someone having a secret love affair, yet there was no sneaking around or lying. Nevertheless, something felt wrong.

I texted Willow letting her know that she can stay with us.

I set my phone down on my desk with a loud thud. It was real now. This would happen. It wasn't going to be some fling or some wild night that Shep and I experienced. We were adding a third.

When Willow and I had been alone that past weekend, I was nervous. When she had sat before me with her black makeup and tube top that squeezed her breasts together, I'd

found her so beautiful. It was similar to any normal tempta-
tion. Like when I admire a sexy person on the street, but I return to my senses and dismiss them as a sexual possibility.
That changed when I'd seen her smile, the way she'd constantly ran her hand through her curly hair, and her freckles
that spotted her arms like a galaxy of stars. There was also her
intoxicating confidence. She seemed so sure of herself, her
body, and her sexuality. She could teach me things that no one
had ever shown me. With every passing thought, my desire
for her pressed stubbornly against the crotch of my pants.

Shep had said it was okay. While his approval felt almost
the same as a betrayal, it also proved how much he cared for
me. He didn't want me to deny my sexual nature. He hoped
that I'd have a partner who would help me explore that part
of myself. It was like Alfred Kinsey. He loved his wife, but he
didn't think marriage had to hold people back from erotic
self-actualization. It's a bunch of mainstream brainwashing
that tells us that exploring other sexual connections was bad
and ruined love. Shep and I were way more mature and
stronger. We could make this work. Then I could have this
amazing sex life without pressuring him to fulfill that need.
And Shep . . . he could have a friend. *Was that enough?*

I messaged Shep that I wanted him to come home earlier
from the Tire that evening because I had plans for us. He
agreed with no questions, which was rather unusual for him.

When he came through the front door, he carried two takeout plates from the restaurant.

"It was Chinese night," he stated. "Spicy eggplant, pork
dumplings, and Peking duck, my specialty."

"Good," I said and pointed at the living room. "Go set it up
in there, and I'll grab some beers."

"In the living room?" He scowled at me. Shep hated any
distractions from his food because he believed that not giving
it one's full attention was blasphemy.

"Just do it," I hollered.

When I came in with the beers, some napkins, and chopsticks, he had the dinner spread out over our coffee table in front of the couch.

"It's going to be difficult eating with chopsticks in here," he commented, pointing at how low the table sat.

"We can sit on the floor, if needed," I suggested. I turned on the T.V.

"So what is this?" he demanded. "You call me home early to veg-out watching T.V. *You* don't even do that."

"I want us to watch this. I think it'll be good for us." I was determined to convince myself that what we were doing was okay. And this was the best idea that I had.

"Watch what?" he asked.

"*Kinsey*, the movie."

"Huh?"

"It's about Alfred Kinsey. He studied sexuality." Shep was educated, so I figured he'd appreciate an outlook on sex coming from an expert.

He groaned. "I'm not asexual because I don't have enough sex education."

"It's not just about that. You'll see."

"Do I have to?"

I smiled and winked at him. "You'll watch it."

CHAPTER FOURTEEN: SHEP

I lost count of how many hours I cried after Elmer's confession of exchanged hand-jobs. Placing my hands on the corners of the bathroom sink at the Tire, I squeezed my eyes shut, chanting to myself, "It's just sex."

While I could be sex favorable at times, for the most part, I was often sex indifferent. While it wasn't my first choice of activities, I could tolerate it like a bad movie, waiting in line, whatever. *So it shouldn't matter if Elmer fucks this other girl, right? Why is sex such a big deal, anyway? It's only bodies touching bodies.*

Despite my efforts, I couldn't shake the dreadful feeling of loss consuming me. I was missing out somehow. Plus, with all the sex on T.V., in movies, in music, in art—it was what everyone wanted. If Elmer had this adventurous sex life with Willow, how was our bond going to compete with that? Bombarded with lust—even in hamburger commercials—sex was *everything*.

Elmer's fascination with the *Kinsey* film didn't ease my anxieties. The way he pointed out all the examples of open sexuality and talked about un-brainwashing ourselves from the monogamous garbage we've been fed all these years was so out of his character. It was like he was all in, and I was staring down at the top of the hill terrified to take the leap after him. *Had I already lost him?*

Elmer made good points, and I was willing to challenge myself for him. There were decades of suppressed sexual desires lurking inside of him that he hadn't felt free enough to

141

explore until now. He was way more sensual in bed, savoring every aspect of my body and loudly vocalizing his outbursts of pleasure. I didn't want to hold him back anymore. Rubbing my temples, I naively wanted for us to have it all.

Friday evenings were the slowest evenings for the weekend. My regular patrons enjoyed table visits from the owner. However, Willow demanded to cook with me at the restaurant. She wanted to smoke some barbecue chicken, a specialty of hers, but she'd never cooked on such a large scale before and needed my help. I agreed that she could serve her dish on Friday instead of Saturday or Sunday in case it didn't work out.

"I thought we'd *all* hang out on her first night sleeping over," Elmer complained that morning. "Not just you two at the restaurant."

"Her pictures look awesome, but in reality, I don't know for sure that this girl can cook. So I'll be damned if I'm going to risk it on a Saturday or Sunday. I get more of my travelers and out-of-towners those days. I can't make a bad impression. I want them to remember the Tire and build the tradition of stopping to eat there whenever they pass through."

"But don't you have other entrees they can choose from in case the chicken's awful?" he asked.

"Yes, but do you think I'm going to waste my chicken? My inventory?" I snorted. "No, we try it out tonight, and if she fucks it up, I can always take it over."

"But you can do that on the other nights, too?" Elmer insisted.

I rolled my eyes. He knew how important my reputation was to me. "Look, I want to do it tonight. I don't tell you how to run your school. Don't tell me how to run my restaurant."

"Okay, okay," he conceded, gulping down the rest of his coffee. "So what's the plan then?"

"I suppose me and her are cooking at the Tire, and you can hang out there, or see us when we get home." I wasn't sure what would make me more nervous. Having Elmer around or leaving him alone.

"I guess I'll see you when you get here. I don't want to tread on your time with her," he mumbled, kicking his feet. He was acting like a spoiled child.

I laughed. "It's *our* time. We're all dating."

Willow's chicken proved to be a success with customers. She preferred a spicy and saucy rub compared to my dry ones. But it tasted succulent, sending squirts of warm juices dribbling down people's chins. I even indulged in several legs myself.

"I told you that I can cook," she teased, as she pinned more breasts on her skewer for the smoker.

"Different technique, but yes, this is quite acceptable." I nodded, wiping grease from my chin.

"Acceptable?" Willow smirked. "This is the fucking bomb."

"No, the Mississippi mud cheesecake was the fucking bomb," I corrected her.

We were alone in the back section of the kitchen where no one could see us. Willow walked over with her gloved hands and her plastic hair cap and laid a big kiss on me.

"All this cooking and this heat is getting me hot," she whispered.

"Okay," I muttered. I never knew what people expected me to do with such information.

She strolled back to the counter. "But I guess Elmer will take care of that when we get home? Is that how this works?"

"Are you joking with me?" I asked, jerking around to glare at her.

She giggled. "You're the one who said that I'm here

because you can't fulfill his sexual needs. So I'm asking how this works. I go grab him and head off whenever we feel the mood. Remember this is my first polyamorous relationship, too."

I grabbed a beer from my cooler, popped off the cap, and took a long sip.

"You drink a lot," she commented.

"Yeah, I guess I do," I agreed, setting the bottle down on the counter. I rubbed my brow. "So you're asking me how this is going to work this weekend?"

"Yes. I told you that I need to be a part of these discussions like you two are. And I certainly don't want to step on any toes. So Shep," she said, coming up to me and placing her hands on my hips, pulling me close to her. "How do you prefer that I seduce your husband for you?"

"Um," I choked, snatching up my beer again.

"Are you sure you're comfortable with this? You seem awfully nervous. Would you feel better if you watch?"

"No!" I shouted, immediately glancing at the front of the kitchen in case I alarmed anyone. I stepped away from her. "If you want to fuck him tonight, then just . . . take him to our bedroom."

"What are you going to do?" Willow asked with a pouty expression.

"I'll watch T.V., read, do something." The idea of me sitting in the living room listening to the sounds of Elmer doing it with someone else gave me the willies. I'd rather make up an excuse to work late and avoid it.

She approached me again, wrapping her arms around my waist this time. "You sure you don't want to participate? It may make you feel better."

"I didn't agree to this so that I had to have *more* sex or sex with *more* people." *I'm such a loser for saying this to someone with such immense sexual ripeness radiating off her body.*

She removed one of her gloves, and lovingly stroked my cheek with her naked palm. "So how will I make you feel special, Shep?"

I shrugged. "I liked having you around tonight. It's been fun cooking and eating drumsticks with you back here." I smiled.

"How crowded is it out there now?" she asked.

I went to the front of the kitchen to peep out the door and surveyed the premises. The crowd was fading, but we had another hour before closing. "It's not packed, but there's quite a bit of people still."

"Good," Willow stated, taking off her other glove and her hair net. "Call Danny."

"For what?"

"Have him watch the kitchen for a few minutes."

"I'd rather have Peggy do that." Peggy was Danny's girlfriend, who was way ahead of him not only in age but also in maturity. Danny did good on the floor because the demands from customers worked well for his ADHD brain, but when it came to the kitchen, he couldn't focus so effectively. He thrived better in constant chaos. Peggy often helped me a lot with cooking, and if their relationship were to blossom into marriage, I'd even be okay with her becoming my next sous-chef.

"I'll be in here," Willow hollered as she disappeared into the back. There was a small spare room at the Tire with a cot and toilet. Over the years, I had a few employees undergoing tough periods who needed a place to crash. So I left it the way I'd found it just for that reason.

I called Peggy in to watch the stoves. The process of handing over these duties was complicated because my cooking times, temps, and any other detail had been planned out precisely. Anything out of those specific formulas, I refused to accept.

145

I walked into the back, and Willow was laying on the cot, sticking her legs up in the air one by one.

"Nice room," she commented. "What's this for anyway?"

"I found it like this and kept it. Sometimes people need a place to crash."

"And you trust them to stay here? At your restaurant?" she asked, sitting up on her elbows.

"I let employees I trust sleep here, yes. No one's disappointed me, yet." I answered, as I sat beside her.

She put her hand on my thigh. "You seem like a really nice guy, Shep. Sending some of my chicken plates out to be delivered to elders. That's very cool."

"Well, the community helps fund that program. It's not all me. The other restaurants here do it, too."

She ran her fingers along my arm. "Don't downplay yourself so much. You let people stay in this room. You get a girl so that your husband can have sex. Not many people are like you."

"Do you now take me seriously when I say that I'm getting something out of it, too? I thought last weekend was great." I placed my hand on her leg and squeezed.

Willow smiled, removed her glasses, and set them on a small table by the cot. "I believe you are, Shep. But I also think you're probably not sure what you're getting into here."

"So you assume it's only to make Elmer happy?" I asked. *Damn! I'm fucking this all up.* I didn't want her to lose interest because of me.

"I think that's a big part of it. You're not as eager as he is. You're very cautious. Careful. Caring." She moved my hand closer to her crotch.

"I'm not going to —"

"That's not what I mean," she interrupted. "Look at how nervous you are right now. You're shaking."

"No, I'm not," I snapped, shoving my hands in between

my legs to hide it.

"We only have a few minutes. I want to do something to make you feel special." She sat all the way up.

"What do you want to do?" I asked. Part of me shook while the other part bubbled with intrigue.

She leaned over and kissed me, grabbing the back of my head. She whispered in my ear, "You don't like partner sex. Do you masturbate?"

"Yeah," I admitted evading her eyes.

"Good." She smiled. "Lay back, and I'll take care of you."

"Wait—" I tried to stop her, holding up my hand.

"Come on, do it," she ordered, pushing me playfully backward.

"Wait . . . I haven't talked to Elm about this," I stammered as she unzipped my jeans and slid her hand into my pants. Her touch sent shivers all through me, and my body welcomed it eagerly.

"Don't worry," she breathed in my ear as she laid on top of me. "It's not full sex. It's only a friend helping you masturbate, right? What's wrong with that? You just have to lay back and not do anything. How jealous can he get?" She shrugged.

"But—" I moaned as her fingers slid between my vaginal lips. My clit swelled with ecstasy. My attempts to stop it surrendered to pleasure.

She kissed me. "You have to explore yourself, too, Shep. If you're going to be able to let Elmer go all the way. But if you really want me to stop, I will." She stared at me with her eyebrow raised. "Do I have your consent?"

My logic argued, but my heart pounded. A warm rush ran through my veins. Plus, everything she said made perfect sense. I needed to explore my boundaries.

"Yes," I replied.

I let my arms fall flaccid. She was right. I'd often preferred it when Elmer and me satisfied each other with hand-jobs rather than intercourse or oral sex. To me, it was like getting a good massage. And I got to keep my clothes on and was able to avoid all the body kissing and petting that I hated.

My clit hardened and seeped out from between my lips, the closest I ever came to having a boner. I grabbed her leg and closed my eyes. My vulva contracted as she caressed my clit, even pinching it between her forefinger and thumb, up and down, like a real penis.

The *Kinsey* movie popped up in my mind. This felt good. *Elmer's still my husband, my one true love. This is only . . . a massage. I should get to experiment, too.* I had worked so hard to be my genuine self. *Why suppress it now?* As Willow said, I needed to discover myself. This was Willow's way to make me feel special. *Just go with it. Try it. Run with it.*

When I was about to climax, Willow leaned down and pressed her lips firmly against mine, causing my breaths to enter her mouth and our eyes to lock into each other's.

There was no turning back now.

CHAPTER FIFTEEN: ELMER

It was Friday night, and I paced back and forth in my living room. I'd considered going to the Tire for dinner and sampling Willow's famous barbecue chicken, but I didn't want to intrude on Shep's time with her.

"I can't be selfish," I said aloud to myself. "This can't all be for me."

An intense greed arose in me. All my life, I had played the good guy. I'd done my homework in school and had avoided the brawls that my brothers often found themselves tangled up in. I'd sat in the corner quietly as I watched more confident guys hit on girls with remarkable ease. I was even jealous of the gay dudes who proudly put themselves out there. The only thing I had ever persistently pursued was becoming a principal and Shep.

But Willow made me feel different. With her, I *wanted* to be indulgent. I'd suppressed so many urges and thus, had missed out on opportunities to experience life by always trying to play it safe. Willow seemed so free. When she'd grabbed my dick, she did it with such dominance. She'd straddled me on the sofa that Saturday evening, with her bare breasts dangling before me and a hungry look in her eyes. When I'd kissed her hardened nipples, her breathing had become louder and deeper. My fingers had worked her from inside, moving in and out of her ravenous wet vagina. I had never been able to awaken a woman like that before.

Now, I yearned for more. I wanted to give in for once. I fantasized about grabbing Willow in my arms and fucking her on a table or against the wall. Some place wild. I day-dreamed about all the different moans I could draw out of her as I penetrated her from various angles. My cock hardened in anticipation, and I put my hand to my nostrils pretending that I could still smell her juices on my fingers.

I opened up my third beer that evening. If it gets awkward with Shep, I can blame it on intoxication. I wasn't as much of a drinker, but I needed to settle my nerves. By the time I finished my fourth, I heard someone at the door.

Hearing the keys on the lock, I assumed that it was Shep and Willow, but I was surprised to only see Willow walking in with an overnight duffle bag. She grinned at me as she dumped it on the kitchen table.

"Where's Shep?" I asked.

"He's cleaning the restaurant. He figured it would be best for me to come on home and hang out with you. You know, give us some alone time." She winked at me.

I tossed the beer bottle in the trash can and fumbled with the ends of my t-shirt. The large-and-in-charge man I was two seconds ago faded away, and now I was the shy insecure coward again.

"Can I get you something?" I asked. "A drink?"

"Sure, I'll have whatever you're having," she said.

I grabbed her a beer, and she motioned for me to sit down at the table. She took a sip and rubbed her forehead.

"Whew." She sighed. "Restaurant work is demanding. I like cooking and all but doing it on that scale is *way* different than doing it for my family or friends."

"How'd it go?" I inquired, placing my hand on her knee.

"Good. *Very* good." She laughed. "Shep might get requests for my cooking now."

After she shared all the praise from the customers about her chicken and discussed her dreams of attending culinary school, she finished her drink and stretched out her legs on my lap. I rubbed her calves for her.

"That feels so good." Willow moaned, resting her head on her hand. "Standing for hours sure is tiring."

"I know that feeling. I'm on my feet at work even though people think I sit at the desk all day." I was glad to have an excuse to touch her.

"Elm, can we talk for real?"

"Of course."

"I've talked to Shep, so I feel like I get a sense of why he's doing this. What are your expectations, exactly?"

"Expectations for what?" I asked, crinkling my forehead. "For tonight?"

"For me and you." She gestured back and forth between us. "What does that look like in your head?"

Despite the liquid courage bubbling in my veins, I froze. *I can't tell her about all the fantasies I was having, can I? Should I? Maybe that's what she wants. What if she thinks I'm a pervert? A sex maniac.*

I cleared my throat. "I want all three of us to, you know, date. Be in a relationship." I chickened out on telling her that I desperately wanted to fuck her.

Willow giggled. "No shit. I think we've established that." She got up and sat on my lap, straddling me. She put her hands on my shoulders. "So Shep's asexual. What I need to understand is how sexual are *you*?"

I flushed. "I'm not asexual if that's what you mean. Not at all." I shook my head.

She moved her hands under my t-shirt and rubbed my chest. "I realize that, silly. You see, I'm a very erotic person, so physical compatibility is super important for me. That's why I prefer to try out the goods early. So . . ." She leaned in to kiss me. "Tell me, Elm, what do you want to do to me?"

"Um . . ." My stomach twisted in a knot, and I started to sweat.

"Maybe this will help." Willow began rubbing against my

groin with her pelvis. "Come on, I've got no patience with shyness. Confess to me what you want."

I'd never taken such a sexual exam before, yet the waves of arousal flooding up from my dick along with the alcohol ignited a fiery urge to let go. *It won't matter what you say. Just be sexy. Speak with authority. Yes, pretend you're at work, and you're taking charge. Do it like that!*

"Hang on a second," I said, and I lifted her off of me. I opened our liquor cabinet that contained a wide array of spirits that Shep only used for cooking. I grabbed the rum, since it was often easier for me to hold down, poured myself a double shot, and gulped it. The burn caused little beads of sweat to pop up all over me. I set the glass down and looked over at Willow. She was now sitting on top of the table, swaying her legs back and forth, revealing her pink underwear underneath her loose black skirt. *Go with it*

I picked up the glass and slammed it down on the floor, watching it shatter all over.

"Whoah!" Willow jumped. "What'd you do that for?"

I walked over to her all wide eyed and shaking. "I needed to ease some tension."

"Well, there's easier ways than breaking stuff. Those looked like fancy liquor—"

I pushed myself in between her legs and kissed her passionately, yanking her pelvis into mine. "I want to fuck you on this table," I told her, mustering up as much tough guy dominance as I could.

"Oh," she whispered.

Keep going. "I want to lay you out naked on this table, and . . ." My mind blanked for a second. "Go down on you."

"You mean you want to eat my pussy?" She grinned, tugging on my crotch.

"Yes."

"Say it, Elm. Say it hard."

I took a deep breath. "I'm going to take your clothes off—

"

"Rip my clothes off," she corrected me.

Ignoring the jitters inside my gut, I forced the confidence out of me. "I'll tear your clothes off, lay you flat, and eat the hell out of your pussy."

"Eat the fuck out of it," she encouraged me like she was giving a pep talk to a football team.

"I'm going to eat the ever-living shit out it!" I yelled. *Did I just say that? What would my students think?*

"Yeah." Willow wrapped her legs around me tight. "Then what are you going to do to me, Elm."

"Then I'm fucking you on this dinner table." She was still rubbing her hands against my cock, causing my body to tingle all over. I melted into the moment.

"Fuck me on this *hard* table," she demanded.

"I'm going to fuck the hardness right out of this damn table." I sounded ridiculous, but she was grinding against me and hiking her skirt up, so I continued.

"Then I'll turn you over and fuck you some more!" I screamed, pressing her even tighter against me.

Willow let out a loud moan and sat back on her hands. "Rip my clothes off. I can't take it anymore."

Wait, should I actually shred them off? She has such nice outfits.

After a brief hesitation, I yanked her skirt down hard, causing her undies to slide off with it.

"Rip it, Elmer," she squealed.

"Okay," I said, and I grabbed the armpit of her t-shirt and tried to tear it. That was when I learned that shirts don't shred as easily as they show on T.V. After a minute of awkwardness, I held my finger up to tell her to wait. I walked over to the kitchen and got a knife.

"Grab a bigger one. The biggest knife you can find," she ordered me as she ran her fingers around her clit.

I snatched up Shep's largest butcher knife, stomped back over, and with a careful but tantalizing motion upward, I sliced off her shirt. She had a black lacey bra on this time with silver cats on the corners.

"Cut it, Elm," she begged.

"It's a nice bra," I argued.

"Do it. I want to feel the blade gently brush my skin."

I snipped the bra in the middle part, watching her plump breasts explode out from its lacey prison. I smiled in my triumph. *Yes, be this forceful assertive guy. Be the principal in bed.*

"Elm?"

"Oh, sorry," I stuttered, realizing that I'd gotten lost in the moment.

With force but not too hard, I shoved her back against the wooden table and yanked her legs apart.

Like a hungry raptor, I went in, gently rolling my tongue around her inner thigh and along her pink smooth vaginal lips. Then I stuck it forcibly inside, sucking and twirling her clit, slowly then fast. I seized her breast with one of my hands, squeezing her nipples each time I heard a heavy moan. Her body twisted and squirmed. I stood up and pulled my clothes off, revealing my eagerly erect penis. I entered softly at first, using the head of my cock to tease her clit more before shoving it all the way in. She gasped. I pushed into her, hard and rapid, savoring all her groans and physical twitches. The sensation of filling a person with pleasure heavily intoxicated me, and I lost myself.

I pulled out of her and plucked her up, turning her so that she was standing but leaning downward against the table. I entered her from behind and moved my hand in front of her, clipping her clit with my fingers. Her moans picked up, and she fingered her nipple while I tapped her.

"Oh, tell me you want me to come, Elm. Order my rabbit to come!" she shouted. "Say it loud!"

"Come, rabbit!" I yelled.

"More!"

"I'm going to fuck you until you come, rabbit. Yeah, you're going to come, you fucking little rabbit!" The more she ordered me, my desire grew stronger, and I pulled her harder into me.

"Yes, yes, yes, uh-huh!" She contracted around my penis as she orgasmed.

Sensing that I was there, she dug her nails into my thighs. "Scream, Elm. Howl while you come."

I let out a yell that didn't even sound like me as intense bliss exploded in my loins and in my brain—all over. Then I fell limp over her, huffing but numb at the same time.

I plopped on a chair, still catching my breath. Willow straddled my lap again with a large grin on her face and sweat trickling down her brow. She looked beautiful.

She kissed me hard. "I knew you could be fun if I got you to loosen up."

"I think that was the best sex I ever had," I blurted out, holding my hand on my forehead as if I might faint.

"You'd be surprised how much of a blast you can have when you let go." She hugged me. "I guess it isn't the greatest when you're with an asexual, is it?"

Shep often shared many articles about asexuals who were sex favorable and some who were even a little kinky. So I didn't feel right assuming that asexuals were automatically terrible in bed. But Shep's indifference didn't make him spectacular, or very great for that matter. And until now, I didn't know what I'd been missing.

"I don't think all asexuals are bad," I informed her. "Not all sexuals are good, either."

"Touché." She laughed. "Sorry, I wasn't bashing Shep or anything. I mean, damn, he's so cute that I assume anyone would want to fuck him even if he laid there."

"He's definitely got the looks in the relationship. I'm old and overweight," I said, rubbing my gut.

Willow pinched my belly. "You were pretty damn sexy tonight. I'm never going to look at that principal picture the
same way again."

"I'm not a total dork?" I asked, running my fingers through
her hair.

"I love men who show a different side of themselves sexually," she replied. "You don't realize dorks are sexual until
you fuck them. Then it all comes out. But it's special because
only *you* get to see that part of them. I think it's hot. It's much
better than guys who flaunt it all the time."

I must have been grinning as big as she was. *She thinks I'm
sexy and hot. I can be those things.* God, I didn't know how I was
going to be able to keep my hands off of her. I could already
feel my dick swelling up again.

"So back to my question, Elm," she said, pressing her forehead against mine. "What do you want me and you to be?"

"I think I could fall in love with you —" The words escaped
my drunken horny mouth before I could stop them. A twinge
of fear jolted through my stomach almost severing my blos-
soming erection.

"Wow," she whispered.

"Sorry, no . . . that just came out. I've been drinking. It's the
moment —"

Willow placed her finger over my lips and kissed me. She
wrapped her arms around me, pressing my head into her
breasts. "That's what I want, Elm. I want us all to be in love.
Not just sex and flings. I need to get inside your heads and
your hearts."

Her words made sense. Why would I think that she should
hang out as my erotic toy or Shep's cooking buddy? What was
in it for her? At the same time, neither Shep nor I had ever
discussed falling in love. *How could we have been so naïve?* Feeling Willow's breaths and the soft warmth of her bosom, how
could anyone *not* fall in love with her? She was so

captivatingly beautiful, sexual, smart, everything. If she walked out on us today, I'd be devastated.

"So do we know where we stand?" she muttered, kissing my cheek.

"Yes," I replied. "I do. I don't know how Shep feels about falling in love, though."

She pulled away and lifted my chin up toward her. "He's a puzzle, but mysteries are exciting. I can't wait to woo him and win him over, but I promise you I will. I can be very romantic."

I kissed her, picking her up in my arms and setting her on the table. "But you're all mine now. And I want to fuck you again."

"You go right ahead, Mr. Principal."

And like that, I parted her legs, shoving myself inside her already wet and ready pussy. This time, she squeezed her limbs around my torso, and we kissed heavily as I moved in and out of her.

That's when it dawned on me that I had completely forgotten a condom.

Chapter Sixteen: Shep

When I'd returned from the Tire on the Friday of Willow's first weekend with us, I wasn't sure what I would walk into. My whole body was tense. Willow had offered to help me close, but my guilt over the hand-job told me to let her go home so that she and Elmer could be alone.

When I entered the house, the lights were off, but I saw the glow of the T.V. in the living room. I grabbed a glass of water before going in. They were cuddled up on the couch.

"Hey," Elmer said, lifting his arm up from around Willow and sliding away a little from her.

"Hey," I replied.

Willow got up. She was only wearing a baggy t-shirt and her underwear. She hugged me, pulling me over to the couch in the process, and snuggling me in between her and Elm.

"We wanted to wait up for you." She smiled. "You must be tired." She rubbed my shoulders.

"That I am," I agreed. "What have y'all been doing?"

"Just taking care of business," Willow teased, kissing me on my ear. I squirmed a little. I hated getting kissed there.

"Yeah, you could say that," Elmer concurred, giving me a naughty look.

"Was business good?" I asked them.

They both grinned like teenagers. While Elmer could convey an innocent boyish-like charm, the foolish grin on his face clashed significantly with his usual demeanor. I felt like an intruder.

"Excuse me for a few minutes," I said as I got up to sneak

into the garage. I found my stash of marijuana vapes, plugged one into my pen, and took a few hits. The door creaked open behind me.

"Shep? What are you doing? Are you fucking smoking?" Elmer scolded me as he stomped over, turning on a lamp to expose my crime. Being a principal, he hated that I smoked weed, so I did my best to hide it from him and only give in occasionally.

"Just a few hits," I assured him.

"I thought you said you got rid of all your weed. You know this can get me fucking fired—"

"I don't need a lecture right now," I interrupted, shaking my head. "I'm careful. Don't worry so much."

"Well, I'm going back in before you turn her on to it," he snapped as he turned to leave.

"So?" I demanded. "You fucked her?"

He froze in his steps before slowly approaching me again. His eyes were red, so I knew he'd been drinking more than usual.

"Are you upset?" he asked quietly, crossing his arms.

"You didn't answer my question." I wasn't sure if I wanted to know. I felt like yelling at him. Slapping him. But I couldn't.

He nodded. "I fucked her. A few times."

My eyes grew wide. "Oh, um, okay." My thoughts raced, and my chest burned.

"She's spending the night," he continued. "I figured we both knew that this was probably going to happen. I assumed you sent her home by herself for that reason."

"Yeah, I did." I took a long drag of my vape.

"Shep, I thought . . . I'm sorry—" He started coming toward me.

I held up my hand to stop him. "You don't have anything to be sorry for. You're right. I agreed to it. We both talked about this. I didn't know how it would make me feel. Walking

in here and seeing you two cuddling with only your underwear . . ."

Elmer pushed my pen away from my mouth and hugged
me. "I'm sorry. I didn't think about it being too much too
soon. I got really into the moment."

"I fucked up," I admitted, forcing the pen up to take a hit.

"Huh?" He moved away with a puzzled look.

"Tonight, at the restaurant, she . . ." I closed my eyes. "I let
her give me a hand-job."

"You let her give you a hand job in public?" He gasped
with his mouth gaping open in horror.

"No." I punched him in the shoulder. "In the back room.
No one saw."

He surveyed me carefully. "What happened?"

"She gave me a hand-job. I didn't do anything. I just laid
there. We kept our clothes on." *Ugh, why am I defending myself
when he fucked her all over my house?*

"I thought you said that you talked about you being ace
with her." He had his hands on his hips, his typical principal
stance.

"I did," I assured him. "I assume she wanted to do it to
level the playing field. I think she figured that you and her
would probably have sex this weekend and didn't want me
to feel left out. I guess she was actually being nice . . . and even
caring."

Elmer fumbled with his nails, and his forehead crinkled up
in thought. "You didn't do anything, though?" he clarified.

"No," I promised him. I didn't want to see him hurt. I took
another hit to ease the guilt.

"Did you like it?" he asked.

I shrugged. "It's an orgasm. It felt good. Yes, I liked it. Did
you?"

"Yeah, I really did. Too much maybe."

"What do you mean?" I asked.

"Nothing," he mumbled. "I don't think you fucked up. It's

not as if *you* had sex with her. You let her . . . pleasure you. And I can see how she may have done that to ease some tension. Do you think it helped?"

"Sure, it did," I replied. Willow and I seemed closer after our small excursion, and she acted more comfortable with me. Yet, it didn't ease the anguish in my chest knowing that someone else was pleasing my husband in a way that I couldn't. Worse, the pain of seeing her make him happy. At the same time, Elmer's double standards annoyed me. *Why is he so entitled to enjoy himself and I can't? I shouldn't have to feel guilty over exploring myself with Willow.*

We went back inside. Despite his insistence on clarifying that I didn't actively participate in the hand-job, Elmer accepted things rather well. I was relieved but also scared.

We decided that we would all share the bed for the night. It felt too awkward to make Willow sleep on the sofa, and even stranger to have one of us with her while the other was banished to the couch.

I imagined waking up to find Willow and Elmer cuddling or even having sex beside me. Much to my surprise, I woke up to discover Willow curled up close with her arms around me, and her face nestled against the back of my neck. I wasn't sure if she randomly got that way. Maybe she was just being attentive to my needs and wanted me to feel desired.

I jumped out of bed early to prepare a breakfast for all of us before I needed to head to the Tire. I sometimes went in earlier on Saturday because there was so much prep work to be done before the weekend rush.

As I prepared some zucchini omelets and blueberry buckwheat pancakes, I envisioned Elmer and Willow giggling and snuggling on the couch. Knowing that they would be alone together while I worked most of the day filled me with FOMO.

The aromas from the kitchen eventually woke the two

161

lovers up.

"This smells great," Willow declared. She still only wore her t-shirt and undies.

"He makes a good breakfast," Elmer confirmed, walking over to hug me as I was getting out the dishes.

"I thought I was going to be the chef in the house," she claimed.

"No, that position is taken," I assured her, waving my hand in dismissal.

"You'll be lucky if he ever lets you make dinner. He never lets me," Elmer remarked as he poured himself some coffee and sat down at the table.

"If you tasted his food, you'd know why," I retorted.

He snorted. "You only let me do it that one time, and I accidentally overcooked the chicken —"

"You burned it," I corrected him, setting out all the plates. "Mealtimes are way too precious to waste on ruined meat. I'd rather be sure it's going to be right."

"You know mine is," Willow asserted, helping herself to some pancakes. "Why don't I cook for you guys tonight?"

"That sounds great." Elmer grinned.

"I have to work," I reminded them. I hated the idea of leaving them alone for another night.

"I guess the downer of being a restaurant owner is you always have to be there. That sucks," she whined.

"That's why the nightly cleanup is the main way we spend time together," Elmer told her. "Otherwise, we'd hardly see each other."

"I take Mondays off," I argued, cutting into my omelet.

"I work on Mondays," he stated.

I shrugged. "What do you want me to do? It's *my* business. I'm not really at the point where I feel comfortable letting one of my employees run it for a weekend. I hope to get there, but we're not there, yet."

"He took off for our wedding," he informed Willow.

I pointed my fork at him. "And all my customers made me promise to never do *that* again. Remember?"

He laughed.

"How'd you two get married?" Willow asked, cradling her coffee mug in her hands.

"We went to a wedding chapel in Vegas and gambled for the weekend. I couldn't pull him away from the Tire for much longer," Elmer shared.

"Not like I could drag you away from the school. We didn't want to make a big fuss with it," I told her. Living in Cloverleaf, neither of us ever felt truly confident being a couple in public. Plus, it was difficult for Snavis or Kicky to take the time off from work to attend a ceremony in another city. I didn't talk to my family other than my nephew who had moved up here because he had needed a job. A wedding didn't make sense.

"Why not?" she asked. "Is the school okay with you two being together?"

"Not really. It's a don't ask, don't tell kind of climate. As long as we don't flaunt it, it seems to be all right. Besides, who'd fire Elmer," I said, gesturing toward him. "He's the best principal they could get for that school. No one's going to invest in it the way he does."

"So what will they think about me?" she asked.

Elmer and I glanced at each other blankly. Neither of us had considered how to handle Willow. We did a good job at keeping our private lives discrete, but nothing ever stopped a small town from gossip. I wasn't sure that he could afford another taboo as the principal.

"Willow," Elmer started, using his professional tone. "We need to keep this secret. Like we must be careful about how much you hang out at the Tire. It's not because we're ashamed of you, and I hate to do this to you. But it's my job, you understand? If I lose my position, I'll have to go somewhere else, and with the Tire . . ." He paused and stared intently at me. "I couldn't ask Shep to abandon it. He's worked so hard. It's too important to the community. In fact, I think the only reason people haven't come after me yet is because of the Tire. They love that restaurant, and they adore Shep . . . as long as he doesn't remind them that he's trans or bisexual."

"I understand," she solemnly agreed. "But that makes it even more urgent to get away. Maybe not right this instant, but for all three of us to go somewhere where we don't have to hide. I want to be able to be your girlfriend in public."

Elmer gave me a look as if he wasn't going to push it but obviously wanted me to give in. I sighed. "Okay, let's see how things go for the next month, and I'll consider taking a weekend off.

"Yes," Willow squealed, hugging and kissing me as I tried to finish chewing the pancake in my mouth.

"Thanks, Shep," Elmer remarked, winking at me.

I worked a twelve-hour shift that day at the Tire. It was game weekend. I'd gotten special permission to serve game meat a few times a year. The menu was full of not only elk, deer, and duck, but also my famous organ dishes of tongue stew, grilled heart, and Indian style liver. I offered tips to customers who wanted to know how to prepare recipes with organs so that they could use the whole animal. Hunting was big in Cloverleaf because many people relied on it to feed their families. I was either running back and forth from the kitchen or providing mini-presentations on preparing organ meat. I had little time to think about what Willow and Elm were doing. After seeing his behavior the previous night, I could only guess that it involved a lot of sex.

When I returned home, Elmer was in the shower, and Willow was sipping wine on the couch, looking at a photo album.

"Where'd you find that?" I asked after peering over to see old pictures of me in feminine form with Tank.

"I found it in the top of the closet in the bedroom. You don't mind, do you? I love photos. It's such a good way to get to know someone. Who was this big guy?" She pointed at Tank.

"My first husband. He died." I sat down beside her.

"I'm sorry." She rubbed my thigh with her hand. "How did it happen?"

"Car accident. Not too long after his mother passed. That's where I got all the money to start the Tire. In fact, this was his mother's house. I loved the kitchen so much that I had to keep it." I leaned back and looked around the room.

"Tank," she whispered. "You and Elm . . . you're both widowers."

I nodded.

"It's weird when things like that happen. If neither of your spouses died, you wouldn't even be together. Isn't that *crazy*?" She sighed. "We can build our life and make this plan with this one person but then it changes. We just go on a different path."

The truth was that I had felt an attraction between Elmer and I long before either Tank or Luna passed. The way he'd hung out with the art club goofing around with the kids had made me wonder if he was there for the students or for me. He hadn't gone to other clubs. Sometimes, we would spend a few hours chatting as we cleaned up the art room. Then there had been those times when he would walk by my classroom or be in the hallway talking to another teacher, and he'd never failed to make eye contact with me. There had been this covert burning desire toward him, a sensation I hadn't experienced with Tank.

"I think there was always something there," I told Willow. "I used to teach at the school. Me and Tank."

"Really?" Her eyes widened. "So you guys knew each

165

other for a while. What's he like as a principal?"

"Pretty much what you can imagine from his *Facebook* picture. Serious. Conservative. Firm." I smiled. "But also caring, funny . . . the students liked him. A lot of teachers did, too."

"I can't visualize you as a teacher." She looked back down at the album, running her finger along a picture of me in feminine form. I was reading a book and laying on a hammock. My long hair dangled toward the ground, my feet were crossed, and my small breasts stuck up from under my tank top. "I can't believe this is you. You seem so different."

"I'm still the same person . . . only a little changed. If anything, more of myself," I insisted.

"Sheppy?"

"Yes."

She took my hand in hers, setting the photo album off to the side. "You see, I'm a *really* sexual person."

"I can see that." I squeezed her hand.

"I guess I've always had a high sex drive, generally. And I know that I don't have the best body. I could lose some weight."

"You're beautiful. You don't need to change anything," I said. I pulled her closer to me.

"I made the decision, even in my teens, that I wasn't going to let my insecurities hold me back. That I wanted to be sexually free. The best part is that sex is what gave me confidence in myself." She teared up. I put my arm around her. "To be naked and feel sexy . . . that's why I'm a little domineering. I get carried away with how it makes me appreciate myself. Not to mention that *a lot* people, guys particularly, seem very attracted to it, which also boosts my self-esteem."

"That makes sense to me," I replied. I knew the difficulties in maintaining a positive body image. After all, I was a masculine person with a vagina.

"So I'm a little stuck with you," she admitted with a

worrisome look on her face.

"Why's that?" I asked.

"I express myself physically, and it seems to fit in perfectly with Elm. You know, you were probably right about getting him a girlfriend. I think that's just what he needed."

I nodded, trying to hide the pain in my gut from that comment.

"But you . . ." She paused a moment. "I guess I'm a little lost about how to get close to someone who isn't . . . sexual, or very physical at all for that matter. You seem so uncomfortable when I touch you."

My temples tensed up, and I removed my arm from around her and rubbed my chin.

"Did I say something wrong?" she inquired.

"You didn't say anything that I don't already know," I confessed. I sighed. "Same as you, I try hard to accept myself for who I am. But it's fucking difficult not to get insecure when the entire world seems sex crazy. It's also hard not to become frustrated."

"Frustrated?" she asked.

"Why does everyone have to make it sound like the only thing people can do is have sex?" I snapped. Tears welled up in my eyes, and my hands shook.

"No, that's not all they do. But I sure enjoy doing it a lot. It's my way of showing love, my love language. So it's hard to figure out how to show you love without getting physical. Honestly, I've wanted to jump your bones from that first night in the restaurant." She gently brushed her hand through my hair. "You're so intriguing."

"Willow, I don't know how to answer you," I said softly. "I'm really in love with my husband . . . and I genuinely like you." While I struggled with jealousy over Elm's relationship with her, I didn't want to get rejected over my asexuality. I questioned if things would work out if I couldn't form a physical connection with her, too.

"That sounds as if you're holding back." She sat up.

I nodded. "Probably." I couldn't see myself falling in love with anyone but Elm. He was a good guy. When we were alone, he relaxed, and he could be pretty funny. He would go from goofy dad jokes to dark humor. When he held me, I felt cherished. I was scared to have that with someone else because I wasn't sure if my feelings for him would remain as intense. I was clueless in how this all works.

"You don't like me?" she asked.

"I like you, Willow," I assured her. I did like her. She was a cool person and easy to be around. "You're fun," I told her. "You can cook. You're beautiful. You're making Elm happy in a way that I can't. But . . . this is so new and confusing. I think I need time."

"You're kind of like demisexual . . . or demiromantic, I guess they call it."

"Kind of. I'm not sure what you want. I know we agreed that all three of us are in a relationship. Is it not possible . . . why can't you and Elmer have your thing, and you and me be close friends for now?" Friend status, at least for the time being, would remove a great deal of pressure off of me.

"I want to be more than friends with you, Sheppy. Elm seems wonderful. But he's a little predictable. You . . . you're special," she whispered, continuing to stroke my hair. "Plus, I don't think it can work with you and me as buddies while Elm and I build this other relationship. That becomes a love triangle. That turns into drama."

"You're probably right," I concurred. "I guess it's hard for me to form a bond, but also, I'm still struggling with this feeling like I'm cheating on Elm. I have to get over that. I need time." Even though my concerns were strong, I believed that I could push through it. I'd read about how some asexuals had open relationships or engaged in polyamory. I wanted to be able to do this.

"Is kissing okay?" she asked with a slight grin.

"Yes," I complied. "We can kiss."

She pulled me to her and kissed me, gentler and slower this time. She placed her hand on my cheek. "We can be friends for now. But friends who kiss and cuddle. If that's what you want."

"Thanks." I appreciated that Willow didn't push it any further. She was a good friend.

She smiled. "I've been waiting to find a treasure. After all, you have to hunt for a jewel. It takes time, but it's all worth it."

We kissed until Elmer appeared from the shower.

CHAPTER SEVENTEEN: ELMER

We had developed this routine of Willow traveling to Cloverleaf on Friday evening, which meant that I had her all to myself those nights. Shep spent time with her after he came home from the restaurant. He acted like his usual self, focused on his alternating menu items and searching for innovative ideas. He would spend hours discussing these with Willow on the sofa after work. Willow and I had all Saturday to lay around, naked and cuddling. We watched old eighties movies, which were her favorite and explored each other with various sensual oils and sex toys that she brought over with her. At night, all three of us would squeeze into our queen size bed, and she would snuggle up against Shep while I cozied up behind her.

But after a month, things felt off. Shep and I worked so much. I still met him a few times during the week to help with closing. But the new academic year brought football games, after school assemblies, and no time to get my paperwork done unless I stayed late. I was frequently exhausted and often went straight home. With focusing on Willow on the weekends, I didn't feel like I had a lot of energy leftover for Shep. A distance hovered in the air.

Shep never asked about my sex life with Willow. But we hadn't done it since she came into our lives. While I didn't think he expected our sexual relationship to end, I hesitated to ask him for it. After all, the whole point of finding someone like Willow was to release him from that burden.

Unsure about the way that their bond was developing, I

broached the subject one evening when Shep was off from work. He made us an extravagant dinner on Monday nights, even though I came home late. I figured he'd want a break from it on his days off, but for Shep, cooking was equivalent to breathing. Besides, he prepared dishes he deemed too risqué for the customers he catered to at the Tire.

The weather was getting chilly since summers fade quickly in Montana. During fall, Shep would prepare any type of squash out there. With it, he'd make soups, hummus, dips, casseroles, fritters, fries—anything. For this evening, he roasted some rosemary lamb with pumpkin grits and spicy collard greens served with sweet potato rolls and gingerbread cake.

As I entered the house, the scents of ginger, spices, and pumpkin filled the air. Every day smelled like the holidays.

"That smells wonderful," I stated, as I walked over to hover over the stove, admiring the cuisine.

"Thanks." He smiled, as he sipped from a glass of rum.

"Thought you didn't like liquor," I commented as I took off my jacket and shoes. "When did you start drinking that?"

"I don't know," he muttered. "Go get undressed. It'll be ready in another fifteen minutes."

We chatted casually about our day as we sat down to eat. I waited until we were on dessert, and Shep had finished his second glass of rum before moving to a more serious topic.

"How do you think things are going? With Willow? With everything?" I asked before taking the first bite of the cake since I knew the taste would completely distract me.

He shrugged. "All seems to be progressing well. We get along. You seem happy." He continued eating his dessert.

"Are you?" I couldn't help but stare at the empty glass of rum. I had never seen Shep drink liquor.

He nodded. "Sure."

"Because I've been worried that things are little

imbalanced," I informed him.

"How so?" he asked.

"Willow can only come here on Friday and Saturday nights. You work on the weekends. I guess I feel like I'm getting all the time with her, and you don't get much." I wasn't clear if the arrangement bothered him or just me. Maybe it was my own guilt. After all, the third was mostly for me.

"I said that I'd try to take a weekend off. It's been hectic." He focused on his plate, not looking up at me.

"It's always busy," I argued. "If you wait for a time that's not hectic, it'll never arrive. Besides, that would only be one weekend. Then we'd return to this routine again." I played with my food with my fork. "Don't you feel like things are off . . . between us?"

He rubbed his chin before pouring another glass of rum. "It seems to me," he said slowly after a long pause, "that *you* think that things are off. Otherwise, you wouldn't ask me that question."

Shep was right, as usual. I had frequently projected my own concerns and emotions onto him instead of acknowledging that they were my own. But I wasn't sure how to respond. We hadn't had sex or been very affectionate lately; however, the anticipation of seeing Willow occupied most of my thoughts. I often texted her throughout the day, and she'd even send me sexy photos. I daydreamed about being inside of her with her body pressed hard against me. I wanted the days to fly by so that the weekend would come, then she'd be mine. I worried that my feelings for Willow were distancing me from Shep. *But I can't tell him that.*

"I don't feel like we're talking anymore, and we're not having sex," I told him. "I mean the goal wasn't for you and me to stop making love altogether, was it? Is it because of Willow?"

"I get you a girl to fuck, and you're still pressuring me

about the sex thing," he retorted with a snort. "Can't fucking win."

His attitude threw me back, but then again, I wasn't used to the effects of hard liquor.

"I'm not trying to pressure you, but you didn't answer my question, and I don't think we clarified this. Is the goal that you and I stop doing it? Is that what you want?" I feared that he'd say yes. Sex with Shep wasn't something I wanted to lose.

He tossed his fork down on the table. "When are we supposed to do it, Elm? We're home so late on the weekdays, and hell, you've been going to bed before I even get here. With Willow here on the weekends . . . what?" He threw his arms up in the air. "I should walk in and take sloppy seconds or something? Knowing her, she'd probably want to watch or join in, and I'm not having that."

"Why are you so upset?" My stomach dropped.

"Y'all fucking is one thing, but Elm, I don't need to see it," he insisted.

"Who said you needed to?" His tone surprised me. Shep usually didn't get so ornery.

"It's too awkward for you and me to have sex when she's over here on the weekend. I'm not doing it," he stated firmly and downed his rum.

"I think you can slow down on the booze," I said, pointing to his glass.

"Fuck you." He smirked, flipping me the finger. He stood up and started clearing the table.

"Fuck me?" I snapped. His words hurt. "What's with the attitude? You don't talk to me like this."

"You want the whole world, don't you?" he yelled. "You get this amazing sex life now, but no, that's not enough. It never is." He threw the dishes into the sink.

"I wasn't saying that at all," I asserted, noticing my own

anger. "Why are you being so sensitive about this? We agreed to discuss concerns. I worry that it's going a little awry, and I want to get it back on track. That's all."

"Don't get her pregnant, man," he ordered me, leaning over the kitchen counter. "You better not do that."

"Wait, what?" I got up and walked over to him, turning him around to face me. "I'm not trying to. Where's all this coming from?" It was like we were in two different worlds. That scared me.

Shep sighed and ran his hands through his shaggy hair. "Maybe you're right. Things have been off. Seeing you with her sometimes . . ." His voice trailed off.

"It's hard for me to watch you with her, too." It was. Even though I didn't see them get affectionate, I hated watching them on the sofa, jabbering nonstop about food. Shep seemed so intrigued with her. It made me jealous.

"It's not the same." He choked up a little.

"Why not?" I asked.

"Because I'm not fucking her," he replied. His hands trembled.

"Hasn't she gotten you off like you told me?" I didn't want to picture them having sex again, but I also thought it'd ease my guilt.

"That was just that one time," he said.

The tension in the pit of my stomach got so intense that I thought I'd vomit. My hands quivered. I cautiously asked, "Do you want me to stop fucking her?"

Shep stared blankly at me for a moment. "No," he mumbled. "You don't have to do that."

"Do you want me to?" I demanded. "Damn it, Shep. Be clear with me."

"No," he said again.

I grabbed a beer from the fridge and sat back down at the table, taking a huge gulp. I wasn't sure I believed him, and I didn't know what to do with this. I had no intentions to stop seeing Willow. But I worried about ruining my marriage. "I'm scared that if things are imbalanced that it'll hurt us. I don't want that. I wish that you and me could have our time together, and you and her to have your own relationship."

"So what do you propose?" he asked.

"I want to ask her to move in," I blurted out. *Fuck. Why did I say this now?*

"Move in? We just met her," he gasped with his bloodshot eyes bulging out.

"It's been a while," I pointed out.

"That's fucking fast," he argued. His face looked tense.

I shrugged. "We already threw ourselves into it, didn't we?" I could tell that he was upset. But I believed that this would fix everything. Or maybe it made things easier for me.

Shep started rubbing his chin again and poured himself another shot of rum.

I walked over to him, lifting myself up on the countertop.

"I figure it will be simpler that way," I pleaded. "You'll have more time with her. And . . . you'll get used to her around, and it won't be such a big deal if we have sex."

"What about her job? We're going to support her?" he asked.

"We can give her a job," I offered.

He shook his head. "I don't have any more room on payroll. The holidays are approaching, and I promised Pam, Danny, and Peggy that they could work additional shifts to make some extra money." He sipped his rum.

I thought for a moment. "She's an office assistant. She might be able to find a position like that around. I might find her something at the school. It won't be much. It can do until we figure it out. Lots of places will be hiring when we get closer to Christmas, too."

"That's two months away," he responded.

"We'll work it out," I told him. I didn't know why he was

so worried about money. Both our houses were paid for, I earned a good salary and still had funds leftover from Luna's life insurance. Shep had invested his remaining life insurance into stocks and bonds. It didn't make sense.

"Did you talk to her about this?" he questioned with an accusatory look in his eyes.

"Not really," I assured him. "We've talked casually about living together one day. Nothing serious."

"I don't know," he moaned. "I'm trying to get used to her with us, and now you want to move her in. You have feelings for her."

"No, I don't . . ." My shoulders tensed up. "Well, yes, I have some. We're in a relationship with her. I don't think we can avoid it if things work out." We hadn't discussed developing a strong connection. I wasn't even sure *what* I was feeling. I didn't want it to hurt Shep, though.

He went to grab the bottle of rum again, but I pushed his hand away from it, picking it up myself.

"I assume you've had enough. What's with all the drinking?" I asked, throwing my hands up.

"I drink. You know I drink. You said you'd rather me do that than smoke weed," he snapped.

"Alcohol is legal," I pointed out.

"So is weed," he insisted.

Shep was right that Montana had legalized it, but there were still many people who were against it. It would be years, even decades, before public opinion felt the same way about marijuana as alcohol. As a principal, I couldn't chance it.

"I guess you're not okay with her moving in." My voice sounded calm, but my heart yearned for Willow.

He crossed his arms and stared at the ceiling. "Let's not rush into anything permanent. I know that she has to quit her job, but . . . let's make it a trial thing. Like, she doesn't need to move *all* her stuff over here. Do you really think that she'll go for it?"

"Yes," I blurted out.

Not to my surprise, Willow was totally game for living with us.

"Yes," she squealed over the phone, almost bursting my eardrum.

"I wasn't sure you'd be up for it," I admitted, trying to hide my own exhilaration.

"Well, gosh, it's better than rooming with Mom. Plus, you have a big house. I get all the delicious food I can ever eat. You think I'd turn *that* down?" She giggled.

"What about your job?" I asked.

"I can probably find something. I got a college degree, so that gives me bonus points."

"That's great." I beamed. "God, I can't wait to wake up with you every day. Maybe we can start our mornings off with a shower together."

"Now *that* sounds perfect," she concurred, laughing. "It'll give me more time with Shep, too. I hardly see him."

"That's what I was thinking, too." I sighed in relief. "I'm so glad we're on the same page."

"So when should we do this?"

I returned to my more serious tone. "I know this seems bizarre, but Shep—we were considering a trial run. Like maybe you bring a lot of your stuff, but we give it a month or so before you completely move in."

"Elm, I'm a young girl who lives with her mother. I don't have anything. Just my clothes, makeup, personal items . . . oh, my art. I guess I can leave that stored here."

"Okay, yeah, store your art there," I agreed. It didn't make any sense, but I convinced myself that by leaving her art at her mother's, then she technically wasn't moving in all the way.

"I'm so excited," she shouted again.

"Me, too." Everything was working out and felt so easy. I envisioned us as one big happy family.

"Is Shep as thrilled as we are? Was this your idea or his?" she asked.

"It was our idea, pretty much," I lied. She focused a lot on Shep's feelings. I didn't want to disappoint her.

"That's awesome. I can be a better girlfriend to him now. Thank you, Elm. You made my day."

"I have to get back to work," I told her. "Go ahead and bring your stuff whenever you resign from your job."

"I can quit this week."

"Oh, okay." I gulped. *This week? He's going to kill me.*

"I don't want to wait," she begged.

After I hung up the phone, I was elated. *Now I can have her every day.* Part of me feared having to inform Shep that she was moving in so quickly, but that worry had nothing against my desire. I wanted her, and that was that.

CHAPTER EIGHTEEN: SHEP

It was Thursday evening. Business had been slow at the Tire due to a snowstorm that produced poor road conditions. While Montanans were used to snow, most were usually smart enough not to drive in it until the roads were plowed. I'd let Pam go home early, so it was only me, Danny, and Randy, my delivery guy. I sat at the bar, sipping a pumpkin ale and making notes for my upcoming Halloween menu. The Tire hosted two events on the Saturday before Halloween. That afternoon was focused on kids' activities. I would set up various cookie and cake decorating stations all over the restaurant where children could garnish them with any toppings or icings they wished. Appetizers were mostly served with finger foods resembling body parts, brains, zombies, bats, ghosts, and many other scary figures. Parents often donated to the event to keep the activities affordable, and there was a small fee paid at the door.

That same evening, there was a second party for adults. Drinks were discounted, spooky music filled the air, and the Tire would stay open until midnight. Tables were set up with various board games, and the winner of our costume competition won a free dinner. Considering there weren't many events in Cloverleaf, Halloween was one of my most profitable holidays.

I bet Willow may have some original ideas for this year. While I enjoyed reserving past favorites, I'd never liked repeating the same menu. Novel items usually boosted my sales. Plus, my sampler options ensured that they could still enjoy the foods they loved while also trying my new dishes.

Around seven, Elmer shuffled in. He wore his long business-like trench coat that hid whatever ugly brown suit was under it. He hung it up at the door, waving to me as he walked over.

"You're here early," I remarked.

"I let everyone go on home due to the weather," he told me, motioning for Danny to bring him one of my beers.

"Anything else?" Danny hollered, as he went into the kitchen.

"What was for dinner tonight?" he asked.

"Get him the pork roast with caramelized mashed pumpkin and wild rice medley," I ordered. Danny nodded and proceeded to the back.

"Good, I'm hungry," Elmer stated as he sat down. "It's been a long day."

"Did you need to talk about it?"

"No, it's only usual stuff. Dealing with parents who don't want to make their kid accountable for anything. How are you doing?" he asked, eye-balling my beer.

"It's been slow. Just making out my list for Halloween," I replied.

He put his hand on my knee. "Are you doing better than the other night?"

I rubbed my chin and tried to bury the tension building in my gut. "Yeah," I muttered. "I'm good."

"I talked to Willow, and she's . . . well, she's cool with moving in." He looked shyly at me.

"Okay," I mumbled. After a long week and now a new roommate, my mind couldn't process it all.

Danny brought over Elmer's drink and some silverware. "Food will be out shortly," he told him.

Elmer started fidgeting with his hands, staring down at his lap.

"What's up?" I inquired.

"She was really eager. It makes sense. She does live with her mom. I remember wanting so bad to move out on my own, too." He laughed.

"That's good," I stated, searching his face. "Why are you so nervous?"

"Well . . ." he started, taking a deep breath. "She wants to move in this weekend."

My mouth dropped open. "What?"

"I know it's fast." He put his hand on my leg and squeezed my thigh.

"I mean you talked to me about it, but I assumed . . . I thought maybe we had a few weeks. That I had more time to absorb another person moving into my house." I finished my beer and motioned for the next. I wasn't ready to see Elmer with Willow every day. It was too much too soon. I was trapped.

"Should you be drinking when you're on a shift?" he questioned with a concerned look on his face.

"I'm not really. It's under control. Don't fucking change the subject, Elm," I scolded him. "You're nagging me about my drinking, and you've got your girlfriend moving in after asking me only a few days ago? Are you sure it's not *you* wanting her to move in so fast?" My face grew hot.

"Maybe we shouldn't talk about this here. We should go in back," he suggested, anxiously glancing around the restaurant.

"I don't give a fuck. This isn't the damn school. It's my place. I do what I want here." I slammed my pen down on the table, causing it to bounce off and fall on the floor.

"Why are you calling her *my* girlfriend?" he asked. "It's *our* girlfriend, remember? Shep, this was *your* idea. Recognize that, too."

"Yes, I'm quite aware of it," I retorted, rolling my eyes. I wanted to slap him for reminding me.

"I thought we were on the same page the other night." His face turned sad. "I know that things seem imbalanced right now. That's why I preferred her to be around more so that y'all would get more time together. Why are you acting all jealous?"

Danny came with the food. We waited for him to walk away before continuing.

Jealous? The word made me cringe. "Maybe I didn't know how'd it make me feel," I admitted, solemnly. I buried my face in my hands for a second. "It's hard . . . like if I was a sexual person, too, then we'd both have the same kind of relationship with her. But watching you two together and knowing . . . I recognize that she's giving you something that I can't. I'm worried that I'm not good enough for either of you." I took some deep breaths.

"Shep—" Elmer started, putting his arm around me.

"I know. It's *my* problem. I've tried so hard to be confident and accepting of who I am as an asexual. But sometimes . . ." I sobbed a little. "It's difficult not to get insecure."

"I understand," he replied, placing his other hand on my knee.

I wanted him to hold me, kiss me, and assure me that I was still number one. I wished that he'd say that a few weeks of passionate sex with a *very* sexual person proved to him that he didn't need it. But at the same time, it'd be hard not to miss Willow.

"This is important to you, isn't it," I asked.

"What is?" He raised his eyebrow.

"This polyamorous relationship. You really want it to work."

He looked more puzzled. "Don't you?"

I sighed, taking a huge slug of my beer and running my hands through my hair. "Elm, I need you to answer me.

Would it hurt you to break up with her?"

His eyes grew wide, and he tilted his head to the side. "You prefer to end it?"

"Damn it, Elm." I covered my face with my hand. "Don't respond to me with another question. I want to know how you feel . . . about her."

He fumbled with his fingers for a moment. "I don't want to end things with her," he answered in a shaky voice.

My heart sunk. "It would hurt you?" I clarified.

He nodded.

"Like heartbroken?"

"Yes."

I trembled and tried to swivel in my seat to hide it. I took another sip of beer, but this time, the taste made me almost vomit. I grabbed my napkin and pretended to blow my nose to disguise my tears.

"I didn't realize you were in so deep," I told him.

"I thought we were all in this. Like all in." He shook his head and squinted at me. "I pictured that it would bother you more if it were only about the sex. We talked about how you would be romantically involved with her, so I figured that meant you would fall in love with her, too."

I froze for a moment. A heaviness engulfed me, and I closed my eyes. "So you love her?" I asked.

He placed his hand on my shoulder. "It doesn't change the fact that I love you, Shep. I'm sorry. I didn't know you were struggling with this so much."

I laughed sarcastically. "I guess I didn't see that you weren't. You don't get possessive of me . . . with her?"

Elmer ate a large bite of roast, chewing and thinking. After a hard swallow, he made eye contact again. "It's a little weird watching you kiss her," he confessed.

"But is that you jealous of her or of me?" I asked.

He glanced down. "It's different. You're not a sexual

person. I guess I figure you don't enjoy any of that stuff, so there's nothing to get envious about."

"So if we were having sex, you'd be upset, but if I romantically fall for her, that's fine with you?" I asked, hiding the desperation in my voice.

"Um—"

"Sex is more important? Is that what you're saying?" I attacked him. I could understand if Elmer didn't want me to develop strong feelings for Willow, but it bothered me that he didn't care about that issue at all. He was only focused on the sex. It felt so superficial.

"No. Kind of. It's hard to explain." He poked at his roast with his fork.

"Well, try," I pushed him.

"Shep . . . I've never been a casual sex person. I haven't even been with many people. Sex is special for me. It's tough for me to picture you with her, and it *not* involve love."

"But *you're* in love with her," I reminded him, slapping my hands on my thighs. His hypocrisy astounded me and certainly only added to my guilt for pursuing my own relationship with Willow. It wasn't fair.

He fell silent.

"Look, you finish your dinner. I've got some things to do in back," I told him as I started getting up.

"Shep." He grabbed my arm. "We can't just leave it like this. It's supposed to be a three-way situation, and you're not participating."

"Okay, well, maybe tomorrow night, I'll go home and fuck her. Will that be enough for you?" I snapped.

"Shhh!" Elmer stopped me, gently pulling my arm downward. "Calm down. Why are you acting this way? Talk to me. We said that we would. Always. That was the goal going in. I feel like you're pushing me away. I can't help how I feel."

"Neither can I." I wiped some tears from my eyes. "There's

all these rules for me and none for you."

"Sit down," he yanked me back down to the stool. "Would it be better if she doesn't move in? Is that what you want?"

"No." I sighed. "She can move in."

"I believe you're not telling me what you need, Shep," he pleaded. I wasn't used to his desperation. I felt guilty.

I took his hand in mine. "It's fine. I'm sorry. I'm struggling more than I thought I would. You're right. It was my idea. I like Willow, too. I should try harder."

"Are you sure?" he asked.

"Yes," I assured him. "I appreciate seeing you happy. Perhaps I can be, too. Be patient with me."

"Okay," he smiled in relief. "I need to try more, too. I'll think more about my issues with you having sex with her. I know it's not exactly reasonable."

"All right," I replied.

Luckily, we had a spare bedroom with a walk-in closet because while Willow didn't have much stuff, she had a ton of clothes and makeup. Fortunately, I still had my old vanity that I used when I presented as feminine that I moved from the garage to the room for her.

The permanency of her moving in didn't settle in at first. It felt like any other weekend with me working all day at the Tire then coming home to her and Elmer snuggled up on the couch. It wasn't until that Monday morning when I realized that for once, we would be alone.

Willow slept late, but I woke up for an early run on my treadmill since the roads were too icy. Afterwards, I made coffee and some sausage, egg, and cheese muffins. The seductive aromas roused her from her slumber.

"This is new," she stated, pulling up a stool to the kitchen island as I waited for the muffins to finish baking.

"What's that?" I inquired, pouring her a cup of Joe.

"Waking up not in my mom's house. And it just being me and you. I think when I find a job, I'll tell them that I can't work Mondays." She winked at me as she sipped her coffee.

"Oh, what for?" I asked.

"So that I can stay at home with you, silly." She grinned. "Man is it hard to flirt with you."

I chuckled. "Sorry. I'm usually so oblivious to it."

"So what do you want to do with me today, my love?" She smiled.

I shrugged. "There isn't much to do in Cloverleaf."

"Do you typically go out on your day off?" she asked.

I shook my head.

"So what do you do then?"

I thought for a moment. Generally, I smoked some weed since I had the house to myself, and I zoned out for a bit in front of the T.V. or from reading a good book.

"I don't do that much, really. Working the Tire makes me so tired that I savor the laziness of my days off." I rubbed my chin in thought. "But I do something that you may like."

"What's that?" she asked.

I checked the muffins then exited the kitchen. I returned with a large folder with many papers protruding out of it. I set it down in front of her on the island and took the pages out carefully.

"I'm not that good," I told her. "But I do these drawings sometimes."

Willow flipped through them. There were sketches of people who were half masculine and half feminine. A collage of various sexual images surrounding a shadowy figure that knelt down on the ground. One image of a man and a woman embracing each other, their nude figures fading into the body of the other while a third silhouette peered from a pit down below.

"These are pretty deep," she remarked. "They're

beautiful."

"Elmer told me you like to paint, so I figured you might appreciate them." I enjoyed having someone to share my drawings with. Art had become a way for me to release my anxiety.

"You do this on Mondays?" she asked, holding up one of them toward the light.

"Sometimes," I said.

"Has Elm seen these?"

"No," I replied. "He knows I do it. He's noticed things before, but . . . I guess I do them mostly for myself. Kind of like a journal."

She stayed focused on the last image of the man and woman embracing over the third character. "Is this us? You, me, and Elm?"

I nodded.

She pointed at the figure in the pit. "Is that how you feel, Shep?"

I tapped my fingers on the counter and clinched my jaw. "What do you think that person feels?" I asked her.

Willow took a sip of coffee and thought to herself for a moment. "It doesn't resemble a polyamorous relationship. It looks like two lovers and a third wheel. We're bright, and you're dark. It seems as if you're fading away."

"Then, yes, that's how I feel sometimes," I admitted. I was scared to tell her, but I also knew that to get closer to Willow, I needed to be vulnerable about my insecurities. And I trusted her.

She looked up at me with hurt in her eyes. "Oh, Shep. I'm sorry. I didn't know you felt that."

"I know you didn't." I hated seeing her upset. She was a sweet person. "You don't have anything to apologize about, Willow. I've had a harder time adjusting to this, especially because our relationship is so different than the one with Elm."

"Oh, but, Shep, you have it all wrong." She carefully placed the drawings back into the folder. She took my hands. "This whole month, I've been yearning for you."

"You have?" I froze.

"Yes. Ever since that first night I met you. You're not in the dark. I haven't figured out a way to . . . I don't know how to explain . . . to open you up." She stared into my eyes.

"But you seem so happy and lovey-dovey with Elm—" I insisted.

"I like sex." She laughed. "And he's very horny. But I often wish that I was doing it with you instead. I know you don't enjoy it, or want to, but I long to make love to you. It would help me feel closer to you. When Elm asked me to move in, it wasn't because of him. It was because I wanted a chance with you."

"Do you not like Elm?" I asked. My forehead crinkled as I tried to process everything.

"Yes." She sighed. "He's great. I have a blast with him. But I'm truly enamored with you. Oh, Shep, that drawing . . . I would do anything to be able to prove to you that it's not reality."

"How would you do that?" I didn't know what to do with her emotions. I'd been too consumed with losing Elmer that I hadn't noticed all the signs that she had feelings for me. I knew that I didn't want to hurt her.

"Please let me make love to you?" she pleaded, squeezing my hands. "At least once. You don't have to do anything reciprocal if you don't want to."

"Uh . . . I don't know," I stammered. *Don't have sex with her.* My promise tormented me. Even though Elmer admitted that he had a double standard with it, we hadn't come to a new agreement. But as I looked at her, she was so beautiful. There was a part of me that wanted to be with her and let myself fall in love.

She gently placed her hands on my cheeks. "I don't want to pressure you," she whispered. "That's the last thing I want. I try to be very respectful of asexuality. I've been reading about it. I don't want you to feel coerced. But you said that you and Elm do it and that you're not sex averse. That's why I need to know if this is possible. But if not, I understand."

Elmer had already crossed so many boundaries. I thought of my drawing. *What if the only way to overcome my insecurities and open my heart more is to make love to her?* I wasn't like Elm. I'd been reserved, holding back. He had let go. I needed to go for it, too.

"Okay," I agreed firmly. "I'm a little intimidated, though." Seeing how forceful she was, I worried that I'd only disappoint her in the bedroom.

"You don't need to be concerned about anything." She smiled and kissed me.

"I don't want to let you down. You seem so . . . good. I'm not," I disclosed. My heart pounded in my chest.

"Shep, I like a lot of different kinds of sex. I experiment. I role play. To me, this is another kind. It's not worse. It's just unique. And it's with you. That's all that matters." She hugged me.

I smiled. She was so brilliant at making everyone around her feel loved and safe. "Okay, I trust you," I told her. I kissed her, pulling her tight against me. My whole body tingled in her arms.

We went to the bedroom, and she laid me out along the bed. She removed her t-shirt and panties and climbed on top of me, straddling my hips. She gently pulled off my shirt.

"What don't you like, Sheppy?" she asked me.

"Kissing . . . on my body, I mean." I replied.

"Is touching and caressing okay?" she asked, keeping her hands on her thighs until getting my full permission.

I nodded. "Yes."

"Can I go down on you?" she checked.

"Yes." I trembled underneath her. I was exposed and vulnerable but also excited . . . and scared.

"Wonderful, my love." We stared in each other's eyes as she gently ran her fingertips on my arms then my chest, brushing up against my top surgery scars. She swiveled them along my stomach and down to my inner hip, sending a shiver up my spine.

"Do you want to lay there? Are you okay touching me?" she whispered.

"I can touch you. Where would you like me to?" I asked.

"My breasts."

I slowly placed my hands over them, cupping them in my palms and stroking my thumbs around her nipples. She let out a breathy moan and leaned down to kiss me. "Oh, Sheppy. I waited for this moment with you."

I moved my palms downward after she sat back up and rubbed my fingers lightly across her clit.

"Are you cool with this?" she checked. "You don't have to."

"I want to. Are you good? It's important to me to make you happy, too," I told her.

"Of course."

She removed my running shorts and boxers and re-straddled me. I returned to stroking her clit and massaging her breast with my other hand. As her excitement grew, she began grinding her pelvis against me, causing my own clit to harden and swell. When she came, her whole body shivered. She rocked forward and backward violently, jerking a moan out of me.

After leaning down to kiss me again, Willow pulled me downward toward the end of the bed and knelt down on the floor. I closed my eyes, and her curly hair tickled my inner thighs as her mouth met my vagina. Her lips were plumper and softer than Elmer's. She pushed my hips upward and moved her tongue ravenously. As I neared climax, I grabbed her curls, twisting my pelvis more into her. Her hands seized mine in a firm grasp, and I clutched them back so hard that my knuckles went numb.

When my body relaxed again, Willow laid down on top of me, tucking her head into my neck. "Oh, Shep," she whispered. "Thank you for giving yourself to me. Are you okay?"

I rubbed her back with my hand. "It's amazing," I said.

CHAPTER NINETEEN: ELMER

Even though Shep acted so anxious about Willow moving in, everything seemed to fall in place. She had accepted a part-time job at the local grocery store, The Clover Shop, while she searched for an office position. We often teased her for her uniform since it clashed significantly with her usual flamboyant style. She specifically requested Mondays off but stayed flexible the other days. Weekends were usually the busiest in retail, but the store closed at ten, so she was home early enough for us to be together before Shep returned from the Tire. Since she was working, we all felt more like a team.

Shep had grown out of his funk and was more open with the whole situation. Now it was me who was returning on Mondays to find both of them giggling and flirting as they were cooking in the kitchen. I'd noticed that they were painting together. On the weekends when Willow's shift started early, Shep and I enjoyed some alone time, which rekindled our own sex life. Everything felt great.

I'd just finished a staff meeting about the school's upcoming Halloween masquerade and was organizing some paperwork when Alice, my secretary, poked her head into my office.

"Yeah, what is it?" I asked her, motioning for her to come in.

Alice shut the door, which alarmed me since it indicated that this conversation must be serious. I put my documents aside and invited her to sit.

"Principal Lee," she stated nervously, "I have something to

tell you. Well, something that I think you should be informed about."

"Okay, go ahead," I encouraged her.

Alice stared at her hands that were clasped together on her lap. "I want you to know that I've enjoyed working with you for the past ten years. I feel that I probably appreciate you more than any other staff member. I see you not only as a coworker but as a friend." She looked up and gave me a slight smile.

"That's very nice, Alice. I consider you a friend, too. You've been an excellent assistant." Alice had her questionable beliefs. She never gendered Shep correctly and was adamant that marriage was between a man and a woman according to God. However, she didn't mistreat me and was actually a great worker. I didn't want her to quit if that was what this conversation was about.

"What's wrong?" I asked her.

Alice bit her bottom lip before answering. "Principal Lee, there's been some . . . rumors, if you will, going around the school. Well, the town for that matter. And I'm afraid that . . . I don't want to see you get in any trouble."

"What rumors?" I inquired. My stomach became unsettled. I despised gossip and had worked so hard to stay out of it even though I knew that people said things about my marriage. I'd been lucky so far that my reputation—or my career—wasn't jeopardized.

"It's so awkward to have to tell you this, but know that I'm telling you as a devoted friend," she said. Her voice sounded shaky.

"Alice, what is it?" I asked again more sternly. Her stalling was killing me.

"People are saying that . . . you and Shelly—"

"Shep," I corrected her.

"I'm sorry," she apologized even though it came across as

more dismissive than sincere. "That you and she—that you both have another girl living with you now. A very young one. She works at The Clover Shop."

Keep your composure. My gut twisted up in knots, and my throat closed in. As a principal, I'd gotten quite skilled at keeping my calm despite whatever was happening inside of me.

"Yes, Alice, that's accurate. Except that it's not *another* girl. We have *a* woman staying with us." I didn't want to lie because it only produced more dishonesty and often made situations worse. It was best to tell the truth and control the narrative.

"Oh," Alice grinned bashfully. "So it is true?"

"Yes. What of it?" I tried to sound annoyed more than scared. "What are people saying about it that has you so concerned to come inform me of it?"

"No one knows who she is, Principal Lee." She had changed into her usual gossipy tone that blended an air of concern mixed in with judgment. "She's obviously not from here. Is she a relative?"

While truthfulness was better, I also considered that saying that Willow was family could be believable and likely pacify any rumors going around town that may expose us.

"No, not mine," I replied. "She was a relative of Tank." *Yes! Someone who's related but distant enough so that we wouldn't be bombarded with a bunch of questions about her.* "She's a niece of Tank, and she needed a place to stay. She was having problems with her mother, and Shep had a good relationship with Tank's family. He didn't think anything of it to let her live with us."

"Ooooh," Alice gasped with a prolonged *o* sound. "That makes sense. I forgot that Tank had a sister." She giggled. "Gosh, what folks will make up."

"What did they say?" I demanded.

"Oh, Principal Lee, it's not important. I don't wish to upset you. You have enough stress."

"Tell me," I insisted, crossing my arms.

"Well . . ." She hesitated. "You know how people always talk about Shelly."

"Shep," I interjected more firmly, tapping my hand on the desk.

"Right." She smiled. "I don't want to hurt your feelings, sir, but it's folks like that . . . they . . . they do things that people like us wouldn't do."

"Like what?" I asked, reclining back in my chair. I kicked my feet as I waited for whatever awful thing she was going to say.

Alice blushed. "I'm sorry, sir, if I overstepped my boundaries."

"It's okay." It wasn't really. But I had to choose how to fight my battles. Too much fuss, and I was sure that the School Board would find an excuse to kick me out.

"But if I can give you some small advice," she stated. I gestured for her to continue. "I would never want to pry into your private business, but I think it's best to let the community assume that you're in some grief-stricken confused period of your life. And to allow them hope that you'll come back to your senses and find yourself a nice woman again. That's better than letting everyone assume . . . you're gay."

"I think you may be overstepping, Alice." I wasn't prepared to discuss my sexuality with my office assistant, nor get into a lecture about how being gay is okay.

"I'm so sorry, sir. It comes from a place of worry. You have to realize that people here are old-school. They might spread rumors, but it's their way of coping with such things, you understand. This hasn't been easy on *anyone*," she emphasized.

"Alice," I said with a slight smile on my face, but I kept my eyes and tone stern. "Thanks for your concern, but my private life is no one's business. Also, we have students who are gay or transgender. So while I respect your views, I ask you to keep those to yourself. This school will not be an environment that's not inclusive for everyone. Do you understand?" I shoved my hands in my lap so that she couldn't see them shaking. While I wanted to defend my LGBTQIA2S students, it was hard because it was so personal to me. I was really fighting for myself and Shep. Worse, I feared that I'd lose.

"Yes, sir. I'm sorry," she agreed, holding up her hand in surrender.

"It's okay," I told her, trying to control my jitters.

Alice got up to leave, but she paused at the door. "Principal Lee?"

"Yes?"

"What about the rumors about your ... Shelly's niece? Should I correct those when I hear them?" she asked.

"It's *Shep's* niece." The more she called him Shelly, the more I understood why Shep left the school. I also realized what a poor job I was doing at making Cloverleaf High a safe space for LGBTQIA2S staff and students. I'd failed.

"Oh, yes, sorry," she apologized again.

"If you feel the need to, go ahead," I told her. It's not as if Shep and I hung around anyone other than Snavis and his family, so I cared less about the rest of the town believing that Willow was a non-blood relative. It felt like a livable lie.

"Okay, sir." Alice left my office.

The rumors worried me, but Alice seemed pretty satisfied with the niece explanation, so I hoped that it would suffice everyone else's nosiness, too. I needed to let Willow know that she was a *relative* now so that she could corroborate the story if ever questioned.

I returned home from work around six thirty, expecting to find Willow there since she'd worked an earlier shift that day. However, the house was empty. I texted her, and she said that she was at the Tire with Shep. I decided to go over.

The Tire was busy considering it was Wednesday, which was burger night. Shep offered patrons their own choice of dough from plain white to honey wheat, garlic and herb, and spicey. Customers got to pick their own toppings and sauces. What made his burgers special was that he mixed ingredients directly into them rather than only adding them on top. When I bit into one, I would taste a variety of flavors and textures. There was the crunch of peppers and onions but also the chewiness of mushrooms or even dried fruit, an ingredient that I was surprised worked in a burger. They were more like meatloaves.

I found Shep and Willow in the kitchen. She was mixing something in a bowl, and he was rolling dough in his hand.

"Why, hello there." Willow winked at me. "It's the boss." She was infatuated with my authority. She often wanted me to dominate over her in sex, which led to her giving me the pet name of *the boss*. My dominance in our sex life was exactly what fueled my newfound confidence. I'd never been able to act so sexually free. Most of all, I loved not having to feel guilty about it. With Shep, I was too worried that I'd traumatize him if I wanted to do more since I knew he wasn't into it.

"I wasn't expecting you," Shep said. "Want a burger?"

"Sure," I told him. "Whenever you get a chance." I noticed that instead of a beer bottle, Shep had a glass of brown liquor next to him.

"Willow?" I turned to her.

"Yes, dear?" She smiled.

"Has anyone asked you about us? About living with us or who you are . . . anything?" I asked.

She shrugged. "Just my coworkers. Maybe a few customers."

"What did you say?" I asked.

"That I'm from Great Falls. I'm staying with you." She

didn't sound concerned, which both relieved me but also scared me. I feared that she may undermine the conservative beliefs of Cloverleaf.

"Did they ask you why you're living with us? Did they act suspicious?" I questioned further.

"I told them we're relatives. Cousins," she responded. "Why?"

I sighed in relief. I said niece instead of cousins. A reasonable error. I could say she's Tank's relative and that I was unsure about the actual relation.

"Good," I replied.

"Is something wrong?" Shep inquired, scrutinizing me up and down.

"No. Alice asked," I told him. He rolled his eyes. He was quite familiar with Alice. "Said some people in town were asking. I said the same thing that she's a relative. A niece of yours . . . Tank's. I figured it'd be easier if she wasn't our direct relative. Fewer questions."

"What were they saying?" he asked.

"I don't know. She wouldn't really say. I speculate that it probably isn't good. But hopefully, now, those rumors will be dispelled. I think I put them to rest." I knew that I was wrong. Being a principal and a restaurant owner naturally made us huge targets for gossip. I'd gotten away with marrying Shep, so I wanted to be hopeful that this would all work out, too.

"Good," he stated. "I've got to go make some rounds with the tables. Willow, can you handle it for a few minutes?"

"Yeah, I've got it." She smiled, blowing him a kiss.

After he disappeared out front, I walked up closer to Willow.

"Sorry, were you looking for me when you got home?" she asked. "I want to learn from Shep, you know? I've dreamed about starting my own restaurant or at least, cooking for one. So I figured why not come study from a professional? Plus, I guess I wanted to see Sheppy. You can live without me for a night, right?"

"Yeah," I agreed. "Um, Willow, can I ask you something?"

"Sure." She kissed me on the cheek.

"Is Shep drinking a lot?" I picked up his glass and smelled it.

She shrugged. "What's a lot?"

"Is he drinking more than usual?" I clarified.

"I don't know," she responded. "He seems to drink heavily since I've known him, so I can't really tell if he drinks more than he used to."

"Is he drunk at work?" While I'd started drinking more with Shep after he introduced me to various beers and wines, I still wasn't what I considered a big drinker. A beer with dinner was acceptable, but I didn't like getting too buzzed. Shep had always drank, but I'd never seen him drink so constantly. I was scared.

Willow squinted her eyes. "He doesn't seem drunk. Or maybe he's just good at hiding it. Why? Do you think he's drinking more?"

Looking back at his drink, I answered, "Yes."

"Oh," she replied in shock. "Really? How can you tell?"

I pointed at the glass. "He doesn't consume liquor. We only use it to cook. And he seems to be drinking whenever I see him."

"I know what you're talking about," she agreed. "He shouldn't drink on the job. You make mistakes doing that. I've seen in the show *Bar Rescue*. People do that, and then they make sloppy mistakes that cost them a lot of money. Is that what you're worried about?"

"No. I mean, yes, that's a concern, too." I sighed, and she must have been able to sense the sadness in my breath. She set her hamburger meat aside and removed her gloves.

"What is it? What's wrong?" She got closer to me, caressing

my cheek with her hand.

"I guess I'm upset because I don't know *why* he's drinking more." My words choked up. I hadn't realized until that point that there obviously was still some distance between me and Shep. It hurt.

"You think it's because of you?" she asked.

"Maybe," I concurred. "Or something else he's not telling me."

She put her arms around my neck and rested her forehead on mine. "Have you asked him about it?"

"Not really," I mumbled. "I've made a few comments, but it seems like the subject changes or the topic we're discussing is more important. Or perhaps I don't know how to bring it up."

"You're sensitive toward him, aren't you?" she asked.

I thought about her statement. Unlike my relationship with Luna, I had a tendency to avoid confrontations with Shep. Despite the fact that he didn't openly show his emotions, he had always been an extremely delicate person. Since he was also transgender and asexual, I'd figured he dealt with enough shit. While I had my battles with my own bisexuality, I'd believed that his problems were on a totally different playing field.

"I worry that he'll assume I don't understand him," I admitted to her.

"Do you think he's drinking because of me?" she asked very cautiously.

I kissed her forehead. "I don't know. What's your relationship with him like? When I'm not around."

Willow's lips protruded out in a pout, something she did when she pondered a question. It was also one of her most attractive expressions.

"Hmm," she muttered. "There's been a few . . . spectacular moments, I would say." She grinned. "He's either so hot or so cold. It's hard to feel close to him sometimes. It's quite different than when I'm with you."

"How would you describe me? Us?" I asked.

"You're easy." She laughed. "No offense."

"I'm easy?" I smirked. I'd always been so reserved. It was a weird compliment.

"Yeah." She pinched my chin. "You're constantly ready to go. It feels like you really wanted this and that you want me. Almost as if you've known me for a long time and had already made the decision that I'm your girl. It doesn't take much to woo you, my dear." She kissed me.

"But Shep isn't?" I inquired further.

She shook her head. "No, he isn't. He's not aloof. But he's not willing to give himself up easily."

"But you've had moments." I reminded her.

"Yes." She grinned with a slight blush. "That's why I'm not giving up on him."

"Has he told you how he feels about you?" The question escaped my lips, sending a shiver of fear through my body.

"He's told me he likes me," she replied with a hint of disappointment in her tone.

"Has he told you the way he feels about me?"

Willow smiled and cupped my chin in her hands. "Elm, he loves you. That I can tell you for sure. Should I ask him about his drinking? Want me to?"

"That'd be great, actually. Maybe he'd talk to you." Relief flooded through me. *He'll speak to her. Because he isn't talking to me.*

"Okay. Can do." She lovingly caressed my cheeks and forehead, tucking small loose hairs behind my ears.

"Willow?"

"Yes, dear?"

"When you say you had these moments, what makes them spectacular?" Spectacular felt like a big word. *Are they having more sexual or romantic occasions than they have with me?*

She kissed me, slipping her arm around my back and pulling me close to her. "Oh, Elm. I believe it's all right if we keep some situations private between us, don't you think? You don't tell Shep about all the stuff we do, right?"

"No, I don't," I admitted. *I wonder if he thinks I'm keeping things from him, too?*

"Then, I guess I'm entitled to a little privacy myself."

"Okay," I agreed.

CHAPTER TWENTY: SHEP

Winter arrived early that year. Since Cloverleaf lies along the plains of Montana, the cold winds were brutal. The sharp sixty plus miles per hour gusts felt like they could cut slices up and down my face, causing my dry cracked lips to bleed. The weather prompted me to add a few spicy dishes to my Halloween menus to get people's blood pumping again.

Willow had some fantastic ideas for the kids' party. She'd designed some marshmallow ghosts with candied eyeballs, gummy worms, donut holes painted with orange icing making them into tiny pumpkins, and cake pops created to resemble bloody fingers. She still had to work that Saturday since it was too early for her to demand time off, but she came into the Tire at four with me that morning to help create all these treats. I'd worked hard preparing miniature meatloaves made to look like brains to be paired with French fries dipped in ketchup.

"What about the food for the adult party?" Willow asked, rubbing some sweat off her brow. "Are you going to have time for that?"

"I've got some individual sized lava cakes in the fridge that ooze a blood-cherry filling. I've got pumpkin cookies, too. I made them all yesterday," I told her.

"Well, that's not as fun as these." She laughed. "The adults are missing out."

"You haven't had my cookies," I informed her, holding up my forefinger. "Trust me. I probably baked a good twenty dozen or so, and whatever they don't eat tonight, they'll be purchasing to take home with them. I don't know what I'd do right now without your help."

I walked over and hugged her from behind. "You've undoubtedly made it a lot easier. Thanks. Sometimes I think people expect me to work hard, but they don't understand how tiring it gets."

She placed her hands on top of mine as they rested on her waist. "You should really hire a manager. Your business seems good enough to afford it. That way, you could take some more time off or just focus on the cooking, which appears to be what you genuinely like doing anyway."

"If I could only relinquish the control that easy." I groaned, burying my face in her back. "I love my employees, but they make mistakes sometimes. I don't need to see the Tire go down."

Willow turned and threw her arms around me. "It means a lot to you, doesn't it? I mean, of course, it's your job. But you put your heart into it. Into your cooking. I can tell you want to make other people happy."

I nodded. "Never thought of it like that before, but you're right. I do enjoy watching crowds devour my food. Life's rough here in Cloverleaf . . . in Montana . . . anywhere. It's nice to be able to bring some joy into people's lives with a delicious meal. Healthy food, too. I do my best to make my stuff fresh and hearty. Financially, it's hard, though. If the house wasn't already paid for and we didn't have Elm's income coming in, it might get rough. Elm's got onto me about that many times."

"About what?" she asked.

"Not focusing as much as I should on profit. Yeah, I'm a pretty lousy businessperson." I chuckled. I loved cooking and so far, kept the Tire afloat. But I knew that my profits could be better. It was too bad that I didn't have someone like Elmer to help me manage it.

Willow smiled and kissed me. "You're such a wonderful person. That's why it's so easy to adore you." She caressed my cheek.

We hadn't had sex again. Willow was good at making love. Not only was she confident, but she was also caring and sensitive. Her attentiveness made me feel safe, and I didn't stress over my performance or that I needed to pretend to be the sexual person that I wasn't. But with her, it didn't feel like sex in a way but just two people cuddling and giving each other orgasms. She didn't appear to enjoy it any less than she would with Elmer. Afterwards, we had laid in bed, telling each other old goofy stories from our childhood and giggling as if we were lifelong friends. Just like now, her eyes sparkled with a glow of passionate warmth.

"I wish you could be here tonight," I told her.

"You like having your little niece around," she joked.

"Willow, I really appreciate everything you're doing. The help at the Tire and how good you are to Elm . . . the way you treat me."

"Have I made you feel like a man?" she asked.

"Yes, you do. But you also make it easy to be myself. Thanks." I kissed her.

"Since we're on a personal topic, Shep," she stated as she walked back over to her decorating station. "I do have a little concern."

"What's that?" I asked.

"I don't want to bug you. I'm sorry if this offends you." She sighed as she leaned against the counter. "But Elm mentioned something about your drinking a few weeks ago. And I've noticed that you drink pretty regularly, but he seems to think you drink more than you used to. He said you never drink liquor, and you've been drinking rum a lot."

I thought about the question for a moment. "Did he ask you to talk to me about it?"

"I offered. He didn't ask," she corrected me. "But it's not just Elm. Are you drinking more because of me?" Her eyes looked sad.

I paused. I hadn't thought much about my drinking. I stared down in shame. I was losing control.

"I shouldn't be drinking so much," I admitted.

"Is it because of me?" she asked again.

I sat down on a stool in the kitchen and rubbed my temples. Willow walked over and pulled up a chair in front of me.

"What is it?" she asked softly. "If it's me, you can tell me."

I groaned. "I have a lot of insecurities."

"About what?"

"About myself. About being trans. About Elm. About being ace. About you . . . about you and Elm. About everything." My anxiety spiked, and I began to tremble.

"That sounds like it *is* about me," she said woefully.

"It's not about you. It's about me," I insisted, taking her hand. "I know that sounds totally cliché. Bringing in a third . . . I worry that I'm going to be the one left out. The third wheel."

"Why? Sheppy, I thought I told you that you shouldn't feel that way. I'm nuts about you," she assured me, squeezing my hand.

I rubbed some tears from my eyes. "Because I can't compete with you or him. I can't give either of you the sex life you need. I know that sex isn't everything, but sometimes if *feels* like it is."

"Oh, Shep," Willow muttered with a slight tremor in her voice. "I would still choose to be with you even if we weren't in this polyamorous relationship. I don't care that you're ace. I can learn to do it in the manner you feel comfortable."

"But you're so . . . exciting," I argued. "You flaunt your sexuality, but in a good way. I wouldn't want to take that away from you or make you think like you have to subdue it." My cheeks grew hot as I realized how much I must have pressured Elmer to suppress his own sexuality.

"I don't have to do that." She leaned forward and wrapped both her hands around mine. "I can flaunt my sexual being. I can still have sex with you, Shep, and be an erotic person."

I'd never considered that we could both be ourselves and express who we are simultaneously.

"You're right," I told her. "I shouldn't feel that way."

"All I've been thinking about since the other Monday is us together again. Sheppy, it was one of the best sexual experiences I've ever had." She smiled and put her hands on my knees.

"Really?" I gasped.

"Yes." She laughed. "Because it's the person that matters the most. You were so . . . delicate. I get tired of all the more aggressive men sometimes. It was fun with you."

"You really have a wonderful way of looking at things. Or you're just good at making me feel better," I joked.

"Shep?"

"Yes?"

"I think I'm falling in love with you. Is that okay?" Her voice resembled a timid child instead of her usual array of confidence.

"You think you love me?" I asked in bewilderment. "I don't understand. I thought you and Elm—"

"I like Elm. I do," she insisted. "He's a lot of fun, and his uptightness makes him more charming. But . . . I feel extraordinary with you." She looked at me eagerly.

"What's different with me?" I asked. I wasn't sure what intimidated me more. Her sexual desire or her romantic feelings toward me.

Her face grew serious. "You're so kind. You care so much about everyone else even to your own detriment sometimes. You're not just a cook. You're an artist with your food, and again, the love you put into it. The joy you want others to get from it. And the caring spouse you are. Who's willing to try adding a third to their marriage because they want to make their husband happy? There isn't anyone like you."

Love and sadness collided inside of me bubbling up to the surface. I let out a long sigh and held her hands.

"Thanks for those words," I stammered through my tears.

"Do you see yourself falling in love with me?" Willow asked.

I grinned nervously. "Um . . . if you keep this up." I snorted.

"I'm being serious. How do you feel about me? About us?" she demanded again.

I swallowed hard. "I don't want to lose you from our lives. But the other week . . . it was difficult for me to open up like that. I move slower."

She looked hurt, but she gave a slight smile. "I understand. This is harder for you. You're so committed to Elm."

"Do you think Elm loves you? Has he said it? Have you?" I asked, changing the subject.

This time, Willow let out a loud breath, pursing her lips as she exhaled. "He hasn't revealed it in exact words, but . . . yeah, I think he loves me. I guess he did from the beginning."

I got up quickly from the stool, grabbed my open bottle of Captain Morgan's, and poured myself a shot. I gulped it down so fast that the after burn sent tears swelling up in my eyes. Willow came up from behind me, placing her hands on my shoulders.

"I'm sorry," she whispered. "I guess I shouldn't have told you that if he hasn't said anything, yet." She turned me to face her, seeing the tears and slight tremble in my body. She took the glass from my hand and set it down. "It's way too early to drink, Shep."

"It doesn't matter," I retorted. "I fucking knew it was going to happen anyway." I covered my eyes with my hands.

"Don't be angry." She pulled my hands away from my face. "Or hurt. Damn it. I shouldn't have opened my big mouth. It's just . . . oh, never mind."

"What?" I demanded sharply. "Tell me."

"I'm jealous," she confessed, starting to sob. "I watch you here, crying and drinking over someone who . . . I'm not saying Elm is a bad guy. I don't see how you can be so upset over him considering how he's dived all into this. I mean, do you know the thousands of texts I get from him every day? The things he says to me. I don't see why you can't let go, too. He's doing it. I don't see him stressed or sobbing over it."

"It's harder for me," I yelled. "I can't move that fast."

"Are you sure you're okay with *him* moving quickly? Because you don't act like it," she stated.

My gut screamed no. But there was no way that I was going to be the downer for everyone. After all, Elmer was the uptight one. I wasn't. I was queer. I pushed through social boundaries. *I've got to be able to overcome this. I believe that I can get there. I can be like them. I can't lose him.*

"I'm okay with him. With you. It's an adjustment for me. I know I can do it," I insisted, rubbing my eyes.

"Shep, are you sure this is what you need?" She placed her hands on my shoulders, staring intently at me.

"Yes," I blurted out. "It's what I want, Willow." I hugged her. "Please don't go tell Elmer about any of this. I don't want to mess things up."

"I won't." She embraced me tightly, and we held each other for a few minutes. Finally, she pulled away and smiled. "Besides, I'm kind of glad to get a side of you that's all mine."

The Halloween events were successful, bringing in even more children and families than any other year. I had always dressed up, and this time, I was caked in massive layers of makeup transforming me into a zombie. I wore an old sweater that I'd sliced holes in and a dirty-looking pair of jeans. I found that when I was in costume, parents were more friendly because it was easier for them to avoid questions like *is that a boy or a girl?* from their kids.

Elmer was busy that same weekend with the school's Halloween masquerade, so all the cleanup was left to me, Danny, Peggy, Pam, and Willow, who had returned after the grocery store closed. By the time we rolled into the house, all three of us plummeted into bed.

We had a few weeks of calm before both Elmer and I had to start planning holiday events. His school presented an annual assembly for Veteran's Day in which local veterans gave speeches to the students. The school also hosted a Thanksgiving community dinner. Before Elmer, Cloverleaf High hosted few assemblies, but he felt it was important to build a strong school-community connection. Like me with the Tire, he put his blood, sweat, and tears into it.

I offered free dinners for veterans on Veteran's Day. Other than that, I only had to plan my upcoming Thanksgiving week menu and fundraising for my food drive. I'd collected donated items and cash that I used to prepare holiday meals for elders. Danny did most of the fundraising. His social skills and good looks charmed many Cloverleaf residents into contributing, especially if they had a single daughter. Danny often returned with cash and girls' phone numbers.

A feeling of intimacy arose for Willow. More than anything, she seemed to genuinely care about me and Elmer. She was friendly and kind. Customers loved her when she hung out at the Tire, even though many of the local mothers tried to fix her up with their single sons. Her laugh and smile could melt away any tension in a room.

I stumbled in early one Wednesday evening, tired and shaking all the snow off my shoes. Elmer was still at work, and I heard the shower running in the bathroom. I changed into my pajama pants and a flannel and gulped a few shots of rum before hearing the faucet turn off. I waited for her to join me in the living room, our usual routine, but after twenty minutes, she didn't appear. I decided to go check on her. I gently pushed the partially closed bedroom door open and saw her laying in bed. I crept over and sat beside her.

"Are you okay?" I asked worriedly, considering Willow never went to sleep early.

"I'm really exhausted," she mumbled. "I'm not feeling too well. I think I'm going to go to the doctor."

"What's wrong?" I placed my hand on her shoulder.

"I feel sick. That's all. I'm sure it's nothing." She buried her face into the pillow. I wasn't used to seeing her so uncomfortable.

"But you need to go to the doctor?" I clarified. I worried that it had to be more than just a cold if she needed a doctor.

"Maybe . . . I don't know," she said.

Her words were hesitant and abrupt, not her usual chipper self. I gently rubbed her back. "If you want to see a doctor," I told her, "I'll pay for it. Don't worry about it. Do you want me to take you tomorrow? We can go in the morning."

"I think I should go by myself," she replied.

"I don't need to be at the Tire until the afternoon. I'll go with you." I hated seeing her ill. Sometimes getting an appointment in Cloverleaf was tricky since it was such a small town, so I wanted to help her.

"Okay," she whispered with a slight smile. "The back rubbing feels good."

"I can lay down with you," I offered. "I'll rub your back some more."

"I'd like that," she stated.

I got up and put away any evidence of my drinking. I texted Elmer that Willow was sick and that we were both going to bed early. I brushed my teeth, and when I went to dispose of my dental floss in the bathroom trash can, the corner of a rectangular box stashed under a bunch of tissues caught my eye. On the front side of it, I saw the infamous white stick with a pink top and digital reader on the front. I picked up the carton, and my fears were confirmed. It was a *First Response* test. Immediately, I searched the rest of the garbage, but the stick was nowhere to be found.

Why does she need to see a doctor? Where's the stick?

My legs weakened, causing me to plummet down on the toilet, and I had to choke back my vomit. *Maybe she's just late. I had that happen before. I took pregnancy tests even though I knew I probably wasn't pregnant. Sometimes, you want to be sure.*

But where's the stick? Why does she need a doctor?

That's when I went into a full panic attack.

Chapter Twenty-One: Elmer

I woke up on Thursday morning to find both Shep and Willow sick. Willow wasn't behaving like her typical bubbly self. She appeared tired. She merely threw on a pair of black sweatpants and a t-shirt, shoving her curls into a baseball cap. At breakfast, she barely picked at her food.

Shep seemed even worse. His eyes looked wild and bloodshot. He was sweaty and pale. Similar to Willow, he wasn't eating. They both had me worried.

"Are you sure you're okay? Is it the flu?" I asked, placing my hand over Willow's forehead.

"It's nothing," she murmured, unconvincingly. "I don't want to miss any shifts at work, so I prefer to go get some medicine, if needed."

Shep glared at her with his arms crossed, but Willow didn't glance up from her plate.

"Is that what you think it is?" I asked him. "You've never had the flu."

"I didn't know you weren't feeling well, too," Willow said, finally looking over at him.

His jaw visibly tightened, and his face turned red.

"Are you sick or is it something else?" I urged him. "You look upset." His behavior was strange, and I was scared that an argument had happened between them.

Shep got up from the table and took his plates to the kitchen. He stood with his back toward us, not answering.

Willow gazed at him with a slight tremor. My stomach tightened.

213

After a few moments, he coolly remarked, "I don't think we're going to the doctor for the flu, are we?"

I glanced at Willow, and her eyes grew wide. She immediately looked down.

I asked, "What are you saying? Is it something more serious?" I didn't know what he could be so upset about. Certainly, they couldn't have had *that* bad of a disagreement.

Shep turned around and sneered at me with a look of complete disgust. "Who the fuck do you think you're kidding?"

"Who are you talking to?" I asked, throwing my arms up in the air.

"I'm speaking to you," he snapped. He went into the cabinet underneath the sink and took out a box. He threw it across the room, and it landed on the table in front of us. It was a *First Response* test.

"You're going to get a pregnancy test, aren't you, Willow?" he accused her.

Willow kept evading our eyes. She sat in silence. My heart jumped out of my chest, and my temples throbbed. I picked up the box, but it was empty.

"Where is it? Did you take it?" I asked her.

"Why the fuck does she need to take a test, Elmer? Huh?" Shep yelled. He was crying.

Willow finally looked up. "I didn't realize that you'd be so mad," she told Shep. "I mean, I think I might be pregnant. I'm over here scared shitless. And you're over there yelling at me?" She started sobbing, burying her face in her hands.

Shep sighed, and I could see him shaking. "I'm not mad at you, Willow. I'm not blaming you for getting pregnant. What I want to know is . . ." He turned his attention on me. "Elmer, how is it possible that she got pregnant? What birth control have you been using?"

My heart started beating brutally against my chest. My throat tightened so hard, I thought I'd choke.

I got up from the table and walked over to Shep. He backed away from me as I got closer. I put my hand on the counter to brace myself. Willow stared at us dumbfounded from the table.

"Shep . . ." I stuttered.

"Well?" he demanded.

"We haven't . . . *I* didn't use any protection," I confessed as my hands shook.

Shep's face writhed in hurt, and he turned away from me again. I went over to comfort him, but he pushed me away hard. I could see the tears streaming down his face and his shoulders moving up and down as he heaved.

Willow got up from the table. "Shep? Are you okay?" She peered at me. "What's going on? I don't understand."

"All I said was no kids," Shep choked out. "I said to use protection. I said not to get her pregnant!" He pounded his fist on the counter.

"I know." I wanted to hold him. But my powerlessness froze me. "I fucked up. I'm sorry. We don't even know if she's pregnant. Willow, what did the test say?"

"It said I'm pregnant," she replied, getting teary eyed again. "That's why I want to go confirm it with a doctor."

"Well, see" — I pointed at Willow — "we still don't know for sure. Those tests can be wrong," I insisted. *If she isn't pregnant, we can fix this.*

"That's not the fucking point!" Shep shouted, still weeping and bracing himself on the counter. "I asked this one thing."

"No, you didn't," I argued. "This whole time you've been against this, yet you were the one who pushed it from the beginning. I think you did this on purpose."

"What? Are you fucking serious?" he retorted.

"You demanded a third to break us apart. You wanted it so that you can make me out to be the villain."

Shep's wet eyes gawked at me in disbelief.

Willow interjected. "I see you're both angry —"

"You're damn right that I'm angry," Shep snapped. He stormed out of the room.

"Don't leave it this way, Shep," I hollered after him. "You go to the doctor, and see if she's pregnant, and we'll all come home early and deal with it. We'll work it out."

He reappeared in the hallway. "Sure, I'll take her and find out if *you're* having a baby. Is there anything else I can do for you?"

"You know, I'm sick of this shit, Shep," I shouted as my temper grew. "I'm fucking tired of you playing the victim in everything. You started this whole thing. I never said that I wanted a girlfriend or a third. It's bullshit!"

"Guys, stop," Willow screamed as she walked over and stood between us. "Calm down. Elmer. Go to work. I'll text you when I know. Shep, relax. You have to drive me."

"That's fine with me," I stated, grabbing my coat. "I'll walk away like the asshole I am, right? I wasn't the one who decided to go find someone else to fuck my husband for me."

"Elmer, go!" Willow ordered. "Stop this!'

I grabbed my backpack angrily. As I got to the door, I turned to Shep. "I took a huge risk to even be with you. The high school principal marries the transsexual. Nothing that I've ever done to show you that I love you has been enough."

I slammed the door behind me.

The hours at work dragged by as I constantly checked my phone for any texts from Willow or Shep. This burning desire to reach out and say something to them bubbled up, but I was scared. Shep and I had never fought that way before. I didn't know why this potential pregnancy bothered him so much. He knew that I had wanted to have a baby, and we both loved Willow. I couldn't ignore the excitement about possibly being a dad.

He'll chill out. He's freaking himself out. It's his insecurity.

I'd never hesitated to text or call my own husband. I didn't want to see him in pain. A tension rose up in my shoulders and temples. *I hurt him.* My guilt hovered all around me like a large black cloud. *Maybe I'd been selfish.*

It was getting close to the afternoon, and I knew that Shep had to be at the Tire by one, so I decided that I couldn't wait any longer. Frantic, I texted Willow to see if she had any news. She said that they weren't able to get an appointment that day, which was typical sometimes in Cloverleaf. While there weren't many people in town, ranchers and residents living outside of the city limits often drove into Cloverleaf for medical care. With few doctors, it could be challenging to get in. Willow mentioned that she was still in shock after that morning. She asked how I felt about the possibility that she was pregnant. I told her that I'd support whatever she wanted to do and that I wanted all of us to sit down and discuss it. After a few minutes, my phone beeped.

Do you want me to get rid of it? Just tell me. It's mine and your baby.

Get rid of it? One of the things that I both loved and hated about Willow was her directness. My mind told me that it'd be best to at least consider an abortion. Shep's behavior that morning indicated that we weren't ready for this. But that didn't feel fair to Willow — or to me. *Lose my baby?* Slightly trembling, I texted that I wanted to have the child.

A few minutes passed with no response. I fumbled with the cuticles on my fingernails so badly that one ripped off and bled. I grabbed a tissue and wrapped it around my finger. Then my phone dinged.

I'm not sure. Still absorbing it all. But I can't really picture myself aborting it.

I responded that I understood and that I'd take care of all of us, regardless of what happens with Shep. But I assured her that he was being insecure and that he'd calm down.

I set my phone down, assuming the conversation was over. Another fifteen minutes passed when it went off again. Willow said that she had something to tell me. I sent a question mark and waited. All I heard was the tick of the clock on my office wall and the cracking of my knuckles. Finally, she replied.

I had sex with Shep.

Chapter Twenty-Two: Shep

The entire shift at the Tire passed in a blur. I wasn't even sure if the food tasted up to par. My heart felt heavy like it was going to plummet into my gut and disintegrate. I chose to stay in the kitchen focusing on the cooking rather than mingling with the customers. I told Peggy to say that I'd had a stressful day since many of my regulars often inquired about me.

I was falling apart from the inside. My thoughts raced so fast that I had a throbbing headache. I didn't even drink the entire evening because everything made me nauseous. Carrying my vape pen on me, I periodically snuck into the back room to take a few puffs just to calm my nerves. The previous evening's panic attack had left me drained but still on edge. The dreaded conversation waiting for me when I got home caused more dismay.

I took off early, letting Pam close the restaurant. I took a few more hits from my vape before entering the house. Elmer and Willow both sat at the kitchen table. Her eyes appeared damp and shiny. His face looked tense and flushed. I didn't say anything but instead, walked over to the liquor cabinet, poured myself a double shot of rum, and gulped it down. I refilled it before joining them.

Our table wasn't large, but the distance between all three of us felt poignant. I evaded eye contact. I fumbled with my glass, tapping it back and forth with my fingers. Every time I glanced up, Elmer's eyes were glued on me.

He was in full force principal mode, something he did

when he wanted to take charge. "We all need to talk about this. And some other things. And without fighting or yelling. We're all in this together. Let's remember that."

Silence. My whole body was stiff like a log.

"Shep, how do you feel?" he asked.

I cringed. "I need to know what you two have talked about already. It's your baby after all. Not mine," I said firmly.

"I'll go first," Willow offered gently. "I didn't plan on getting pregnant. I mean, I want kids, but I wasn't thinking about having any right now. So this is all new and scary to me."

"I understand," I muttered, glancing over at her. I didn't want my heartache from Elmer to cause any pain to Willow. I wasn't angry at her. Watching her act so shaky and not her usual chipper self made me feel ashamed of how I'd acted that morning.

"I need some time to make a final decision. I've only had a few hours to really think about this. But talking to Elm . . . if I am pregnant . . . I guess I want to keep it." Her eyes met mine as if she was seeking my permission.

"You do," I stated flatly. I couldn't breathe.

"I think so," she replied, giving me a slight smile. I could tell that she desperately wanted my approval. "It's one thing to think about having a baby. It's different when you actually realize that you have one inside of you . . . or at least, I think I do. I know my job isn't the greatest right now. But even if I had to do this without either of you, I could go back to Great Falls and live with my mother. I may even be able to get my old position back. I can take care of myself. I want you two to know that. I don't need you to feel pressured like you have to change your whole lives for this."

Willow running back to Great Falls to have a child alone was too depressing. She didn't deserve that. "That's nice of you, Willow," I told her. "But I can't fathom that Elm would let you walk away and raise a baby—*his* baby—all by yourself." I slowly turned my gaze toward him. "Is that right, Elmer?"

He nodded. "You're right, Shep," he confirmed. "I couldn't *not* take care of my own baby."

I took a deep breath. "So what is it that you want?" I demanded.

Elmer looked hurt. "Like Willow, I haven't had much time to process this. But I've always wanted a child. You know that, Shep. I didn't think I'd ever get the chance. It feels as if . . ." He put his hand on his chest. "I don't think I can just walk away from it." He glanced down as if he was ashamed.

"That leaves you, Shep," Willow chimed in. "What do you want to do?"

I gulped down my rum, feeling the burn in my head and the throbbing in my temples increase. Averting my eyes, I replied, "I want you two to be happy."

"That's not a direct answer, Shep," Elmer claimed. "What do *you* want? Do you want us to have it or not? We need to hear from you."

I shrugged, clenching my jaw to fight back tears. "If y'all want to have it, I support you."

"Are you sure?" he inquired. "You're going to be okay with an infant in the house?"

My heart broke. My hands shook. I realized that I had to tell the truth. "I'm cool with you having a kid. In terms of me and my place in this, I don't have that figured out, yet." I trembled. I knew there was no way that I could talk Elmer out of his dream of being a parent. But I was also aware that this would create a bond between them that I could never be a part of. Sure, I could be the second dad, and we could be this cool hip family with two dads and a mom. But that wasn't who I was. I couldn't give Elmer sex or a child. And I was too insecure to see someone else provide those for him.

"Well, we'd all be together, of course," Elmer assured me.

"The baby would have three parents. We'll figure it out." His gaze looked frantic. I hated that. I didn't want him to feel guilty about getting what he wanted.

"I'm unsure about that," I told him.

"Shep," Willow interrupted. "Elm knows that we had sex."

My eyes grew wide, and I gasped.

"Sorry," she continued. "After your . . . both of your reactions this morning. I don't think we should keep any secrets. I think after tonight, we should start anew."

My cheeks became hot. "It was just one time," I confided to him. "I thought . . ." I buried my face in my hands. "I believed if I did it that I'd feel more like you about this."

"About sex?" he asked.

I rubbed some tears from my eyes. "About . . . this polyamorous relationship . . . well, about Willow. I expected it would help me. I don't know . . ." My voice trailed off.

"Did it?" he questioned. His tone sounded calm but hurt.

I saw Willow surveying me closely. My hands started shaking even more, and my body became numb and tingly. I took a few slow breaths to try to soothe myself. But I couldn't stop the tears from leaking out.

"No, it didn't," I admitted. "It did. I . . ." I looked over at Willow again. "I have feelings for you. I really enjoyed being with you."

She covered her face with her hands, and I heard her give a slight sniffle. Elmer sat there, fiddling with his thumbs.

"Willow," I said, leaning toward her. "The sex wasn't bad . . . it was good . . . it was great. You made me feel so comfortable. It was one of the most positive sexual experiences I've ever had. And just being with you afterwards . . . I loved it."

"But you don't love me." She wept.

"Willow, I care about you a lot. I do." I tried to convince her. I hated seeing her cry. Willow was like a saint to me.

"But you don't love me?" she asked, uncovering her eyes.

"It's not that. I . . ." I turned to Elmer who sat watching me very closely with a blank stare. "I can't do this. I'm sorry."

"Do what?" he asked.

"This three-way relationship," I replied. "Fuck!" I started crying. "I know it was all my idea . . . I really, really tried." I glanced over at Elmer. "Seeing you adapt to it so easily . . . I didn't want to tell you. And Willow, I wanted to avoid hurting your feelings. But . . . I care about my husband too much to love someone else. I don't want to spread my love between two people. I'm monogamous."

"You want to break up?" Willow blurted out in surprise.

I wiped some tears away. I ran my finger along my silver wedding band.

"Wait," Elmer interjected. "I know you've had a harder time adjusting to this. But is this coming up because she's pregnant? Would it be different otherwise?"

I paused for a moment. I didn't think I could keep lying to either of them. "I don't know, Elmer. I love having Willow around, but . . . I'm not happy."

"I'm not sure how to react," he stammered, shaking his head. "You want us to split up? You prefer that Willow return to Great Falls and raise the baby on her own?"

"No," I choked out. "I want you and her to do it."

"Then what about you?" he asked, leaning forward.

I took a deep breath and let out what I had been considering all afternoon. "I think it's best that . . . that I leave."

Elmer stood up abruptly, nearly knocking his chair down behind him. He knelt down in front of me, pulling my hands away from my eyes.

"Wait a fucking minute. No," he stated firmly with his voice shaking up. "That's not an option. No one wants you to go."

"I know you don't want me to, but . . ." I tried covering my eyes again, but he yanked my hand away. "I can't give you what she can. You've been so happy these past few months. Like a teenager. I've never seen you so giddy. Now, you're going to have a baby. You shouldn't fuck this up."

"Why can't we all have the baby? It's all of us together," he pleaded squeezing my hands in his.

I groaned. "We were fooling ourselves. Or I guess I was."

"Shep, I never wanted to break up your marriage," Willow remarked, rubbing her eyes. "You can't leave. I don't want to be here without you."

"It's okay. It's better this way," I insisted. My heart ached inside. I clinched my fists to give me the strength to let it go.

"No, it isn't," he snapped. "You're my husband. I fought hard for us."

"Yeah, you reminded me this morning," I blurted out. Hearing Elmer refer to me as a transexual — or even an asexual felt dehumanizing, even though I knew he was just upset. He had taken a risk in the career he was in.

"I didn't mean that," he mumbled, looking down.

I gently touched his chin and pulled his gaze upward. "Elm, I know you love her. You do, don't you?"

He paused for a long moment, glancing over at Willow before turning back to me. "Yes, I do."

"You both care for each other. You're having a baby. I'm happy for you. I really am. Even though this hurts." I sobbed a minute. "But I can't do this with both of you anymore. I realize that you have this liberal hip vision of all three of us parenting, but . . . it's not me. It's only right for you two to be together for the kid. And I know you'll make a great father."

"Shep," he whispered. His eyes stared at me with longing. "What can I do? What do you want? You can't leave me." His voice broke up as he began crying.

"Don't go, Shep," Willow begged from across the table. "I'll leave. I can't let you do this."

"I can't do it," I answered solemnly. "I can't go back, Elm. I think it's best for me . . . for all of us."

"No—" he started.

I pushed Elmer aside and stood up. "I'm going to pack some things and stay at the Tire."

"You're staying at the restaurant?" he asked.

"In the back room," I said. "Just until you have time to move back into your old house. The one you had with Luna."

"My brother's wife's sister and her family are living there," he pointed out.

"Look, there's no rush," I replied holding up my hand. "I basically live at the Tire anyway. I'll be fine until you figure something out." At that moment, I wanted to run away, and the tiny room at the Tire suited me.

"You want me to move out? Are you going to divorce me?" he questioned, placing his palm over his heart.

"I wasn't planning to draw up the papers tomorrow. One step at a time. Let me grab my things." I started walking toward the bedroom.

Elmer walked up from behind me, throwing his arms around me tightly. I could feel a slight tremor from his body and hear the anguish in his voice.

"Don't do this, Shep," he cried. "Please, please don't do this. I can't live without you. You're breaking my heart."

"I have to," I told him. The unbearable pain of heartbreak shot up through my chest. *Let him go. Let him be happy.*

"No, you don't. We can work this out."

I turned to face him. I wiped some tears from his eyes and hugged him. He squeezed me back so hard that I could hardly breathe. I pulled away and placed my hand gently on his cheek.

"I know it's tough, Elm," I told him. "But you'll see that this is better. Besides, you can't have it all. I thought we could, but we can't. I'm sorry. Maybe it's all my fault. I shouldn't have suggested a third."

"Why didn't you tell me?" He held onto my shoulders.

"Because I loved seeing you happy. Even if it wasn't me doing it. I couldn't bring myself to take it away." I despised how stupid it all sounded now. But the damage was done.

I kissed him, and he engulfed me in his arms again, causing me to have to squirm to escape his embrace. "Goodbye, Elmer."

I packed some clothes and personal items in a duffle bag. When I returned to the kitchen, both Elmer and Willow sat hunched over at the table. I went over and leaned down to hug her. She didn't respond. Elmer avoided my gaze.

Just like that, I walked out into the cold wintry November night.

Chapter Twenty-Three: Elmer

I wasn't there when the doctor informed Luna that she had stage-four cervical cancer. I'd known that she was seriously ill. But it was the beginning of the new school year, and as principal, I'd felt like I couldn't miss the first day. Looking back, I should have been there.

When she had called me, my heart dropped. I'd dreaded hearing about the diagnosis, and perhaps that was part of the reason that I had avoided going to the appointment with her. When I answered, all I heard was gasping and sobbing on the other end. My wife was dying. I felt emasculated for not being able to help her, as well as powerless and alone. There's nothing worse than preparing to lose someone I love.

When I'd woken up in my bed only feeling the soft brush of Willow's leg beside mine and no Shep, my heart sank. All the familiar dark feelings of losing Luna flooded through me as I realized that he was getting taken away from me.

"Elm," I heard Willow whisper as she gently shook my shoulder. "Don't you have to get up for work?"

My whole body felt like a blob of putty. I responded by turning over on my side.

She softly rubbed my back and rested her chin in the crevice of my neck. A heavy sadness radiated off of her. A few moments later, a few tears hit my cheeks.

"I'm scared," she muttered with a tremble in her voice.

I knew the right thing to do was to roll over and wrap my arms around her, assuring her that it would be okay. That I would take care of her and our baby. That I loved her.

Waves of grief engulfed me. *I can't handle this kind of loss again.* Instead, I buried my head in my pillow.

Willow eventually got up to get ready for her shift, and I heard my cell phone beeping and ringing. Yet, I couldn't move.

When she was leaving, she sat down beside me on the bed. She lovingly stroked my hair away from my face. I kept my eyes closed.

"I answered your phone," she said into my ear. "It was your secretary calling. I told her that you were really sick, like vomiting and stuff. I said that you may not be in if you don't get better. I hope you're not mad. I didn't want you to get in trouble."

I didn't reply.

"Elm," she started before stopping to breathe through another crying spell attempting to surface. "I hope you're not upset with me. I'm so afraid that you hate me. That Shep hates me. I never wanted any of this to happen. I love you and Shep. I think I ruined your marriage. And I know that you're hurting right now, but . . . could you please say something to me? I don't know what to think. I feel abandoned . . . and scared."

"I'm sorry," I grumbled. "I just need to be left alone.

She wiped her tears, leaned over, and kissed me on the cheek. "Okay," she said.

I stayed in bed most of the day even though I wasn't sleeping. I refused to get up and walk around Shep's house. Having to go into the kitchen without the aromas of whatever sensational culinary masterpiece he had cooked for breakfast felt too painful. Knowing that there'd be no more evenings where I sat on the bar stool listening to him explain all the spontaneous additions he was making to a recipe. The realization produced a poignant hole of emptiness that I hadn't experienced before or at least, since Luna's death.

Despite the dread in my body, I forced myself up around two in the afternoon. I didn't bother getting dressed but proceeded to pour myself a shot of whiskey and grab a loaf of bread before slumping down on the couch in the living room. As I gulped down the liquor, I twirled the glass in my hand.

This is why he's been drinking so much. Because of me.

I shoved an entire piece of bread in my mouth to fight back the tears in my eyes. I knew Shep so well, yet I had failed him. I'd gotten lost in Willow, the sex . . . I'd gotten carried away with the sex.

I recalled the early days of toying with the idea of a third and how awkward it had all seemed when Shep proposed it. I hadn't needed to have sex with anyone else. I only wanted Shep. However, I'd spent so many years not exploring my sexuality. I'd heard lots of stories from Snavis and Kicky about their various sexual adventures, so it had felt good to be able to explore myself with Willow. To let go. But I had never thought that it would replace my marriage.

Now I had what I always wanted, a baby. All those years that Luna and I had tried desperately to conceive, and it finally happened. I would have a family.

Willow returned home around eight that evening. I knew her shift ended at six, so I wasn't sure why she was late, nor did I really care. By that time, I was sprawled out on the couch in nothing but my boxers and an empty bottle of whiskey on the floor.

My eyes stared blankly at the ceiling until a familiar fragrance hit my nostrils, causing me to jolt up. I heard rustling in the kitchen. Stumbling to my feet, I walked into the room, seeing Willow laying out some plates. A brown paper bag from the Tire was on the bar.

"Shep thought you'd be hungry," Willow stated flatly. "Why don't you sit down, and I'll get your stuff ready."

"You talked to Shep?" I asked eagerly, nearly tripping and falling as I entered the kitchen. "What did he say?"

"Just have a seat. I'll tell you."

I plopped down on a bar stool. My stomach immediately burst into life as the aromas of the food penetrated the air. The familiar scents filled me with joy and a painful nostalgia that caused my chest to ache more. Willow came over with two plates and laid one in front of me. I examined the perfectly pink succulent prime rib next to a mound of wheat berries that were fragrant with toasted pine nuts and fresh figs. A couple of parker house rolls with melted butter oozing down them sat on top. Instinctively, I shuffled heaping forks into my mouth. Willow set a glass of water on the table.

"I think you could use some," she remarked. "You don't look good."

"What did he say? What happened?" I mumbled with a mouthful of rib.

She took the seat next to me and pinched off a piece of a roll. "I went over after work to talk to him. I thought maybe I could change his mind. Assure him that you still love him . . . that I love him."

"What did you say?" I demanded, pounding my fist on the table.

She finished chewing her bread. "I told him how you were this morning and that you didn't even go to the office. He was surprised by that. That's why he gave me the food. He seemed worried about you."

"Does he want to talk to me?" My eyes were so wide I thought they would pop out of my head.

She glanced at me sadly. "He says he doesn't want to speak to either of us."

My heart dropped again, this time taking my throat down with it. I froze, letting the fork in my hand fall onto the plate with a loud clang. Tears welled up, and I shoved my face into my hands to hide them.

"I know," she whispered, leaning over and rubbing my

thigh. "It was hard for me to hear that, too. I thought he and I had something." She wiped away a few tears from her face.

"How can my husband not want to talk to me!" I screamed desperately. I jumped up, picked up my plate, and smashed it down on the floor. Rib, bread, wheatberries, and glass flew everywhere. Willow flinched. I stumbled over to the wall, as if I could burrow myself into it. I fell to my knees.

Willow stood up and slowly knelt behind me, resting her hands on my shoulders.

"I'm hurt, too, Elm. I know you're suffering. But I need to know what this means for us? Do you still love me?"

"Why did he say that he's doing this?" I cried. "Why didn't he change his mind?"

She let out a deep sigh. "Because he doesn't love me." She paused to sob. "He loves you. He wants you to be happy."

"But I'm happy *with* him," I argued. I wanted to race over to the Tire and shake Shep until he realized what a mistake he was making.

She nodded. "I know you are. I can't convince him of that. But . . . it's more complicated now. I don't think Shep wants to share you, or love someone else besides you. But now, I'm pregnant . . . or might be. I have an appointment to find out for sure. I guess he feels like . . ." She shook her head. "I'm unsure what he thinks. But I don't expect he's going to change his mind."

"I fucked it all up." I wept, still hiding my face from hers.

She hugged me from behind. "Elm, I can't help but to feel like the other woman here. But that's not how this was supposed to be. We were *all* in a relationship. I know you're hurting, but I feel very alone right now. He broke my heart, too."

I took a few deep breaths and turned around to look at her. She sat cross-legged on the floor behind me. Her cheeks sparkled with fresh tears.

"I'm sorry," I stuttered. "I'm not going to abandon you if

that's what you're worried about."

"I know that you wouldn't do that." She smiled. "We don't have to be together for you to be a father. But I do have feelings for you, Elm, and you said that you love me. So on my end, I'm open to being with you if you want to be with me."

"Monogamously?" I asked.

"Yes. I've been in monogamous relationships before. It's not like I'm incapable. Again, I know we're both in pain right now, but ... I'm sitting here by myself, and I don't know what's going to happen with us, or if there is an *us*." She looked down, and her hands trembled.

I could see the stress that strained her face that usually was so youthfully bright. I recalled all those days that I fantasized about her eyes, her smile, and holding her against me. I took her hand in mine.

"Willow, I'm willing to try it. I don't want you to feel alone or abandoned."

"Do you really love me? Like you said?"

"Yes," I lied.

Chapter Twenty-Four: Shep

M any people wouldn't appreciate waking up to a tiny closet-like room in the back of the Tire, but sadness overwhelmed me to the point that I didn't care. If anything, it was comforting because it felt safe. I had my own private locker to hide away in.

What agonized me the most was anticipating questions from my customers or even my staff. Not many people in Cloverleaf acknowledged my marriage. It was a classic *don't ask, don't tell* situation where folks could let us be as long as it was never mentioned. Nevertheless, gossip spread quickly in the small town, so I wondered if people's curiosity about our separation would surpass their homophobia.

I had to fight the urges to take a shot of rum as soon as I woke up. Elm's concerns were right. I had been drinking too much, and I couldn't let our split fuel the behavior any more, or it would get out of control. I'd had previous bouts of heavy alcohol use in my past when I struggled with my gender identity and sexuality that teetered on the brink of alcoholism. So I knew I had to resist.

I welcomed the slowness of the day even though it also gave me more moments alone with my thoughts. Danny sensed that I was off, frequently stopping to question if I were sick or okay. Finally, after the umpteenth time, I conceded just to get him off my back.

I pulled him aside in the kitchen, making sure that the dining room was managed enough for him to step away.

"Look," I told him flatly. "Elm and I split up."

"You broke up?" Danny gasped so loudly that I thought the whole restaurant could hear it.

"Shhh!" I silenced him. "Yes."

"When?" His mouth still gaping open.

"Last night." I fought back tears. I didn't need to cry at work.

"Why? What for? What happened?" Danny asked.

I didn't want to tell him the truth. At the same time, I figured it wouldn't be long before Willow was showing, and everyone would find out anyway. I sighed.

"You know Willow, right?"

"Yes," Danny responded. "Oh god! He fucked your cousin." Danny's eyes bulged out in horror.

I had to chuckle. "She's not my cousin or my niece."

"He fucked Tank's cousin. That bastard," Danny said, pounding his fist into his hand.

I rolled my eyes. "She's not anybody's cousin. Elm and I . . . we got a girlfriend. Willow's our girlfriend . . . or was our girlfriend."

Danny's squinted at me in confusion. "Huh?"

"It was a polyamorous relationship. We all dated each other." I realized for the first time how awkward it sounded, or at least to those outside such circles.

Danny's bewilderment didn't ease. "But . . . I thought you two were gay?"

"Not gay, bisexual. We both still like women," I corrected him.

"You and her were with each other?"

"Yes," I clarified. "And Elm and her were together, and me and Elm were together. We were all together." I made a circle with my hands.

"I've never heard of that," Danny said, rubbing his chin in thought. "So what happened?"

"She's pregnant."

"You got her pregnant!" Danny shouted.

I punched him in the shoulder. "No, you idiot. I don't have sperm. Elm got her pregnant."

"Oh," Danny replied. "So why do you have to break up? If you're all in the relationship together, what's the deal?"

"I'm asexual." I wanted to run away from this conversation. It was bad enough explaining polyamory. Now I had to educate Danny on asexuality.

He shrugged. "So?"

"So I can't satisfy Elm like he wants."

"I never saw Elm unsatisfied," Danny stated.

"Do you want to know what happened or not?" I snapped.

"Sorry."

"Elm wanted a baby and he's going to have one, and I . . ." A lump formed in my throat causing my voice to trail off.

"You what?" Danny asked.

"Nothing. That's it. Let's get back to work."

I managed to get through the day, taking control of the cooking and occasionally visiting with my regulars. I was in the kitchen, preparing some fresh dinner rolls when Willow knocked at the entrance.

"Sorry," she said as she stepped into the room. "Danny said it was okay to come on in. He figured you had your hands full."

I didn't stop rolling the balls of dough in my palms. I motioned for her to enter with a jerk of my head.

"Shep, can we talk?"

"Go ahead," I told her as I kept working on the rolls.

She walked over, placing her hand on my arm, and forcing it downward. "Can you quit for a minute?"

"I can't get behind on our supply of dinner rolls. We ran out unexpectedly. Customers are waiting," I insisted, pushing my arm back up and vigorously rolling another clump. "I didn't make enough this morning."

She stared at me with hurt in her eyes. "Why are you acting like this?"

"Because this is better for everyone," I told her. I was thankful to have the food as a distraction.

"Better for who? You?" she accused me, putting her hands on her hips.

"What do you mean better for me?" I snapped. "I'm the one who's sleeping at the restaurant so that the two of you can shack up in *my* house."

"You chose to leave," she retorted.

I focused my attention back on the food.

"I want to know why, Shep? Why does the baby change things?" she demanded.

"I don't owe anyone an explanation," I grumbled. I took a few deep breaths to avoid breaking down again.

Willow grabbed the dough from my hand and threw it down. She jerked me by the shoulders, twisting my body around to face her.

"Damn it," she pleaded. "You do owe. Why are you running away?"

"Because I can't compete with it!" I yelled, immediately regretting it for fear that my patrons heard. I took her by the arm, leading her to the spare room.

"Listen, I can't, okay?" I told her. "I can't contend with the sex you two have or with the family y'all are starting. I'm the third wheel!"

"So it's fine for me to be the third wheel and not you, is that what you're saying?" Willow stated with a sharp look of pain in her eyes.

"That's not what I mean—"

"No, I think it *is*," she accused me. "You thought that I would be here to have sex with your husband on the side while you remained Elm's number one, right?"

I stared down in silence.

"That *is* it," she claimed with tears emerging. "You never opened yourself to me at all."

"That's not true," I argued. "Having sex with you is not something I just do. That was hard for me."

"That's the whole point!" she shouted, throwing her arms up in the air. "You forced yourself."

"It wasn't like that," I corrected her. "I wanted us to have a bond similar to you and Elm. I tried. It was wonderful."

"But you don't love me." She sobbed. "God, do you even like me?"

I took a deep breath to calm myself. "I like you. I love hanging out with you. Gosh." I rubbed my forehead. "I didn't want to make you feel bad, Willow."

"But not in that way." She wiped her eyes. "I assumed you and me were going to have something special."

I crossed my arms and shook my head. "You thought you'd be able to transform me into someone who likes sex?"

"No," she replied. Then she paused a moment. "Well, I guess I expected you'd learn to enjoy it with me. Okay, yes, I'm sorry. Maybe I did think that after a while, you'd feel differently. But don't hold that against me when you got all of us into this when you never even wanted it."

I clenched my fists so tightly that my knuckles turned white trying to fight back tears. Willow grabbed my cheeks, holding my face up to look at her.

"It's true, isn't it? This was all one big bluff," she said.

"I didn't . . . it's not like that," I pleaded. "I thought it could work. I did."

"But did you want it to?"

"I don't know," I whispered under my breath. I'd wanted to believe that I could be cool with this. That I could be that kind of guy. But maybe I wasn't.

Willow removed her hands from my chin and stepped back. "Shep," she muttered under an obvious tightness in her throat, "I'm a person, too. I came in here with nothing but high hopes, and I fell in love with you. But it was all a ploy because you can't handle your own insecurities. I don't deserve to be treated like this."

She covered her face with her hands and sobbed, her shoulders heaving up and down. I wanted to reach out and comfort her. But she felt too distant in that moment, and my own shameful guilt kept me frozen.

"I think you should talk to Elm," she choked out.

"I don't want to," I said, turning away from her.

"He's hurting, Shep. He's in bed. He won't speak. He didn't go to work —"

"He didn't go?" I asked, jerking my head back around. Elmer never missed work.

"No, he's really in pain. And I am, too," she told me.

I hadn't thought about Elmer heartbroken and picturing him lying around and not going to work bothered me. But I couldn't face it. "I can't," I responded.

"You need to tell him that you're insecure," she continued. "And that you didn't want this —"

"I can't!" I yelled.

"Why not?" she asked.

"Because it's what's best for him." I stopped, rocking my feet back and forth on the ground. Then I proceeded gently, "I think he'll be happier. With you. I haven't ever seen him the way he is with you. He loves you. Besides, he wouldn't have gotten you pregnant if that wasn't what he really wanted."

"We're not sure if I'm pregnant. My appointment is next week. You're making a mistake, Shep. Don't walk away."

"I'm sorry, Willow. But I have to."

CHAPTER TWENTY-FIVE: ELMER

I finally forced myself back to work after two days of laying around the house either sleeping or drunk. My eyes were red with bags underneath, and everyone assumed that I must have been ill when I returned to the office. I had never called in sick, so the excuse was successful.

Normally, working became an easy distraction. There was always something that needed to be done, offering me a plethora of excuses to work late. The holidays were approaching. We had a Christmas concert planned and a play.

However, my mind either blanked or raced with so many thoughts that I could hardly think. I stood there at meetings, giving one of my principal speeches, yet it felt like I was hovering over myself just observing. Everything was surreal.

I knew that I couldn't allow my own grief to impact Willow. If she was pregnant, she required less stress. She had missed her doctor appointment because the grocery store was short-staffed and needed her to come in. But I also suspected that she was avoiding it. I'd offered to let her stay at home so that she didn't overexert herself at work, but she refused. She said that she wanted the extra money. I was eager to confirm the pregnancy because I wanted to get her on my insurance to pay for her childcare. Unfortunately, the only way to do that was to divorce Shep and marry her. I wasn't ready to go through that ordeal. At the same time, I hated the idea of her applying for government aid when I had the means to cover her.

The Thanksgiving holiday passed. Willow had invested

even more hours at the store since it paid her overtime. Despite her procrastination to see the doctor, I knew that I couldn't put off talking to Snavis about getting his wife's sister to vacate my house so that Willow and I could move in. Shep had already spent the holiday alone in the tiny room at the Tire. I wasn't going to let him stay there during Christmas. I needed to at least suggest that Snavis' sister-in-law start searching for housing.

I walked over to Snavis' trailer one Saturday afternoon since it was only a few blocks from my house on the outskirts of town. Not even the frigid cold and blistering winds of Montana could keep Snavis indoors. As usual, he sat outside on his porch with a heater, beers, and a large winter coat with a hood pulled up over his head.

"Oh, look who it is," Snavis hollered. He banged on the trailer. "Belle, come here. It's my bro."

His wife Belle appeared in the doorway, barely cracking the door to avoid letting the frigid air in.

"Hey, Elm," she said, and I could hardly make out a slight grin on her face as she peered out. "Sorry, it's too cold to step out."

"That's okay, Belle. Good to see you," I greeted her, as I pulled up a chair as close to the heater as possible.

"Want a beer?" Snavis offered, holding out a can to me.

"Sure." I grabbed it and took a few sips.

"Well." Snavis grinned. "You must need something. You never show up over here unless you're helping me or you need something."

I frowned. "Oh, I'm sorry. I didn't mean it to be like that."

"I'm just teasing you, bro," Snavis jeered as he slapped my shoulder. Only Shep and Snavis did this thing with hitting or punching me in the shoulder when they poked fun at me.

"Um." I took a drink. "I hate doing this, but I need you to ask Beth to find another place. I have to move back into the house."

Snavis lit up a cigarette, inhaling and blowing out a large cloud of smoke. "That sucks. There ain't many places to rent here. Going to be hard to get something. Why are you moving back?"

I took a deep breath. "Shep and I . . . we split up."

His eyes looked both surprised and hurt. He leaned forward, resting his elbows on his knees, and scrutinizing me. "What happened?"

"I got Willow pregnant. Well, she might be pregnant. He left." Snavis was the first person that I had told. Hearing the words made it feel more permanent. I picked at my fingernails.

Snavis stared at me, smoking silently.

"I thought things were going great," I continued. "But . . . it's the pregnancy thing. Shep warned me to be careful, but I didn't listen."

"So you were trying to have a kid?" he asked.

"No . . . I don't know. I guess maybe there was a part of me that didn't care if it happened." I rubbed my temples with my hand. "I didn't think it through."

"So you're moving into the house with her?" Snavis confirmed.

I nodded. "Yes. I'm staying with her."

"But not with Shep?" he asked.

I shook my head.

Snavis gulped down the rest of his beer, throwing his cigarette butt in it and tossing it into the trash can. He sat back, running his fingers through his shaggy brown hair.

"Bro, I admit that we've always teased you about being . . . different. Calling you a pansy or queer." He looked sad. "But we love you. You're our brother."

"I know." I never saw him get sentimental. I smiled. It felt good to hear that he loved me even though I wasn't anything like him or Kicky. At the same time, it was a little awkward since I wasn't sure how to react to the mushy side of Snavis.

"I thought you and Shep were really happy. I hate to see you throw it all away." He stared down, shuffling his feet around. "I kind of envied you."

"*You* envied *me*?" My eyes widened.

"Yeah." He looked shyly at me. "You're a good guy, Elm. Lots of folks here respect you. And you followed your heart. You never listened to what me or anyone else thought."

"That's not true," I asserted, shaking my head. "I'm terrified of what other people think. I'm still scared."

"I like Shep. Why would you want to leave him?" he asked me.

"I don't. He left me." I put my elbows on my knees and buried my face in my hands. "He won't talk to me or see me. He doesn't answer my texts or calls. What am I supposed to do? Willow's pregnant, and I'm not going to abandon her or my kid. She's a great person."

"She isn't Shep, though, is she?" he remarked, holding up his forefinger.

I couldn't keep my tears back. "There's nothing I'm able to do. I'm heartbroken from all this."

Snavis placed his hand on my knee. "Then go get your husband."

"It's not that easy," I argued, throwing my hands up in the air.

"Yeah, it is. He's just over there." He pointed over my shoulder. "See, you can see the top of the Tire sign in orange right there."

"You don't know Shep," I insisted. "We can't come back from this. He's too stubborn."

"Elm, don't ruin your life because you're afraid of not marrying a girl you got pregnant. You can still be a good dad. I'm damn sure that you'll be a great dad. Go get your husband.

You know you enjoy you some dick."

"Shep doesn't have a dick," I corrected him.

Snavis leaned over and socked me in the shoulder.

"Ouch!" I yelped.

"You know what I mean, bro," he said. "You like men. I always knew you liked you some dudes even when we were kids. You'd be happier with Shep."

"Look, Snavis, I appreciate everything you're saying right now. But seriously, I need the house. Shep's staying at the Tire until we move out. I can't let him be there too long. He doesn't deserve that."

He groaned loudly. "Okay, bro. I'll start helping them search for a place. I'll let you know when something shows up."

"Thanks," I said.

I had mixed feelings about waiting to hear back from Snavis. I knew that finding another rental in Cloverleaf would be challenging, even impossible this time of year. I hated thinking of Shep stuck at the Tire for that long, yet I also feared getting the call that I could now move out of our home. This house, this dream, was over.

One night after work, I parked my car in the garage and decided to take a walk. Willow was working the evening shift, so I figured a stroll would prevent me from falling into a massive heap of despair.

After about ten minutes, a strong familiar scent hit me through the cold crisp air. The Tire.

I walked over to the restaurant. Cars packed the parking lot that had rows of Christmas lights all around it. A large inflatable Santa Claus swayed back and forth in the wind near the entrance. Shep loved Christmas. Every season, he tried to perfect his holiday dishes, spending hours at home experimenting with new ingredients or flavors. And the town gratefully showed up to consume whatever revised or original concoctions that emerged. The place was crowded this time a year.

I crept up to the front window and peered in. I saw Danny carrying stacks of entrees through the crowds, and Pam pumping out drinks at the bar. The smell of spices like cinnamon, nutmeg, and cloves, along with pumpkin, bacon, and molasses tickled my nose, filling my belly with a warmth of comfort. Then I noticed Shep.

Shep loved putting on bar tricks for the guests. He stood in the center of the dining room, wearing a black Santa hat and a *Nightmare before Christmas* sweater, tossing various glasses in the air and catching them. He threw one behind him where Pam caught it. The crowd cheered and clapped. He smiled and gave a loud whomp, stomping his feet on the ground.

Patrons waved him over to their tables. He grinned and chuckled with them. If he was hurting, he didn't look like it. His grin widened from ear to ear, exposing his bright white teeth and the dimples in his cheeks. He looked beautiful.

"Hey!"

I jumped, turning to see Steve, another one of the waiters, standing behind me.

"Sorry, Elm. Didn't mean to scare you," he said, putting out a cigarette. "I'm coming from my break. What are you doing out here?"

"Nothing," I replied. "I was taking a walk. I wanted to check out what's going on."

"Why don't you come in?" he asked.

"Um . . . I better not," I mumbled.

"Elm, I know you guys are broke up or whatever." He rolled his eyes. "But get inside. Shep would never turn someone away from this place. Come on. He won't care." He waved me over.

I shook my head. "I shouldn't, Steve. He doesn't want to

see me."

He stared at me like an arrogant teenager with his hands on his hips. "It's bullshit, man. This thing you guys are doing. It's bullshit."

"What are you talking about?" I asked.

"You two breaking up. It's bullshit." He stepped closer to me and leaned against the wall. "You should figure this shit out. He's in there crying. You're out here peeping at him from the window. Just go in there and deal with it, man."

I smiled nervously, moving farther away from the entrance. "It's not that easy."

"That's too bad, man," Steve said, shaking his head as he headed for the door. "People like you two split up, guys like me have no hope. No hope, man." He vanished inside the Tire.

I glanced inside and Shep's gaze met mine. My heart sank.

I held up my hand to wave to him. He returned his attention to the drinks in his hands. He carried them to one of the tables and returned to grinning and laughing with the guests.

Tears welled up in my eyes as a tight pain shot through my chest. I moped back to the house.

A week later, my secretary, Alice, knocked timidly on my door. I welcomed the interruption since I'd been staring blankly at my computer screen in a daze all morning.

"Yes?" I greeted her without looking up.

"Hi, um . . ." She shut the door behind her. She walked toward me with her hands clamped together in front of her. Her face solemn.

"Principal Lee, people are saying that you got that girl that's staying with you pregnant. I don't mean to upset you, but I thought you should know about these rumors."

I leaned back, motioning for Alice to sit. She scooted a chair close to the desk and sat. Her voice shook.

"Is that true?" she whispered.

I had no idea how news traveled around Cloverleaf so quickly. Shep had taken her to the doctor that morning when they were unable to get seen. Maybe people assumed? Of course, if Danny knew that Shep was sleeping at the Tire, the whole town was probably aware of it by now. He wouldn't keep his mouth shut.

"Yes, it's true . . . or it might be. We aren't sure if she's actually pregnant, yet." There was no way to lie. If we would be living together and raising the child, I had to tell everyone eventually. And I didn't want to dismiss the rumor only to have to admit the truth later. I realized that my job was in jeopardy. I trembled.

"Oh, no," Alice said disappointedly. "You're going to be in trouble, Principal Lee. What will people say? The principal being gay was hard enough, but you've always been so discrete that everybody lets it go. But a girlfriend . . . a young girl, and you got her pregnant out of wedlock. It's way too scandalous. The town will never accept it."

I stared down. A deep hopelessness burned in my chest. "I don't know what to do, Alice. My husband left me. You're telling me that I'm losing my job . . ." I started crying.

"Oh, I'm so sorry, Principal Lee," she said in a motherly tone, getting up to put her arm around me. "We all make mistakes. You're such a good principal. No one's going to do what you do. But there's nothing you or me can do. There's already a petition—"

"A petition?" I gasped, jerking my head up.

She nodded. "Yes, sir. Some parents got a wind of it . . . some of the ones that I guess don't like you, and they're coming after you. But when they tell everyone what for . . . I think they'll turn a lot of folks against you."

"Fuck my life!" I screamed. I plopped my head down on the desk with a bang.

"Shhhh," Alice covered her lips with her fingers. "Principal Lee, we're at school. Don't add fuel to the fire."

"What do I do, Alice?" I asked her frantically.

She stood up and knelt beside me. "I think it would be good to resign. That way, you're in control. It would be the best approach to protect your privacy. Maybe they'll stop spreading the rumors to get the petition signed if they hear you've quit."

I hadn't considered leaving my job. I'd worked my whole life to be a principal. I had devoted countless hours to this school and even sacrificed being myself to play the role. In one moment of shortsightedness, it was gone.

I picked up my golden name plate with *Principal Elmer Lee* sketched into it. My throat tightened as if someone was strangling me as all my dreams vanished. I hadn't mourned the loss of Shep, and now, I was no longer Principal Lee. I caressed the plate as I fought back a wave of tears.

Chapter Twenty-Six: Shep

I wasn't miserable sleeping at the Tire itself because I was safe from the world. The prospect of seeing Elmer or Willow made me want to vomit. However, being so suddenly cut off from Elmer inflicted me with a painful yearning inside. The thought of letting him go proved too overwhelming.

Then that one night, I saw him outside the Tire. His expression looked so sad and pitiful, not his usual professional collectedness. When our eyes met, a shiver ran down my spine, but I couldn't bear to talk to him. I knew that I had to end it. It was for the best.

I was cleaning up after closing when I heard a quiet knock on the window. Turning, I saw Elm.

It was snowing outside and quite cold, so I let him in. He rushed inside, shivering and kicking snow off his feet.

"Sorry, I'm making your restaurant dirty again," he stuttered.

"It's okay. Go sit at the bar. I'll get you some hot cocoa," I offered, walking toward the kitchen.

"Coffee is better," he mumbled.

"No, you like cocoa," I insisted.

"I'm trying to watch the calories," he asserted. "You know how I gain weight this time of year."

I returned a few minutes later with a large mug of fresh cocoa with molasses and chocolate whipped cream on top, just the way he liked it. I set it down firmly. He rolled his eyes.

"You'll drink it," I said.

Elmer took a small sip, licked his lips, and hungrily gulped more down. I chuckled.

"Yeah, you're always right," he conceded, smiling.

"So what are you doing here?" I asked. I continued wiping off the counters as a way to hide my nervousness.

"I needed someone to talk to." He stared down at his mug.

I threw down the cleaning supplies and sat down on a bar stool beside him. I nudged him sharply with my elbow to push him to speak.

"I resigned."

My mouth dropped open. "Why? You love the school."

"I had to," he told me. "There was a petition out to get me removed. It's because of Willow. They know she's pregnant or that's the rumor."

I slapped my forehead. "Shit moves fast around here. Has the doctor confirmed it?" I held my breath. The reality of the pregnancy still terrified me.

"No, she missed a few appointments due to work. It's the holidays, and they got short-staffed," Elmer stated, choking on some tears. "I don't know how I could've been so stupid. I was so blindsided by you leaving that I didn't even think about something like this."

"What's this petition?" I inquired. I wasn't used to seeing him so shaken. He'd been the calm one in the marriage. My heart broke for him.

"Well, apparently, it doesn't look good for the principal to be gay," he quoted the word gay with his hands. "Or have a side chick and get her pregnant. And she's only 20 years younger than me, too."

"It's not 20 years—"

"It doesn't matter, Shep." He sighed as he rubbed his temples and wiped his eyes. "It's done. I'm over."

"Why would you walk away? You're better than that. Fight it," I encouraged him, but I could tell the defeat hung heavily in his soul.

"That'd just put me, you, and Willow on parade for all to see. I'd have to justify and defend all these questions." His voice cracked again. "I can't do that to us. This way, I get to leave without having to answer anything."

"Clover people are still going to gossip. You resigning probably confirms whatever wild idea they have in their mind." I hated seeing him give up. Perhaps he'd learned it from me.

"It doesn't matter." He swallowed down the rest of his cocoa. "They've always gossiped about us. At least I don't have to answer anything. I guess speculation feels better than invading our privacy. Plus, Snavis claimed he'd beat up anyone who didn't let the rumors die out."

I chuckled, causing Elmer to glance over at me. He laughed.

"You know Snavis," he said in a lighter tone. "It's good to have a crazy brother who has your back, especially when you're a square like me."

"Square?" I slapped him on the shoulder. "No, Elm, I think you've managed to graduate from being boring. Bisexual exploration, a side chick, and a baby. You're pretty wild now. You can change your boring *Facebook* profile to match your exotic lifestyle."

He giggled some more. I could typically tease him a little to get a chuckle out of him, especially when he was sad or angry. I hated witnessing his pain. It was a major reason that I'd refused to talk or see him this entire time for fear that his anguish would cloud my own judgment.

Elmer's face grew serious again, and he fumbled with his empty mug, staring off blankly.

"What are you thinking about?" I asked.

"That I can't swallow," he replied. "Or breathe. My whole life is just a bunch of grains of sand that are slipping through my fingers, and I can't stop it. Like a tragic hero."

A pinch of guilt tightened in my stomach listening to his despair. I'd never seen him so distraught and hopeless, and somehow it felt as if it was all my fault. I'd brought Willow into our lives. If she wasn't here, he'd still be a principal, and we'd still be married.

I pulled him close to me, and he put his arms around me. He cried into my shoulder for a few moments. His body slumped heavily against me. My heart ached as it absorbed the pain that he was carrying. I squeezed him tight.

He moved away, drying his eyes with a napkin.

"I'm so sorry, Elm," I told him. "I know you loved your career."

"Yeah, I'm sorry, too. It sucks."

I took a deep breath. "In a way, I feel like it's all my fault. It was my idea, and I fucked everything up."

"What do you mean?" he asked.

"I brought up the whole let's find a girlfriend thing. If I'd never pushed things, you'd have a job."

"And we'd still be together," he blurted out, gazing up at me.

I paused. "Yeah, I guess so," I agreed.

"If you think it got fucked up, can we not fix it?" he asked gawking at me pitifully. "Why can't we resolve it, Shep?"

I stood up and walked back behind the counter with my arms wrapped protectively around me. *You have to let him go.* This event had proven to me that Elmer wanted a family, and I couldn't give it to him. I loved him too much. I preferred for him to be happy.

"Wait, wait, wait," he pleaded. "Don't say anything. I want to know if you would see a counselor with me."

"A counselor?" I snapped. Elmer didn't seem like the kind of person to see a counselor. The whole image of being enclosed in a room where we must discuss our feelings horrified me.

251

"Yes, all three of us, actually."

The *three* stabbed my heart, and I turned away again.

"Wait!" Elmer yelled. "It's not like that. Trust me, please. It's about us. Are you willing to sit down, one meeting, and talk? Please . . . that's all I'm asking."

I went back over to him. He sat still and quiet as if he was holding his breath.

"I only have to do it once?" I asked hesitantly, placing my hands on the counter to balance myself.

"Yes, just once. I'll do whatever you need to do afterwards. I promise. You want a divorce from me? Okay, I'll do it for you. Do this for me."

"What's the point? What for?" I demanded.

"Because we can't let this end this way. You won't talk to me. I bring it up here, and you immediately start running away." He teared up again. "I thought this environment would give us a place to get things out. I have to know why you left me, Shep."

My body started to quiver, and my stomach grew tight and nauseous. Too humiliated, I couldn't make myself tell him about how my debilitating insecurity sabotaged my marriage and our polyamorous relationship.

"Okay, I suppose I can make time for it," I muttered, evading his eyes that were pressed on me.

"Thanks," Elmer said. "Are you okay over here? I talked to Snavis, but it's a tough season to find a place quickly."

I nodded. "I know. It's fine. Keeps me from having to mingle much outside the Tire. I never liked that."

"You didn't do it anyway. If you're not here, you're home." His words trailed off with a melancholic tone when he said *home.*

"I guess I better get back," he remarked as he stood up to put his coat on.

After putting on his gloves and hat, he opened the door. A

gust of crisp, frigid air blew in, sending shivers up my spine. His foot stepped out, but then he turned to face me.

"It's not home without you, Shep," he said with misery radiating from his eyes before walking out into the wintry night.

A few days later, I was in the restaurant alone, prepping for that day's lunch and dinner items. A loud knock interrupted me from preparing my spicy turkey meatballs. I peeked out into the dining area and saw Willow by the front door. I waved at her, washed my hands, and let her in.

"Hey, Shep." She smiled as she entered. It wasn't her usual bubbly grin but carried a hint of tiredness to it.

"Hang your coat up," I said as I walked back to the kitchen. "You hungry? I can lay out some hummus."

"No, just some water. I'm feeling sick to my stomach. In fact, Shep, can you come here and sit down?"

I stopped and turned around. She held her abdomen and appeared forlorn. I went over and sat in front of her.

"Are you okay?"

"I can't get a hold of Elm. He ran out somewhere with his brother. I can't get in touch with my mom," she said frantically. "I didn't know who else to go to. I'm scared."

"What's wrong?" I asked.

"I've been cramping since last night. I've had an upset stomach, but the cramps are bad." She started sobbing. "I don't know what to do. I'm afraid that I'm having a miscarriage."

"So it is confirmed that you're pregnant?" I inquired.

She grimaced. "No . . . I've been too anxious to go to the doctor." She put her head down and cried. "But now I'm terrified that I'm losing my baby."

"Okay, okay," I replied, placing my hands on her knees. "Let me get some warmer clothes on, and I'll take you to the doctor, okay? What's your doctor's number? I'll call and inform them we're on our way."

"Okay," she said, and she pulled up the number on her phone and held it out for me.

I called the doctor's office and told them that we were coming in and that I suspected a possible miscarriage. I messaged Pam to ask her to open for lunch in case I didn't return in time and called Danny and Peggy to come in to finish the prep work. Since it was Christmas, they were more than willing to jump at the opportunity for extra hours and thus, more money. I then helped Willow into my car, and we proceeded to the doctor.

CHAPTER TWENTY-SEVEN: ELMER

Snavis' trailer had some leakage in the bathroom, and I often offered to be an extra handy man on such jobs. Snavis and Kicky joked that it was the one *manly* thing I did. Our dad had us jump in and help with any repairs growing up, so I was quite accustomed to it.

It was getting dark when we finished. I washed my hands and face then checked my phone. I saw a list of texts from Shep. I immediately opened them.

Please come home when you get this. It's an emergency.
Elmer where are you? Please get home now.
I'm with Willow. She's not pregnant. Come home.

My heart sank down to my feet, and I grabbed my coat and gloves, hollering out to Snavis that I had to go.

"What? No beer, bro?" I heard him yell after me, but I was already hurrying out the door. I ran all three blocks to our house, bursting in so fast that I almost fell to the floor.

"Willow! Shep!" I shouted frantically, searching each room until I found them in the bedroom.

Willow was lying down in the bed with a wet rag on her forehead. Shep lied down behind her, rubbing her shoulders. He sat up when I entered.

I didn't move. I wasn't sure what to say or do. Fortunately, Shep took charge, something I know was new for him.

"We'll be right back," he whispered to Willow, kissing her on the cheek. "I'll bring you some honey tea."

He walked over to me and motioned for me to leave the room. He shut the door behind him as we exited and pulled me into the kitchen. He instructed me to take off my coat and shoes while he made some tea for all of us.

"She came to the Tire and told me she was cramping. So I took her to the doctor," he began, pouring water into a kettle. "I figured she was having a miscarriage."

"Did she?" I clinched my fists and held my breath.

"No," he replied, turning to me. "They don't know if she was pregnant or not. They said that sometimes the pregnancy process starts and sends out some hormones that the tests capture. But if there was one, it didn't take. The cramping was from her period."

My mouth gaped open. "So she was never pregnant?"

"There could have been something, Elm. But it ended pretty quickly," he told me as he got the honey out of the cupboard. "But I guess it scared her since she thought she was."

Again, I froze. Mixed feelings raced all through me. My baby was gone. I would no longer be a father, a dream that I'd always wanted. But at the same time, Shep was in the house, and I needed to savor every moment he was there. I didn't know what to feel.

"How is she?" I asked after a few moments of silence. "Is she okay?"

"She's upset, understandably. She's hurt from it all. How are you?"

I tried to swallow, but my mouth was dry. A numbness infiltrated my whole body.

"I don't think I can take any more," I muttered hopelessly. "I'm not even sure how to begin to process it."

Shep moved closer to me. "I'm sorry that I wasn't comfortable talking about this with you. You wanting to be a father. It was a subject we didn't discuss."

I nodded.

"How did you feel when you thought Willow was pregnant?" he asked.

I fumbled with my hands and nails, staring down. "At first, I was shocked and scared, but also excited. There was going to be three of us taking care of it, so I dreamed that we'd be this big happy family. It felt good." I tensed. *I shouldn't have told him that.*

"You really wanted to be a father," he acknowledged with a sad look on his face.

"Yeah," I concurred. It was true. I wanted to have it all. "But then you left me. That's not what I hoped for. Everything changed."

Shep gazed out the kitchen window with his palm resting on the counter. "How do you feel now? Knowing the baby's gone?"

I ran my hand through my hair. "Like I lost another grain of sand through my fingers. Like all my dreams have been stripped away. I guess after losing you and the job, the baby was the last thing I had to hold onto. Now I have nothing."

My hands trembled. I pulled my hair tie out, letting my hair fall to my shoulders.

"I don't even know how equipped I am to comfort her right now," I admitted solemnly. "I feel so demoralized."

Shep put his arm around my shoulders and hugged me. "I'm really sorry, Elm," he said. "I had no idea that all this would happen. I really wanted you to have this."

"Even though it broke us up?" I asked, pushing him away so that I could see his eyes.

"I left because I wanted you to be happy," he stated. "I hoped that you'd get to be a father. I couldn't give that to you."

"I know." I sighed. "How do I comfort Willow? I don't even know how to soothe myself."

Shep walked back over to the stove to remove the kettle. He poured the water over the tea bags and added drops of honey and fresh lemon juice. He placed two mugs in front of me.

"Go in there and talk to her. Tell her how you feel. Let her share how she feels. There's nothing else you can do . . . or need to do really," he told me.

He went to the door and began putting on his jacket.

"You're leaving?" I asked raising my eyebrows. I wanted to snatch him up in my arms so that he could never go. Also, I needed him right now.

"Yes, I have to get back to work. I already missed the entire day almost. Besides, this is between you two. I'm not in this relationship anymore," he replied with a slight smile.

"Shep, I want to do that counseling appointment. Maybe after things here die down. Are you still willing to do it?" I pleaded.

"Okay," he agreed. "Just text me. And Elm?"

"Yes?"

"Whatever you do when you talk to her, be honest with her and with yourself."

He opened the door and went out into the night.

I returned to the bedroom with the two mugs of tea. Willow was sitting up with the lamp on beside her. Her face looked forlorn and lost. Her eyes red from tears. I set the mug on the nightstand and pulled up a chair.

"Shep told you?" she asked, still not looking at me.

"Yes, he did," I said with a nod.

"What are you feeling?"

I took a long drink of the tea. The warmth of the lemon and honey soothed my dry throat and eased my nervous stomach. I motioned to her to have some. She picked up the cup and sipped.

"With everything I lost lately, I guess I'm more numb than anything," I admitted. "I don't even know if I can mourn anymore. Maybe I'm grieved out. That probably sounds pretty awful, doesn't it?"

"Perhaps it hasn't hit you, yet," she suggested.

"Possibly. Has it hit you?"

Willow drank the tea in silence and leaned back with a groan. "I've got a whirlwind of emotions going through me. I go from being numb one minute to overwhelmed the next. I guess I already had my mindset on a baby, you know? Even though I know that things have been strained with me and you lately, I figured it would all work out after some months passed. At least, by the time the baby arrived, I guessed we'd be a family."

"You and me?" I clarified. I had wanted the child, but I hadn't truly pictured my future household without Shep.

"Yes. I know you're heartbroken. I knew there'd be a divorce. That there'd be gossip in town. That we'd take time to get over Shep. But after all that smoke died down, I thought we could come back together." She took my hand. "You're a good guy."

"I guess I wasn't even thinking about that," I confessed. "I was trying to accept the divorce and find out what I was going to do for work. The baby seemed far off but yet, it gave me something to hold onto. Something that would bring me joy when it got here."

"But you weren't sure?" she inquired, finally making eye contact.

I thought hard for a moment before responding. "I guess I wasn't. I don't think I ever got a chance to be happy about it. I've been too depressed and devastated with everything else."

"Over Shep?" she asked.

I clenched my teeth and nodded. "And now my work," I added. "I'm sorry, Willow. I've been so self-absorbed. That's not who I am."

"It's okay, Elm. Your husband walked out on you. I know how you loved the school and the job. Those are some major blows. I understand."

I placed my hand over my heart. "You do?" Willow really was a saint.

"I realize this probably isn't the most opportune time to discuss this, but I think nothing can really hurt me worse right now," she stated, twirling a lock of hair in her fingers. "When you said you loved me, did you mean it?"

I swallowed hard, looking down. "I don't know," I mumbled.

"How do you feel about me?" she pushed.

I took a deep breath, setting my mug on the nightstand. I leaned forward, resting my chin on my hands. "When I said it then . . . I *felt* like I meant it."

"What are you saying?"

I hated to tell her the truth. But Shep's words hung over me. I needed to be honest.

"I was in love with you," I stated. "I had feelings for you. I still do. You filled my days with sexual excitement. I don't mean that in a shallow or dismissive way. I buried so many of my sexual passions for most of my life. I hid my bisexuality. And I was afraid to let go in bed." I took her hand and squeezed it. "You drew that part of myself out of me. It wasn't just the sex. I was freer. Like I could let loose more instead of worrying about my image or what others think. You're so sure of yourself, Willow. It inspired me. I thank you for it. I really do. Despite all that's happened, I appreciate everything you've taught me about myself. It's all because of you, and I want you to know that even though losing Shep and the job hurts, I have no regrets.

"But you don't *really* love me? Is that it?" she asked. She stared at me, but I couldn't decipher her emotions.

I looked down in shame. "I think if it was me and you, then yes, there are enough feelings to grow into love. And things were certainly heading in that direction."

"But it's not only you and me." Her tears were dried, and her face was stern.

I contemplated her words, glancing down at my socks that were moist from the snow on my shoes.

"Elm? How do you feel about Shep?" she asked, pulling her knees up to her chest and wrapping her arms around them.

The emotional numbness receded, and tears welled up, causing my hands to tremble.

"I can't verbalize it," I blurted out with shakiness in my voice.

"Tell me. I need to know," she insisted. She touched my shoulder to encourage me to go on.

I closed my eyes and breathed. "I always fantasized about being with a man. Shep's the first man I've ever been with. It feels more natural to me. Plus, he's mesmerizing. He's so beautiful. His food, and the way he loves his work and his customers. He's so much more confident than I am, really. I've never been able to be myself with anyone else like I can with him."

"You love him," Willow said.

I wiped the tears from my eyes and nodded.

"You don't want to lose him," she noted.

"No," I replied.

"And you don't *really* love me."

I broke down. My whole body heaved, and I just let it all out.

Willow moved to the edge of the bed and placed her hand on my back. I tried to speak, but waves of agony seized control. I could hear some muffled cries from her.

After what felt like an eternity of sobbing, I finally exhausted myself. She handed me some tissues from the nightstand. I blew my nose hard.

"I shouldn't be the one getting comforted," I stated when I

could talk again. "You need it right now. I'm so sorry, Willow. I'm making this all about me. You must be so devastated."

"We both deserve support right now," she affirmed, rubbing her hand up and down my back. "It was both our loss. The baby. Shep. Us."

I looked up at her. "I'm sad about also losing us."

She smiled. "I know you are. I am, too."

"I *was* in love with you. Who knows? That could've turned into something as spectacular as it is with Shep." I couldn't help but imagine what giving up Willow would have been like if Shep had told me to end it. I could have easily been just as distraught. But when it came to losing Shep or Willow, my heart clearly chose Shep.

"I don't want to see you hurt this way. I hate seeing anyone in pain," she whispered.

I grinned. "God, you're one of the nicest people I've ever met."

She smiled back at me. "So are you."

"Willow?"

"Yes, dear."

"Do you love me?"

She paused before responding. "I think it was more what you described. A feeling of being in love. You were a fun lay." She giggled, finally causing a laugh out of me. "You were so awkward but sexy at the same time. But to be honest with you, Elm . . ." She grew sad. "I was more in love with Shep."

"Really?" I asked, my eyes widening.

Willow nodded. "Yes, for all the reasons you stated. But I realized that he wouldn't return those feelings because he was too in love with you. Plus, I thought somehow that I would turn him into a more sexual person if I just gave him enough good sex or loved him the way that he wanted. But that was more about me than it was about him."

"You fell for that, too." I laughed.

Willow chuckled. "Yes, I did. That wasn't fair to him. Or to myself, really. I guess I got hung up on it because he was so insecure about you and me. I thought by us having a sex life, it'd fix that."

"I know what you mean." I sighed. "All this time, I was so focused on changing him that I didn't stand back and appreciate him and the way he loved me."

"I didn't, either," she agreed. "That's exactly what makes him so elusive."

I slapped my forehead. "He *is* so elusive! Gosh! I never thought that I was pushing him away."

She took my hand again. "But you don't have to, Elm. You can repair this. I know it. I feel like I ruined your life."

I leaned forward. "Willow, you did nothing wrong. I promise you. You helped us so much in ways we haven't even realized, yet. You're amazing. You're a free spirit who isn't afraid of anything. It's been your bravery and confidence that's brought out the best in us. Don't you ever blame yourself."

"But you guys are broken up," Willow argued, waving her other hand in the air. "How did I help?"

"Because you helped us see what's really important. And it's not sex." I grinned and squeezed her hand. "I mean, don't get me wrong, sex is big. And with you, it was fucking fantastic! I'll masturbate on it for years to come."

Willow giggled. "Yes, it was quite memorable, my Elm."

"But sex doesn't have to be like that to be good. It can be great if it's different." I fumbled with my wedding band. "Shep may not feel the same way about it, but he's done tons of things to show me that he loves me. But I never saw it so clearly until now. I'm ready to be the honest person with him that I'm being with you. And maybe it still won't work out. As much as that hurts, I don't regret anything."

"Are you saying that you're going to try to get him back?"

she asked.

"I'll do my damnedest." I wasn't willing to give up on Shep. He hadn't convinced me that he didn't love me anymore. I also knew the negative thoughts that often consumed him when his anxiety got bad. I needed to reassure him.

"Good," she said with tears in her eyes. "I want to see you two resolve this. I wouldn't have entered this relationship if I thought it would split you up."

"What about you?" I asked. "One minute we're having a baby and moving into another house, and the next ... what are we doing?"

Willow gave me a sad smile. "Well, I hope you're not totally abandoning me. We can all still be friends, right? No benefits this time, though."

"But—"

"No buts, Elm," she said firmly. "I'll be fine. I'll move back to Great Falls with my mother, and when I come to visit my sister, I expect royal service at the Tire and a good old-fashioned sleep over with my buddies."

"It doesn't feel right to just—"

She held up her palm to stop me. "I'll be cool, Elm. Trust me. I will be. You two taught me a lot, too. For one, be careful about getting into polyamorous relationships with people who aren't ready for them."

I laughed.

"Yes, sorry, but you guys are a hot mess." She placed her hand on my chin and lifted my face up. "No, seriously, I'll be fine, and besides, our relationship is only changing status. It isn't ending, so don't feel like you're abandoning me. Yeah, I wanted the baby. But that was after I thought I was pregnant. I'm disappointed and sad, but it's no one's fault. It just is. But I also didn't want our relationship to break anyone's heart. You two seem to really love each other. So I don't recommend that we continue this polyamorous relationship. I think you guys are better off monogamous."

"Well, I'd prefer for you to stay here a little longer until you're feeling well. You know, before moving back to Great Falls." I didn't wish to lose Willow from my life. She was too important. But I couldn't see Shep ever being able to handle polyamory. After experiencing such a distance between us, I never wanted to share him again.

"I would appreciate that. I don't foresee my mom taking as good of care of me as you two do. But Elm, I'll stay on one condition."

"What's that?"

"That I see you work things out with Shep before I leave."

CHAPTER TWENTY-EIGHT: SHEP

M y heart really ached for Elmer's loss. As difficult as it would have been to see him around town with a family, it hurt knowing that the opportunity alluded him again.

I texted Willow a few times to check on her. She said that she was doing okay and mostly resting. She quit her job at the grocery store to take some time for herself. I made a point of getting Steve to drop off at least one delicious meal daily to her and Elmer, and she sounded grateful for the fresh food.

Christmas came and went. I normally focused on Christmas Eve and closed the Tire for Christmas day. However, I decided to open for lunch for anyone who needed a place to eat and managed to convince Danny and Peggy to come in for some additional pay. I prepared an apple walnut stuffing, smoked turkey and ham, honey butter biscuits, spicy bourbon cranberry sauce, fried okra, black-eyed peas, and sweet potato latkes. It didn't get busy, but we had some incredibly appreciative patrons who proceeded to order extra dishes to take home with them.

The following week, the Tire hosted its traditional New Year's celebration in which it stayed opened until midnight, serving various cocktails and finger foods to keep the guests occupied. Since people loved a public place to socialize and drink, it was a successful night.

I was putting away the holiday décor and brainstorming my next menu when the weight of the previous year's events hit me. A pang of loneliness flooded through me.

It was etching closer to mid-January when Elmer texted me about counseling. He'd scheduled it a month before, but in a tiny town like Cloverleaf, no one ever got an appointment quickly. It was the following Thursday morning. He'd ensured it was early to allow me ample time to return to the Tire. I said I'd be there.

The whole thing terrified me. I had no idea what to expect. I figured Elmer needed closure, and it was only fair to give it to him. I'd worked so hard these past months to get it together. I didn't feel confident that I could maintain my composure trapped in a room with Willow and Elmer staring at me. It felt too painful.

I spent the days leading up to the visit with millions of thoughts racing through my head.

What will he say?

What will she say?

What will I say?

The counselor's office was on the top floor of a clinic. I didn't want to arrive too soon and have to deal with the awkwardness of sitting with Elmer and Willow in the waiting room.

Are they going to be holding hands?

Where do I sit? Away from them?

I entered the reception area and informed the receptionist that I was present. She said that she would let Dr. Bowen know.

I sat in the cramped space, cracking my knuckles so loud that the receptionist gave me a glare. Fortunately, it wasn't long before a short petite woman with curly brown hair and large glasses greeted me and invited me back to her office.

When I walked in, Elmer and Willow were on a black sofa at a reasonable distance apart. They both looked at me, Elmer with a slight smile and Willow with a typical warm grin. I took a seat on an armchair directly across from them, and Dr

Bowen sat between us.

"So welcome, Shep," Dr. Bowen said.

"Hi," I muttered, avoiding any eye contact with Elmer or Willow.

"As you know, Elmer arranged this meeting. He's been in to see me a few times to give me the background of what's been going on."

"You've been seeing a counselor?" I asked him with wide eyes, finally glancing at him.

"Yeah, I have," he replied.

"He thought that in an environment like this, it would be easier for you to discuss some things," Dr. Bowen continued.

"It's the only way I could get you alone, or to even talk about this with me," he asserted.

"Shep, are you open to having a conversation about what's happened?" Dr. Bowen asked kindly.

"I said I would already," I agreed. My gut bubbled with nerves. I shoved my hands in between my legs to hide their shakiness.

"I would like to go first, Dr. Bowen," Elmer interrupted, holding up his hand. "I can't wait any longer."

Dr. Bowen nodded. "Okay, Elmer. Shep, are you willing to listen to what Elmer has to say? I don't want you to worry about responding right now. Just listen. Can you do that?'

"Yeah," I said.

"I would like for you to look at Elmer when he speaks to you, and Elmer, make sure you talk directly to Shep."

We both acquiesced.

He took a deep breath. His eyes met mine. It reminded me of our days of hanging out as friends when we had this perpetual yearning in our gazes.

"Shep," he began, "I've rehearsed this so many times in my mind, ever since you walked out." He shook his head and teared up. "I'm so sorry that I made you feel like sex was more important than you. That you thought our sex life wasn't good enough. I'm sorry that I became carried away with it. Because I did. I got lost in it, and I neglected us."

It was all I could do to force myself to keep staring at him. My hands trembled. I clenched my jaw to suppress the intense sadness brewing up in me.

"I learned a lot about who I am these past five months," he continued. "About myself as a sexual being. A man. A person."

I sighed.

"I always wanted to be a dad. You know that. And it's been painful for both me and Willow to deal with us not being pregnant."

I nodded. *He needs to say this, as hard as it is to hear.*

"But, Shep, just because there's things that I want like a child and sex . . ." — his shoulders shook — "none of that compares to how I feel about you."

I couldn't hold back anymore. I covered my eyes to hide my tears. Elmer got up and sat on the small table in front of my chair and gently pulled my hands away from my face.

"I never wanted to give up on us for any of that other stuff," he told me. "And you know what?"

"What?" I whispered.

"I'm glad I resigned from the high school." He squeezed my hands. "Because that place treated you and Tank like shit. They were shitty to me, too. And if they're not going to honor people like you and me who invested our hearts into it, if it makes us feel ashamed of who we are . . . then I don't need it."

"But you loved the school," I argued. I couldn't picture Elmer as anything other than a principal. I didn't want him to give up himself for me.

"I care for me and you a lot more," he assured me.

"What about finding another principal job? You'll have to

move away — "

"No," he said firmly. "Because I love the Tire just as much as I cherish you. I love it because the Tire *is* you. I treasure your food because it's you, Shep. It's your heart and soul. I want you and the Tire more than anything."

I looked over at Willow who watched silently but in awe with tears in her eyes and a touched smile on her face.

"I don't understand," I jabbered. "What about you two? Aren't you in love?"

"Shep," Willow chimed in. "Yes, Elmer and I have feelings for each other like you and me do. But it's not near what you guys have, and it's not going to be. I think y'all are better together without a third."

"But — "

"I'm moving home to Great Falls. I'm leaving on Monday," she said.

My mouth hung open.

"Don't worry, it's fine." She waved her hand in the air. "Elmer and I have talked a lot these past weeks, especially since he's been home with me all day. I'm in a good place. We'll keep in touch."

I turned back to Elmer. "Are you sure?"

"I'm so fucking sure," he said.

"Shep?" Dr. Bowen interrupted. "Do you have anything to say to Elmer?"

I rubbed his hands with my thumbs and cleared my throat.

"I'm sorry, too, Elm," I told him. "I brought up this whole scheme because I didn't think you could be happy with me. It was all because of my insecurity. Before I realized it, the idea became a reality. I assumed I knew what was best for you, and I thought I could handle it and even enjoy it. I really wanted to be *that* kind of person. The truth is, I didn't like seeing you with somebody else. Someone who could give you things that I can't. I got more insecure."

"You struggled with it that much?" he asked.

"Yes," I admitted. "So many times, I wanted to say stop or tell you to quit."

"I wanted it to end, too," he confessed with wide eyes.

"You did?" I gasped. "But you were so happy and so in love—"

"I know," he stated, looking down. "But the whole time, I was worried about you and me. Something didn't seem right. I knew in my gut that I was losing you. I just struggled to believe it. And I wasn't ready to lose Willow, either."

"I'm sorry, Elm. I wasn't brave enough to say anything. We promised that we'd talk about any issues that came up. I let all three of us down."

"How do you really feel, Shep?" he insisted, leaning closer to me.

Be honest. "I don't want a divorce."

He started crying. "Neither do I."

"I want to be with you, Elm, like I've never wanted to be with anyone. You're the one for me. You're that love that everyone searches for."

Elmer kissed me hard, forgetting about the fact that we were in a counseling office with two others watching us. I kissed him back as if it was the last time that I would ever hold him, so I needed to savor every moment.

"You're my only one, too, Shep," he whispered. "You're the love that I always wished for."

I heard Willow sniffling in the background. Elmer pulled away and blushed.

"Sorry," he said shyly but with a massive grin on his face. "My apologies, Dr. Bowen."

"Nothing to be apologetic about," Dr. Bowen stated with a smile. "If anything, it looks like it's going to be a good session."

We all laughed.

271

"I'm so happy for you two," Willow said. It was nice to hear the typical enthusiasm back in her voice.

"Can we cut the session short now?" Elmer asked Dr. Bowen.

"If that's what you want," Dr. Bowen replied.

"Yes," he insisted, standing up and holding his hand out to me. "I need to take my husband home and let him show me love in any way that he wishes."

I smiled, took his hand, and rose. "I think it's a good occasion for some sex."

ABOUT THE AUTHOR

Carey PW is an author, college instructor, and mental health counselor. Carey currently lives in Montana and identifies as nonbinary, transmasculine or AFAB and panromantic asexual. Due to the lack of resources in rural communities, Carey has discovered that writing about his lived experiences is a therapeutic outlet for him and hopes that his readers relate to his own personal struggles and triumphs shared through his characters' narratives. Carey is particularly interested in exploring relationship conflicts around sexuality and gender differences. He has also worked as a high school and college writing instructor, earning a B.A. in English Literature, a M.Ed. in English Education, and a Ph.D. in Social Foundations of Education all from the University of Georgia. In 2020, Carey earned his second M.Ed. in Counselor Education and works as a licensed clinical professional counselor, LCPC. He has a strong passion for working with the unique mental health issues of the LGBTQIA2S+ community. Readers can learn more about Carey from his blog, www.careypw.com. When he is not writing, Carey is busy training for marathons, parenting his six cats, sharing his culinary talents on social media, serving on the board for the nonprofit Center for Studies of the Person or CSP and learning photography.

www.ingramcontent.com/pod-product-compliance
Lightning Source LLC
Chambersburg PA
CBHW070800200626
46811CB00023B/199